THE FIRST TIME

"You don't need to do this tonight," he said.

"I *want* to do this." Amber pressed herself against his body, entwining her arms around his neck. She drew his head down, her lips capturing his in a smoldering kiss.

Her gesture surprised Miles. She wanted him. There was no mistaking the passion in her kiss.

Amber lifted her lips from his and stepped back a pace. Holding his gaze captive to hers, she slipped the straps of her chemise off her shoulders, letting the garment pool at her feet. And then she stood only in her silk stockings, garters, and shoes.

The princess could not possibly know how arousing she looked.

"I want no barriers between us," Amber whispered, her eyes glazed with desire. "Remove your mask and make love to me."

Miles froze. "I cannot—"

"We will snuff the candle."

"You fear the dark."

"I fear nothing with you."

Miles kissed her again and then removed his jacket, waistcoat, and shirt.

Books by Patricia Grasso

TO TAME A DUKE

TO TEMPT AN ANGEL

TO CHARM A PRINCE

TO CATCH A COUNTESS

TO LOVE A PRINCESS

Published by Zebra Books

TO LOVE A PRINCESS

Patricia Grasso

ZEBRA BOOKS
KENSINGTON PUBLISHING CORP.
http://www.kensingtonbooks.com

First Printing: November 2004
10 9 8 7 6 5 4 3 2 1

Printed in the United States of America

Chapter 1

Stratford-upon-Avon, 1820

He hated days like this.

Trees colored themselves green, flowers bloomed in the sun's warmth, chirping birds flew across a cloudless sky.

The world was too damn happy.

Miles Montgomery, the fifteenth Earl of Stratford, turned his back on the nauseatingly cheerful sight outside his study window. He shifted his gaze to the portrait over the hearth. Sweet Brenna, gone in the flash of a midnight fire.

Out of habit, Miles reached to close the drapes and shroud his study in comforting darkness. He stopped himself, though, remembering his guests. John Saint-Germain, the Duke of Avon and his brother-in-law, and Prince Rudolf Kazanov had several business ventures in the offing and wanted to include him.

Business ventures. Miles twisted his chiseled lips into the ghost of a smile. Since the fire, business ventures had filled his empty existence.

Miles touched the mask that covered the left side of

his face. His love, his face, his life had died on the fateful night of the fire. Now he needed to wait for his heart to stop beating.

"My lord, His Grace and His Highness have arrived," the majordomo announced.

Miles touched his mask again. "Send them in, Pebbles."

"Come on inside," Pebbles called, his hands cupping his mouth.

Both the prince and the duke grinned at the majordomo as he passed them on the way out. Pebbles inclined his head as if he were the aristocrat and they the servants.

Miles met the two men in the middle of the room. With a smile of greeting, he shook the prince's hand first and then the duke's. Both men were as tall as he, a couple of inches over six feet.

Located on the second floor in the west wing of the manor, the earl's study sat at one end of the Long Library. Floor-to-ceiling windows bathed the room in afternoon sunlight when the draperies were open, as they were now. Thousands of volumes filled the bookcases, and a thick red Persian carpet covered the floor. Over the main fireplace mantel hung an enormous portrait of a woman.

"Brenna, my wife," Miles said, seeing where the prince's gaze had drifted.

"She was a beautiful woman."

"Shall we get down to business?" Miles gestured across the chamber. He sat behind his desk while the other two men took the chairs opposite him.

"Caroline misses you," John said.

"I will visit her soon."

"I'm surprised to see the drapes open," his brother-in-law continued. "Normally, you sit in the dark. I was beginning to wonder if you were a vampire."

"I opened the drapes for you," Miles told him. "Normally, you comment on my sitting in the dark."

Prince Rudolf chuckled, drawing their attention. "You bicker like my brothers and me."

"We are not bickering, Your Highness," Miles said. "His Grace prefers to mind *my* business instead of his own." Though he spoke with the hint of a smile, his tone held a hard edge.

"You need a wife," the duke said, undeterred by his brother-in-law's sarcasm. "If you die without an heir, Terrence the Weasel will inherit."

Miles wished he could be in his family's company without listening to their comments regarding his life. Why should he care if his cousin inherited his title?

"I finished with the wife business when Brenna died," Miles said, his weariness with the topic apparent. He glanced at the prince. "Do you see the nagging inflicted upon me?"

"The nagging will cease if you remarry," Prince Rudolf said.

"No woman can ever replace Brenna." Miles touched the masked side of his face. "Besides, what woman would consider marrying a scarred beast?"

"Georgiana Devon looks especially well," John remarked. "She asked about you the last time I saw her in London."

Miles shrugged his shoulders with indifference. "I left Georgiana behind a long time ago."

"As I recall the gossip, you dropped Georgiana in favor of Sarah Pole," John said. "You did know Sarah's husband was killed at Waterloo, leaving her a wealthy widow? Weren't you on the verge of offering for her?"

Miles gave his brother-in-law a pointed look. "You know very well that I was considering Sarah when I met Brenna."

"Vanessa Stanton lost her husband," John said. "She always favored you, and you enjoyed her company."

"Vanessa enjoyed everyone's company. She sought her pleasures when I had a whole face," Miles replied. "I prefer living alone to wearing horns."

"What would you do if a virtuous woman did want to marry you?" Prince Rudolf asked.

"I would marry and plant a dozen sons inside her," Miles answered, hoping to drop the topic.

"Consecutively, I hope," John quipped, making the other two smile. "Come to London and look over the latest crop of hopefuls."

"I retired from society four years ago," Miles refused. "If you have seen one debutante, you have seen them all."

"Damn it, Miles," John snapped. "Brenna is dead but you still live. Do you think she would want you to hide in shadows?"

Miles said nothing, and an uncomfortable silence descended on the three men. Why, in God's name, did John and Isabelle need to solve his problems? Why couldn't they leave him alone in his misery?

"I couldn't reach her in time and lost half my face for nothing," Miles told the prince.

"I am sorry for your loss," Rudolf said. "I cannot imagine the horror of losing the woman you love."

Miles inclined his head, accepting the prince's condolences.

"John is correct, though," the prince added. "You need to return to the living."

"Are you going to nag me, too?"

Prince Rudolf held his hands up in a gesture indicating he would say no more.

"I told you how pigheaded he is," John said. Before Miles could reply, he added, "Shall we get down to business?"

Miles lifted his gaze to his wife's portrait. He knew

they were correct about living while he could, but his wife was gone. And the woman who equaled her had not been born . . . .

Moscow

"Princess Amber, we will make beautiful babies together."

Amber laughed, a melodious sound that complemented her sweet expression. Looking at her companion, she became almost mesmerized by his piercing gray eyes. With his handsome features and midnight black hair, Count Sergei Pushkin looked as if he had stepped out of a maiden's dream. And his heart belonged to her. For the moment.

"Sergei, you should not voice such thoughts," Amber scolded him, her expression flirtatious. "I do not think your mother would appreciate the sentiment."

"What about you, Amber?" Sergei asked, fingering a lock of her silver-blond hair. "Would you appreciate my planting a child inside your body?"

Her alabaster complexion deepened into an embarrassed scarlet. "I refuse to continue this improper conversation. Tell your driver to take me home. Uncle Fedor will be annoyed if I am late."

Sergei lifted her chin and waited until she raised her disarming violet gaze to his. "Amber, I promise we will make babies together. I love you."

"I am fond of you, too, but look for another woman to be your wife," Amber said, her practical nature rising to the fore. She harbored no silly illusions about a future with the man beside her. "Your mother will never approve a union between us."

"My mother *will* approve," Sergei said. "You are the czar's daughter."

"I am the czar's unacknowledged bastard," Amber corrected him, her voice mirroring her weariness with the same old argument. Why did he refuse to understand? They had discussed this several dozen times.

"The czar sends you a gift each year, which is unofficial acknowledgement."

"I would appreciate the gift of a public acknowledgement."

Nobody understood how difficult life was for those born on the wrong side of the blanket. She supposed that particular heartache had brought Cousin Rudolf and her closer. Though a dozen years separated them, they had always been two of a kind. Only Rudolf understood her suffering.

Amber stared into space, her small white teeth worrying her bottom lip. Recently, Uncle Fedor had been making comments about her being a grown woman of twenty, an age to begin a loving relationship with a gentleman.

The important word was *loving*. Amber feared her uncle would force her into an illicit relationship with the wealthiest aristocrat who offered to take her. She didn't want to be a mistress. She wanted to be a wife and mother.

"Where have you gone, my princess?" Sergei teased her.

Amber focused on him. Too bad she had been born a bastard. She would have enjoyed being Sergei's wife.

"I have returned to you," she said, forcing herself to smile.

Sergei drew her close before she could escape. "One kiss, my love."

Amber turned her face away and pressed the palm of her hands against his chest. "My kisses belong only to the man I marry."

"Surely one kiss cannot hurt," he coaxed.

"One kiss led to my being born a bastard. I will not be painted with the same brush as my mother."

"Very well, princess." Sergei called instructions to his

driver, who turned the coach around and headed in the opposite direction.

Reaching her uncle's home, Amber peeked into the deserted foyer. She paused to remove her shoes and, on silent feet, dashed up the stairs.

"I wish to discuss the princess . . ."

Amber heard her name spoken as she neared the second floor office, her uncle having neglected to close the door tightly. She didn't recognize the voice. The gentleman sounded older, sophisticated, cultured. Had someone decided to offer for her?

Curiosity getting the better of her, Amber leaned against the wall and listened to their conversation. The longer she listened, the faster her heart pounded, the sharper her panic grew.

"Do you wish to court my ward's affections, Count Gromeko?" Uncle Fedor was saying.

Count Gromeko? Amber had heard his name whispered somewhere.

"With her platinum blond hair and violet eyes, Princess Amber is unusually beautiful," Gromeko said, ignoring her uncle's question. "Unfortunately, the princess is a bastard and unacceptable to the best families."

"My niece will marry a younger son or make a firstborn's devoted mistress," Fedor replied.

"God forbid she should be wasted like that," Gromeko said. "Her beauty can bring us immense wealth."

His statement confused Amber. She had no money, no dowry. All had been spent on her living expenses since she had come as a child to her uncle's home. How could she possibly bring them wealth?

"As you know, I deal in high-quality slaves," Count Gromeko was saying. "The moment I saw the princess, I knew I must have her. Not for my pleasure, of course.

"I own a slave with the identical coloring. If the princess and he mate, their children will be born with the same coloring, which commands the highest prices in the Ottoman markets. God willing, she could produce a child each year for the next fifteen or twenty years."

Shocked and revolted and frightened, Amber struggled against a swoon. Her knees wobbled, and her hands shook as if she had the palsy.

Her uncle remained silent. He could not be considering the devil's offer.

"Princess Amber will live in relative luxury as befitting her station," Gromeko continued. "The princess is too rare a flower to be abused or neglected. I guarantee that, once breached, she will enjoy my stud. His member is large, his seed is potent, and he has sired a dozen babies in the past two years. He will, however, service the princess exclusively until she gets with child."

"I don't feel—"

"I will give you fifty thousand rubles for the girl and ten percent profit on each of the babies sold."

"Do you wish to take her tonight?" Fedor asked.

Amber could not believe it. Her uncle was selling her into sexual slavery, a broodmare for profit.

"Do or say nothing to alarm her. Frightened women do not easily conceive," Gromeko warned her uncle. "My business keeps me in Moscow another month. In a day or two or three, tell the princess you have had an offer for her hand in marriage. Then I will join you and your niece for dinner and charm her into feeling comfortable with me. As the month draws to a close, we will tell her that I am escorting her to her betrothed. I need the princess calm and content."

"When can I expect—"

"You will sign a bill of sale giving me the princess," Gromeko told him. "I will give you twenty-five thousand rubles and pay the remainder on the day I take her away."

"About that ten percent profit . . ."

Amber sneaked up the stairs to her bedchamber.

With tears streaming down her face, she leaned back against the door for support. Her heart pounded, and her legs still trembled.

Struggling for composure, Amber wiped the tears from her cheeks. Her uncle was not easily duped. She must remain calm or all would be lost.

Should she ask Sergei for help? He had no legal authority to thwart her uncle. Besides, his mother would see this as a way to get rid of her permanently.

Perhaps she should appeal to the czar. No, she would never gain an audience. Her uncle would tell the czar she was a stubborn chit who was refusing a perfectly acceptable marriage offer. His lie would be more believable than her truth.

She needed to leave Russia.

Cousin Rudolf would protect her. She needed enough money to get to England and a good disguise.

A black dress and widow's veil would allow her freedom of movement. No one would recognize her, and strangers would assume she was older than twenty.

A sob escaped her, and an involuntary shudder shook her body. Amber forced herself to take several calming breaths. There would be time enough to break down when she reached England. If she broke down now, Fedor and Gromeko would win.

London, Six Weeks Later

Amber looked at the brick town mansion and then glanced at the address on her cousin's last letter. She had finally arrived at Montague House, her cousin's English inheritance.

Lifting her valise, Amber climbed the front stairs. The door opened before she could reach for the knocker, and the majordomo looked down his nose at her travel-bedraggled appearance.

"May I help you?"

"I must speak with Rudolf Kazanov," Amber answered. "Is the prince in residence?"

"Are you seeking employment?"

"No." Amber tried to move past the man, but he blocked her way.

"State your business with His Highness."

This last obstacle to safety brought tears to her eyes. With a strength fueled by desperation, Amber shoved the man out of the way and darted past him into the foyer.

"You are trespassing on private property," the majordomo warned her. "I will call the authorities if you do not leave immediately."

"Please announce Princess Amber," she said, ignoring his threat.

"Princess?" His tone implied disbelief.

Amber yanked the black widow's headdress off, revealing the silver-blond mane cascading down her back, and prepared to win this battle. She had traveled too far to be turned away. "Rudolf," she shouted, nearing hysteria.

"You are disturbing the peace of this household." The majordomo caught her arm and dragged her toward the door.

"Rudolf!"

Behind the struggling duo, someone cursed loudly in Russian and then switched to English. "Bottoms, what is happening?"

"Tell your man to release me."

"Cousin Amber?"

Bottoms dropped her arm as if it had scorched him. Amber dashed across the foyer, threw herself into her cousin's arms, and wept uncontrollably.

"Prepare a bedchamber with a hot bath," Prince Rudolf instructed the majordomo. "Then serve my cousin a hot meal in my study."

The majordomo hurried away.

"Protect me from Fedor," Amber sobbed.

Prince Rudolf held her close. "Is Fedor with you?"

Amber shook her head. "I have run away."

"You traveled across Europe alone?"

"I dressed like a widow so no one would bother me," she said. "Fedor will come after me. You must hide me."

"I will protect you," Rudolf promised, guiding her across the foyer.

With his arm around her, Rudolf helped her up the stairs to his second-floor office. He led her to the settee near the hearth and then poured a shot of vodka.

"Drink this," he ordered. "You will feel better."

Amber gulped the vodka, shuddered as it burned a path to her stomach, and then set the glass down. "I need a husband. Can you find me one?"

"Start at the beginning, and leave nothing out," Rudolf said, putting his arm around her. "Then we will speak about husbands."

"I overheard a conversation between Fedor and Gromeko," she began.

"Count Gromeko?"

"Do you know the count?"

"I have heard of him."

"Gromeko persuaded Fedor to sell me to him," Amber said, her eyes blurring with tears, her complexion scarlet with embarrassment. "The count owns a slave with my coloring. He proposed to mate me like a broodmare with this slave and sell my babies."

"Sweet Jesus, I regret not taking you with me when I left," Rudolf said, his grip on her tightening. "You are safe now. My brothers will also protect you. Wait until I tell them—"

"Do not tell anyone," she cried. "I am too ashamed."

"The shame does not belong to you," Rudolf said, "but we will keep this our secret for the present."

"I will not feel safe until I am married and pregnant," Amber told him. "Can you find me a husband?"

Rudolf gave her an indulgent smile, as if she were still the little girl he pampered. "When you recover from your journey, my wife and I will take you into society, where you will find your own husband."

"I need a husband now," she insisted. "Fedor and Gromeko will come after me."

"I do know an earl who needs a wife," Rudolf said, "but the gentleman's face was badly scarred in a fire."

Amber lifted her chin and looked him straight in the eye. "Scars do not frighten me. I will marry this earl if he will take me."

Chapter 2

"My lord?"

Letting the drapes fall into place, Miles turned at the sound of his majordomo's voice. The overcast day conspired with the drapes to shroud the Long Library in darkness. Even the hearth fire in the middle of the room failed to throw light to the far ends of the chamber.

"Yes, Pebbles?"

"Prince Rudolf Kazanov requests an interview."

"Escort the prince to me."

Walking toward the door, Pebbles shouted, "Come on inside, Your Highness."

Out of habit, Miles touched his mask and started to cross the library. A smile of greeting lit his expression when he saw the prince.

"Good to see you," Miles said, shaking his hand.

"You did not expect to see me so soon," Rudolf said with an easy smile.

Miles inclined his head. "You must have ridden through the night to reach Stratford by noon."

"I arrived late yesterday but passed the night at the Black Swan Inn."

"You should have come directly to Arden Hall," Miles said, ushering him across the library toward his desk. "I would have welcomed an overnight guest."

"In that case, I regret my decision not to intrude on your privacy."

Miles gestured to the chair in front of his desk. The Russian prince sat but then hesitated, as if searching for something to say. Such hesitations boded ill, Miles thought.

"I hope you carry no bad news," he said. "We haven't lost our shirts in speculation?"

"Our profits are rising with each passing day," Rudolf assured him. He paused a long moment before continuing, "I need your help with a personal matter."

The prince's statement surprised Miles. His own "personal" life had ended in a fire four years earlier. How could he help someone else with a "personal matter" when he couldn't even help himself?

"I will help you if it is within my power."

"Princess Amber Kazanov, my cousin, recently arrived from Russia," Rudolf began. "She needs a husband, and since you need an heir—"

"*No.*"

"I promise there is nothing wrong with her," the prince continued, smiling at the negative response. "All Moscow hails Amber as its most beautiful woman."

"Why would such an acclaimed beauty marry me?" Miles asked, his tone bitter. "Is she pregnant?"

Prince Rudolf looked insulted. "My cousin is a virtuous woman."

"Beauty and virtue mixed into one woman?" In spite of his sarcasm, Miles knew the prince would not lie about his cousin's virtue. A spark of curiosity flickered to life, surprising him, misery having been his constant companion for four years.

"Amber has lived with my father since the deaths of

her parents," Rudolf told him. "She ran away from a disturbing situation and landed on my doorstep."

"The princess traveled alone across Europe?" Miles asked, surprised.

Rudolf inclined his head.

The spark of curiosity fanned into a flame. Miles knew no woman with the courage to do that.

"What kind of disturbing situation?"

"The choice to share the reason belongs to Amber," Rudolf answered. "The situation is quite serious, though."

If she wasn't pregnant, what could be so serious? Had her uncle disappointed her by refusing to increase her pin money? Young females were notoriously flighty, but no well-bred woman traipsed across Europe on a whim.

"My answer is still *no.*"

"Every man wants an heir to carry his name and make him immortal."

"I died four years ago," Miles said. "I am acquainted with my own mortality."

"Your loss is immense," Rudolf sympathized, "but surely, speaking with the princess will do no harm."

"As a favor to you, I will speak with her," Miles relented, trying to put an end to the topic of remarriage. "Bring the princess to Stratford in a couple of weeks."

"There is no need for that." Rudolf grinned. "Princess Amber waits in the corridor."

The wily Russian had outsmarted him. Miles didn't know if he should laugh in amusement or shout in anger. Though irritated, he couldn't keep his lips from twitching with the urge to laugh. On the other hand, he did want to satisfy his curiosity about this royal beauty offered to him in marriage.

"Does the princess speak English?"

"I taught her myself."

"Then I will speak with her. Alone."

Miles touched his mask when Rudolf stepped into the corridor but then realized the princess would be unable to see him in the dark corner. He would frighten her and send her running from the library. That would effectively put an end to this foolishness.

Still wearing her hooded cloak, a petite woman stepped into the library and paused when she saw no one. She whirled around, startled, when the door clicked shut behind her, the hood of her cloak slipping off her head with the sudden movement.

Miles sucked in his breath. Cascading to her waist like a curtain of silk, her thick mane of silver-blond hair captured his attention.

Princess Amber peered into the enormous chamber's dark corners. "My lord?" She sounded uncertain.

Miles liked her voice. Soft. Musical. Seductive. Like silk caressing flesh.

"Walk to the hearth, princess," Miles instructed her. "I want to see your face."

The princess crossed the library to the hearth. She moved with the easy grace of a dancer. Her poise in the face of uncertainty spoke of her cultured upbringing, her confidence in herself, and her royal station in society.

Miles stared at her perfect features. Framed by her hair, her angel's face was delicately sculptured and heart-shaped. He wondered what color her eyes were.

Miles felt a tightening in his groin. He could almost see that silky mane splayed across his pillow. This was a woman who would heat any man's blood.

"My lord?" the princess called softly.

Though her expression remained placid, Miles noted her hands fidgeting at her sides as if she didn't know what to do with them. First he would frighten her and make her weep. Then he could return to the comforting solitude of his misery.

"My lord, did you wish to speak with me?" she called again.

"Are you pregnant?" Miles demanded in his sternest voice.

His question shocked her but not the way he expected. "I am a virtuous woman," Amber announced, her anger apparent. How dare this disembodied voice accuse her of immorality. What gave this man the audacity to assume she possessed no honor? The earl possessed a low opinion of himself if he believed only a woman of low character could possibly seek a match with him.

"I apologize for offending you."

"You do not sound sorry," Amber said, lifting her chin a notch.

"Why do you need a husband?"

"With all due respect, my lord, that is none of your business unless we reach an agreement."

She heard a smothered chuckle from a dark corner of the library. Relief that the earl had not taken offense swept through her.

"Tell me about yourself," he said.

"I am the only child of Prince Rozer and Princess Natasha Kazanov," Amber said. "People tell me I resemble my mother."

"That merely identifies you," Miles said, purposely prolonging their conversation before he sent her running in fear. More perfect than an artist's idealized masterpiece, her beauty compelled him to keep her with him, beguiled him to study her face, beckoned him to step closer.

He controlled himself, though.

"I do not understand what you want to know, my lord."

"Tell me something personal about yourself."

Amber knew she needed to close the distance between them. If he remained hidden in the darkness, he would never marry her.

"I dislike dust, Christmas, and speaking to disembodied voices," she told him. "Show yourself. Please."

Hearing movement from the darkness, Amber doubted the wisdom of her request. The man had been scarred by fire. She needed to keep her face expressionless. If she cringed, he would know, and all would be lost.

Her heartbeat quickened at the sound of him crossing the room toward her. A large form took shape just beyond the light cast by the hearth fire. The earl was a tall man.

"Princess?"

Relieved that he had paused in the shadow, Amber wet lips gone dry from nervousness. The earl sounded like a normal man. Which encouraged her.

"Your height startled me."

"Why would my height surprise you?"

"You fit very neatly in that dark corner." The hint of a smile touched her lips, and she sensed him smile, too.

"How old are you?"

"Twenty. And you, my lord?"

"Thirty-two . . . I understand the reason you dislike dust," Miles said. "Why do you dislike Christmas?"

Amber stared into the shadows and wished she could see him. "Christmas makes me feel lonely."

"A beautiful young lady like yourself would celebrate with family and admirers."

How could she reply to that without revealing too much of herself? She needed to be truthful, but the earl might decline to marry her if he knew her sordid origins. On the other hand, withholding information was not a good way to begin married life.

"My father murdered my mother on Christmas," Amber told him, her voice barely louder than a whisper.

"Then he killed himself. I lived with Rudolf's father after that."

An awful silence filled the library while the earl digested what she had said. Amber worried her bottom lip with her white teeth. Was the earl watching her? What was he thinking?

"Had your father become unbalanced?"

"My father murdered my mother because of *me*," Amber admitted. "He killed himself to escape punishment."

Miles couldn't credit what she had told him. "Why do you blame yourself for your father's actions?"

Amber squared her shoulders and lifted her chin a notch. "I am not Rozer Kazanov's daughter but the unacknowledged bastard of Czar Alexander."

"And?" He sounded almost bored.

And what? Amber wondered in confusion. What did he want to know?

"No secrets should exist between a man and his wife." Amber hoped her words were the correct approach to earn his respect and, perhaps, a marriage proposal. "I wanted you to know my shame before you made a decision."

"The shame does not belong to you," Miles said, his sentiment encouraging her.

"I have told you what I dislike." Amber gave him a tentative smile. "Do you want to know what I like?"

"I will live on tenterhooks until I do."

Sarcasm tinged his voice, but Amber missed it. "I love the feel of silk, the scent of grass, and the sound of children's laughter."

"How about the sight of hideous scars?"

Amber had no idea what to say to that. At a loss for words, she decided that silence was the best reply.

"Is there anything else you would say to me?"

"I dislike people who hide in shadows when I speak

to them," Amber said, knowing all would be lost if he refused to show himself to her.

"Ah, a woman with wit."

"Do you like women with wit?"

"I *dislike* them immensely."

Silently, Amber cursed her mistake. What should she do now? Gauging his mood was impossible unless she could see him.

"How do I know what I will be getting?" Miles asked.

"I do not understand, my lord."

"Your face is perfection," he said, "but what are you hiding beneath your layers of clothing?"

Without saying a word, Amber shrugged her cloak off and let it fall to the floor. She reached around to unbutton her gown to the waist and then pushed one side down, baring an alabaster shoulder.

"*Stop.*"

Her hands stilled in an instant.

"What are you doing, Princess?" Amusement tinged his voice.

Amber felt her face flaming with her embarrassment. "I am showing you what will be yours."

The dark shape stepped into the light and became a man wearing a mask on one side of his face. He had handsomely chiseled features, full lips, a straight nose. The corner of his mouth on the masked side of his face drooped slightly.

Amber noted all of that in less than a second and then looked into his eyes. Dark and intense, his gaze held hers captive. She stood motionless when he reached to touch her bare shoulder. Merely a hair's breadth from her skin, he dropped his hand to his side.

"Cover yourself," the earl ordered in a hoarse voice.

Another mistake. Amber dropped her gaze and adjusted her gown.

"Are you afraid of this face?"

Amber lifted her gaze to his. "No, I fear you will reject me."

Something flickered in his dark eyes and then vanished. "I can never love you."

Amber felt like weeping. All she had ever wanted was a husband's love and children, a family of her own. She would live without love if he married her. What choice did she have? She could almost feel Fedor's and Gromeko's breath on the back of her neck.

"You may remain at Arden Hall," Miles said, his invitation surprising himself. "We will decide later if you go or stay permanently. Is that acceptable?"

Amber smiled with relief and inclined her head. She felt safe for the first time in months.

Miles lifted her hand and pressed a kiss on it. His lips were warm, making her tremble with excitement. Several men had kissed her hand before, but she had never felt like this.

"Do you fear my lips on you?" he asked, gazing into her eyes as if he could see into her soul.

"I have never kissed a man," she confessed.

Miles cocked his head to one side. "No young swain has stolen a kiss?"

"I protected my honor with vigilance." Her pride was evident.

"Beautiful, intelligent, and virtuous," Miles said, a sardonic edge to his voice. "My luck must be changing."

Amber missed his sarcasm. "A bastard must be especially careful about her reputation. If not, someone will paint her with the same brush as her mother."

"Call your cousin, and tell my man to attend me," Miles said, dismissing her. The princess was much too beautiful and amenable. He needed to distance himself, or his body would betray him.

Prince Rudolf returned to the library, the majordomo following behind.

"You will be passing the night here?" Miles asked the prince.

"I regret I will begin my journey to London within the hour," Rudolf answered, glancing from the earl to his cousin.

"Princess Amber will be staying," Miles told his majordomo. "Escort her to a bedchamber and send Molly to help her get settled." He looked at her. "Go with him, Your Highness. I am certain you will want to refresh yourself."

"Thank you, my lord." Amber turned to Rudolf, who drew her close. "Cousin, thank you for your help."

"You are safe for the time being." Prince Rudolf dropped a chaste kiss on her forehead. "I will see you soon."

Amber followed the majordomo out of the library and up one flight of stairs. He led her into an enormous bedchamber, much larger than her room at home.

The chamber was light and airy and smelled of lilacs, its mullioned windows overlooking the garden. A four-poster bed, its textiles in shades of blue and white and gold, stood along the wall opposite the windows. On the wall to the right of the bed was the hearth.

"Where does that door lead?"

"His Lordship's chamber."

"You should not have given me the chamber intended for his countess," Amber said, a heated blush rising on her cheeks.

"If we settle you now," the majordomo told her, "we won't need to move you later. The late countess never slept here."

Amber inclined her head. Apparently, the man thought she would remain at Arden Hall permanently.

"You have already lit a fire in the hearth," she said. "How did you know I would be staying?"

"Prince Rudolf and I enjoyed a conversation while you spoke with His Lordship," Pebbles answered. "The household has waited a long time for your arrival. Molly has already hung your gowns in the dressing room over there and stored a few items in the highboy. Shall I bring you a pot of tea?"

"No, thank you, Mister—?"

"Just Pebbles, Your Highness."

"Thank you, Mister Just-Pebbles."

Pebbles left the bedchamber, a broad grin on his face.

Safe, at long last. Amber felt her body beginning to relax after the tension of the previous two months. Wandering across the chamber, she looked out the window to the garden below. Mist, sheer as a bride's veil, laced the air. After closing the drapes, she removed her gown and climbed beneath the bed's coverlet.

Gruff but kind, the earl was an enigma. What was the best way to appeal to him? She had no real flirting experience. Gentlemen had always been attracted to her, but she had avoided friendship with all but Sergei, whom she had known since childhood.

Perhaps no strategy was best. She needed to be herself. Anything less than complete honesty would be unfair and lead to an unhappy marriage.

Amber closed her eyes and drifted into a deep, dreamless sleep. Hours later, she awakened to the sound of humming. She saw a young woman fussing with one of the gowns her cousin had bought her.

Thinking of Rudolf made her smile. Her cousin had purchased a complete wardrobe, telling her, "To catch a husband, you must wrap yourself like a pretty package for sale."

"What is your name?" Amber asked the woman, who, startled, cried out and whirled around, her hands flying to her breast.

Amber sat up and moved to the edge of the bed. "I apologize for startling you."

The woman recovered herself enough to curtsey.

"My name is Molly, Your Highness. His Lordship said I'm to take care of you."

"Is that so?" Amber shifted her attention to the gown.

Molly followed her gaze. "I took the liberty of choosing a gown for you," she said. "If you'd like another, I'll start on it now."

"The blue is acceptable," Amber said. "Tell me about the earl."

"You could never find a more devoted husband," Molly answered, her attention on the gown again. "His Lordship needs a woman who can see past his scars." She turned around to look at her. "Everyone at Arden Hall is hoping you're the one."

"The countess must have been a special woman to have won the earl's devotion." Amber felt inadequate. She was a bastard. How did she dare intrude upon the earl's life and expect marriage?

"Arden Hall was filled with laughter in those days," Molly told her. "After the fire, a cloud of gloom settled over the house. Perhaps Heaven sent you to bring sunshine back to His Lordship."

Amber doubted she was up to the task of bringing sunshine into anyone's life but said, "Miracles happen every day."

"His Lordship doesn't need a miracle," Molly said. "Love will cure what ails him."

Love would cure what ailed her, too.

An hour later, Amber inspected herself in the cheval mirror. She wore the blue silk gown with rounded neckline and short, puffed sleeves. Following her cousin's advice about pretty packaging, Amber left her hair loose instead of pinning it up. Gentlemen had always been entranced by her hair. She hoped the earl would also become captivated.

Amber walked down the stairs to the foyer where a footman waited to escort her to the dining room. The earl stood alone and stared into the hearth's flames while he awaited her.

"My lord?"

Miles turned at the sound of her voice. His dark gaze drifted from her face to her breasts to her waist.

"You look lovely." He crossed the dining room.

Amber gave him a smile filled with sunshine. "Thank you, my lord."

The dining room had carved ceilings and an ebony floor. Two crystal chandeliers lit the twenty-five-foot mahogany table. On the opposite wall from the sideboard stood a white marble fireplace with red tapestries on either side. A portrait of a dark-haired woman hung above the mantel.

Miles seated Amber at one end of the long table and took his place at the opposite end. His gesture was significant. If he had been any farther away, the earl would have toppled out the window.

"I trust you had a good rest," Miles said, watching the majordomo pour the wine.

"The bed is quite comfortable. My eyes closed as soon as my head touched the pillow."

"How unusual for a young lady to fall asleep so quickly in a strange house."

"I feel safer in your house than I ever did at my uncle's." Amber wished she could see the expression in his eyes.

"That is surprising."

Amber gave him a rueful smile. "You do not know my uncle."

"If he is anything like Prince Rudolf, then—"

"To liken Rudolf to Fedor is an insult to my cousin," Amber interrupted, her tone mild but with a bitter edge.

"Your uncle did provide a home for you," Miles reminded her. "Your dislike of the man does not make him cruel."

"Fedor Kazanov does not possess a kind bone in his body," Amber told him. "He never gave me an encouraging word or spent a coin of his own on me." She paused a long moment while Miles digested that. "Uncle Fedor locked Rudolf's mother in an insane asylum when she had passed her childbearing days. She remained there for fifteen years until Rudolf rescued her."

Miles fell silent. Even the servants stood as if frozen, stunned expressions on their faces.

"Have I shocked you?" she asked.

Miles inclined his head. "I understand the reason you feel safer in my home."

Amber decided there was too much distance between the earl and her. She needed to get closer or he would never marry her.

Summoning her courage, Amber stood and walked the length of the table. She sat in the chair on the earl's right. From this angle, his face appeared uninjured.

"I want to sit near you," she said by way of an explanation.

His dark gaze met hers. "So I surmised."

The majordomo carried the princess's plate, silverware, and glass the length of the table. He set them in front of her.

"Thank you, Mister Just-Pebbles."

Miles smiled. "What did you call him?"

"Mister Just-Pebbles. That is his name, is it not?"

"Yes, Princess, that is his name," Miles verified. "By the way, do you always get what you want?"

"Nobody gets everything she wants." Amber arched a perfectly shaped brow and asked, "Do you see me as a pampered princess?"

"The thought had crossed my mind," Miles admitted, another smile flirting with his lips.

"Your assumption would be incorrect," Amber told

him. "Uncle Fedor is not the cosseting type. I dislike shouting down the length of the table and need to see a person's expression when I converse. Why do you not eat?"

"I prefer taking my meals alone."

"Why?"

Miles toyed with his wineglass before answering.

Amber dropped her gaze to his large hands with their long fingers. If he took her to wife, the earl would caress her naked flesh with those hands. That thought heated her by several degrees.

"Eating is more comfortable without the mask," Miles said finally.

"Please remove your mask and eat with me."

"If I did that, Your Highness, you would not eat for a month."

Amber stared at him for a long moment, carefully keeping her expression placid, knowing he was watching her reaction to his words. She decided to ignore what he had said.

"You may call me Amber," she told him, sounding like a young queen granting a favor. "May I call you Miles?"

He inclined his head.

"If you take me to wife, Miles," Amber said, lowering her voice so only he heard, "I will expect you to remove your mask and dine with me. Otherwise, you do me a disservice."

Miles stared into her violet gaze for a long moment. Relaxing back in his chair, he said, "I will keep that in mind, Amber. Tell me more about yourself."

"What do you want to know?"

"I cannot believe a beautiful woman like you had no admirers."

"Well, there was one," Amber admitted. "Count Sergei Pushkin and I have known each other since childhood, but his mother would never have approved a match between us. The circumstances surrounding my family prevented her from accepting me as her daughter-in-law."

"Do you love him?"

In truth, Amber didn't know what her feelings for Sergei were. Somehow, she had always known they would never marry. And perhaps being childhood friends had prevented her from caring for Sergei romantically.

"There are many different kinds of love, Miles." Amber shrugged her delicate shoulders. "Will I have duties to perform?" she asked, evading his unanswerable question.

Miles gave her a look of amused speculation. "Where do your talents lie?"

"I garden and bake." Her pride in her accomplishments was evident. "I speak several languages and play the mandolin sweeter than birdsong." She gave him an embarrassed smile. "I confess to being hopeless with numbers and sewing."

"Gardening and baking?" Miles echoed, his tone sardonic. "Twenty years old and already a famous housewife."

Her smile drooped. Was he insulting or teasing her? "I know you have gardeners and cooks." Amber wished he would look at her instead of the woman in the portrait. "Perhaps you would like me to play the mandolin while you work at your desk. I would be happy—"

Miles stood abruptly, silencing her, and stared down at her. "I would like you to leave me alone." At that, he quit the dining room.

Amber dropped her gaze to her plate. Why had he turned on her so suddenly? What had she done? The earl did not want to marry her, did not even want her here. She was wasting her time and should return to London.

Setting her napkin on the table, Amber stood to leave the dining room. Then she realized the servants had witnessed all. Humiliation stained her cheeks. "I apologize for upsetting your service," Amber managed, her bottom lip trembling as she fought back tears. "Please give my compliments to the cook. Just-Pebbles, tell Molly to come to my chamber in the morning to help me pack. Please secure a coach for my return to London."

"But Your Highness—" the majordomo whined.

Amber held a hand up in a gesture for silence. "His Lordship wants me gone. There is nothing to debate."

With her head held high, Amber left the dining room. Upstairs, she changed into her nightgown and then dragged her trunk out of the dressing room. She emptied the highboy and packed her belongings in the trunk but left the gowns in the dressing room until morning. Then she slipped into bed, saddened by the thought that she would be leaving Arden Hall. The earl would mourn his wife until he died; she had not found a safe refuge. Her cousin had been mistaken about wrapping herself in pretty packaging.

These Englishmen were odd. One moment the earl smiled at her; the next moment he snapped like a dog. She did not want to pass her life with an unpredictable man. If she discounted the scarred side of his face, the earl was a handsome man, but his injury and the loss of his wife prevented him from moving forward with his own life.

The earl needed her as much as she needed him. Too bad he could not see what was in front of him. She would have been a devoted wife until she died, but competing against a cherished memory would have been impossible. Her life could have been different if only she had been legitimate issue or publicly acknowledged by the czar.

Amber thought of Fedor and Gromeko and what awaited her in Russia. She prayed Rudolf could find her a gentleman not only willing to marry her but brave enough to protect her from her uncle.

It was a long time before Amber found release from troubled thoughts in sleep.

The Earl of Stratford paced his bedchamber like a caged beast, his thoughts as troubled as his guest's. *By what right does she invade my privacy? She flutters those violet eyes at me and smiles like she bathed in sunshine every day. Her parents should have named her Princess Sunshine.* He had not invited her to Arden Hall, yet the princess behaved as if she was an honored guest. That meddling Russian had given him no choice.

How dare the princess barge into his home and dance around him with her sweet words and shy blushes and sunny smiles. Given a choice, she would never pick him for her husband, and he had no desire for a wife who cared nothing for him.

His pacing brought him to the door connecting their chambers. Miles stared at it for a long time before donning his mask. He wanted to look at her beauty before she disappeared from his life.

Miles opened the door and stepped inside the bedchamber. She had left the bedcurtains open and a night candle burning on the bedside table. Noticing the trunk in the middle of the chamber, he inspected its contents and then approached the bed.

Princess Amber looked even more beautiful in sleep. Her silver-blond hair was splayed across the pillow, and her pink lips were parted slightly.

Miles felt a twinge of guilt. He had behaved badly and hurt her feelings, but he could not allow her to pry his heart open.

Brenna lay in an early grave. That was enough of love for him.

The princess had meant no harm, though. She had merely been charming him as any guest would.

Miles reached to pull the coverlet up. One plump

breast had escaped the nightgown's skimpy bodice. His gaze drifted lower to her slender waist and the soft curve of her hip, the sheer material exposing her nakedness beneath the gown.

An ache grew within him. Deep. Primal. Touching his soul.

Longing filled him, a yearning to take her nipple between his lips—kissing, licking, sucking upon it. Awaken her with an insistent throbbing between her thighs. Bury himself deep within her moist softness.

Steeling himself against temptation, Miles snuffed the night candle and slipped out of her chamber as quietly as he had slipped in. He decided to wait a few days before returning her to London.

Chapter 3

Lilacs scented the air. Amber awakened to their distinctive perfume, her favorite. Someone had snuffed out her night candle and placed a vase of lilacs on the bedside table.

A parchment lay beside the vase. Only two words had been written on it: *Forgive me*.

A weight lifted from her heart. The earl's pain had incited his outburst, and now he regretted his words. From this moment, she would remember that his situation demanded her patience.

In spite of his injury, Miles Montgomery attracted her. The earl was a handsome, virile man. An aura of mystery surrounded him.

He needed her.

She needed him.

He would protect her.

She would heal his pain.

Together, they would build a life and raise a dozen children. In time, love would blossom between them. All she needed to do was convince the earl to marry her.

Amber took special care with her appearance. She chose a petal pink morning gown because men adored women in pink and brushed her hair away from her face, securing it at the nape of her neck with a pink ribbon.

Inspecting herself in the cheval mirror, Amber pinched her cheeks for color. Then she left her bedchamber and walked to the dining room.

"Good morning, Just-Pebbles," Amber greeted the majordomo. She noted the earl's absence and wondered where he was.

"Good morning, Your Highness." The majordomo rushed forward and escorted her to the chair she had occupied the previous evening.

A white rose and a red rose lay crossed on the table in front of her. She stared at them, a soft smile on her lips.

"Are these for me?"

"His Lordship left those before going for his morning ride," Pebbles answered. "In the language of flowers, crossing a white and red rose means unity."

"What do lilacs mean?"

"Lilacs represent the first stirrings of love." The majordomo smiled. "I hope you are hungry, Your Highness."

"I am famished." A blush heated her face when she added, "You need not send Molly to pack my belongings."

At the sideboard Pebbles filled a plate with baked eggs, ham, and a roll with butter. He served her a cup of coffee but paused before returning to his position at the sideboard.

"Your Highness, may I say how very pleased I am that you will be staying with us."

"Thank you, Just-Pebbles."

"The earl—"

"What about me?" Miles asked, walking into the dining room.

"Her Highness asked if you would be joining her for breakfast," Pebbles lied, and winked at her.

Amber watched the earl crossing the room. She admired his broad shoulders tapering to a lean waist and his well-muscled thighs in the breeches he wore.

Miles nodded to her and walked to the sideboard. He poured himself a cup of coffee and then joined her at the table.

"Good morning, Amber."

"Good morning, Miles."

"I trust you slept well."

"Yes, thank you." Amber gave him a shy smile. "Thank you for the flowers and the note of apology."

The earl registered surprise before shuttering his expression. He shifted his gaze to the majordomo.

"I have forgotten the preserves," Pebbles mumbled, and hurried out of the dining room.

Amber blushed with embarrassment and dropped her gaze to her plate. The earl had not left her the flowers or the note of apology. His servants had felt sorry for her. They had meant well, but she despised being pitied.

"A ruble for your thoughts," Miles said, his tone teasing.

Feeling like a fool, Amber managed a polite smile. "You did not leave me the flowers or the note." She set her napkin on the table. "Please, excuse me, my lord. I must finish my packing."

Miles reached out and his hand covered hers. "Don't leave. I want you to stay and become better acquainted."

Amber felt confused. His touch on her hand sent anticipation skittering down her spine, every nerve aware of his masculinity. Sergei had touched her hand many times, but she had never felt like this. If they made love, his body would cover hers as his hand now covered her hand. She felt a melting sensation in the pit of her stomach.

Though unable to put a name to her feelings, Amber knew she wanted this man to be her husband. And her wanting had nothing to do with her desperate situation or her inexperience with men.

"I *did* leave you the flowers and the note."

Amber looked into his eyes and saw no pity in his expression. She knew he was lying but loved him for it.

"I will stay if you dine with me instead of watching," Amber told him. "You need not wear your mask, either. I do not fear scars."

Miles inclined his head, acknowledging her sentiment though not agreeing to it.

"Since my eighteenth birthday several men have sent me flowers," Amber said, pretending to believe his lie, "but none have meant as much as yours."

"Why should my flowers be special?" Miles asked, skeptical amusement appearing on his face.

"Your gift is special because it comes from you." Amber saw that she had caught him off guard.

"You scarcely know me."

"We met only yesterday," she agreed, "but I feel as though I have known you longer." Amber knew she had spoken too boldly when he lifted his hand from hers. "Will you take me on a tour of your home?"

"Some pressing work requires my attention," Miles hedged. "You may wander wherever you will."

"Can you not even spare one hour? We can become better acquainted. I promise to keep you no longer than an hour."

"Very well." His reluctance was obvious, but she didn't have time for a long courtship.

Miles spoke of inconsequential matters while she finished her breakfast. Then he stood and offered his hand as if inviting her to dance.

A twinge of excitement shot through her. She placed her hand in his and rose from her chair.

"Shall we start on this floor, Your Highness, and work our way up?"

"I want to see the kitchen," Amber said.

"The kitchen?" He sounded surprised.

"Baking relaxes me." Amber wondered, not for the first time, why people were always surprised to learn that royalty enjoyed simple pleasures. "Princes and princesses do not pass their lives wearing crowns and marching around palaces."

"Thank you for enlightening me about that."

Large windows flooded the spacious kitchen with light. Set with cook's equipment, an enormous pine table stood in the middle of the room. There were stoves and ovens and an open hearth, complete with drip pan and cauldron and kettle. On a side wall hung copper pots and pans.

The staff stopped working when they walked into the room. Cooks and maids and footmen stared in obvious surprise at the earl and his guest.

"Your Highness, I present Arden Hall's head cook, Mrs. Meade," the earl said.

The woman curtsied to her.

"I thank you for the delicious meals you have prepared for me," Amber said.

"Her Highness didn't eat very much last night," Mrs. Meade said, giving the earl a pointed look.

Miles grinned. "The fault belongs entirely to me."

The friendly relationship between the earl and his servants surprised Amber. *Pleasantly.* If her uncle's cook had spoken to him so familiarly, Uncle Fedor would have beaten the woman.

"I wonder if my invading your domain would create a problem?" Amber asked the cook.

Mrs. Meade looked puzzled.

"Baking relaxes the princess," Miles explained, drawing surprised looks from the staff.

Recovering herself, Mrs. Meade smiled. "Your Highness is welcome here."

"I would like to bake something special for His Lordship. Tomorrow, perhaps?"

"We will look forward to your presence."

"We'll go this way," Miles said, his hand at the small of her back, guiding her out of the kitchen and down the corridor. "The painter's passage leads to the south drawing room."

"You know your kitchen staff," Amber remarked.

"Of course, I know them." Miles gave her a puzzled look. "Mrs. Meade has been in Montgomery service since I was a boy. I also know the footmen, maids, gardeners, coachmen, and stableboys."

"Uncle Fedor never bothered to learn the names of his servants."

The passage was a wide corridor, its floors uncarpeted hardwood, its walls sky blue with white trim. Marble busts and statuary stood on both sides of the passage while ornate portraits hung on the walls.

Amber recognized the busts of Julius Caesar, Aristotle, Zeus, and Socrates. "This appears to be the corridor of the gods," she said. "Where are the ladies?"

"You think I need a few images of women?" Miles asked, amused.

"Aphrodite, Helen, Cleopatra, and Dido would make attractive additions."

"Why do you choose those women?"

Amber cast him a flirtatious smile. "History does not remember well-behaved women."

Miles laughed out loud, his first in four years. He put his arm around her in easy camaraderie and led her into the south drawing room.

Amber gave him a sidelong glance. She liked the feel of his arm around her but would keep that thought to herself.

Oriental carpets, woven in red and gold and ivory, covered the hardwood floor. Upholstered chairs sat in cozy clusters, and neutral beige walls emphasized the artwork.

Next on the tour came the two-story salon, large

enough for a country ball. It had hardwood floors and a carpeted stairway that led to the second floor. At one end of the room was a white marble fireplace. A piano had been set near the hearth.

"Originally, this room was the inner courtyard of the Elizabethan section of the house," Miles told her. "My grandfather enclosed it when he was making renovations."

Amber gestured to the piano. "May I?"

Miles inclined his head.

Settling herself on the bench, Amber flexed her fingers and gave him an apologetic smile. "I have not sat at a piano for months."

She played well, wisely choosing an uplifting song. The melody held a jaunty air and irresistible rhythm. Her music conjured elemental forces—a playful breeze, a chuckling brook, a dancing sunbeam.

Miles applauded when she finished. Falling in with his mood, Amber rose from the bench and curtsied to her audience of one. She stepped closer, a smile on her face, her violet eyes sparkling.

"My lord, will you honor me with a waltz?"

"We have no music."

"We will make our own music."

"I haven't danced in years."

Amber stepped into his arms. "I trust in your ability."

Miles placed his hand in the center of her back. She placed her left hand on his arm and gave him her right hand to hold.

Humming the tune of a waltz, the earl and the princess swirled around the ballroom. He danced with the ease of a man who had waltzed a thousand times. She felt comfortable in his arms and followed his lead as if they had danced together for years.

When their waltz ended, Amber dropped him a throne-room curtsey. Miles bowed and placed a kiss on the back of her hand.

He gestured toward the stairs. "Shall we go to the second floor?"

Amber held out her hand. Miles hesitated for a fraction of a moment and then, to her relief, took her hand in his.

The salon's second level had upholstered benches and chairs placed along walls covered with artwork. Another portrait of the dark-haired woman hung in a position of honor facing the stairs.

"You saw the library yesterday," Miles said, his hand on her back as he guided her toward the corridor.

"I must confess," she said, blushing, "I felt much too nervous to notice anything."

"In that case, welcome to my library."

Amber stepped inside. At one end of the library stood the earl's desk. A giant, five-foot globe rested on a wooden stand, marking the end of the library and the beginning of the earl's office. Over the great hearth's mantel hung still another portrait of the woman.

"My library contains more than forty thousand books," Miles told her. "That includes one Gutenberg Bible and one Shakespeare folio."

"I love reading," Amber said. "Without ever leaving my chair, I can travel to faraway places and long-ago times. Reading eases a person's loneliness for a little while."

"Have you ever felt lonely?"

"I have felt lonely my entire life."

Amber took a fortifying breath and walked across the library. The time had come to face her competition for the earl's affection. Stopping in front of the hearth, she looked up at the portrait. "This woman's image hangs in every chamber."

"Brenna, my late wife," Miles said, his voice suddenly choked with emotion.

"She was very beautiful."

"Yes, Brenna was a beauty."

"Tell me about her."

"Why?"

Amber heard the suspicion in his voice and shifted her gaze to the earl, but his eyes had fixed on the likeness of the other woman. "Your wife must have been special to have inspired such love and devotion," she said. "You cherish her still."

"We met at a ball and fell in love," Miles told her, his gaze on the portrait. "I suppose we were devoted to each other the same as other couples."

"I have never witnessed marital devotion," Amber said, drawing his attention. "My father murdered my mother, and Uncle Fedor locked his wife in an insane asylum."

"I am sorry," Miles said. "This Sergei must have been devoted to you, though."

"I told you last night I would never have married Sergei," Amber reminded him. "My unacknowledged bastardy made me unacceptable to his family. They would have approved of his taking me as his mistress, I suppose."

"If he loved you," Miles said, "Sergei would have defied his family to make you his wife. Forget him."

"That is one reason I left my homeland without bothering to ask for his help."

"Why *did* you leave home?"

Amber gave him an ambiguous smile. "You will know the answer to that if we reach an agreement."

"Tell me why you fear the dark."

She looked at him in surprise. "I do not fear the dark."

"You sleep with a night candle burning and the bed-curtains open."

"I prefer the light," Amber said, "but that does not mean I fear dark, closed places."

Miles cocked a brow at her. "I never used the word *closed*, Princess."

Amber faltered, momentarily at a loss for words. She had good reason to fear dark, closed places but refused to share that weakness with him.

"You will never finish your ledgers if we linger," she said, changing the subject.

"The third floor has the bedchambers, which you have already seen," Miles said, ushering her out of the library.

"Where does that go?" she asked, pointing toward the dark end of the corridor.

"The state bedchamber and the nursery. The fire destroyed the whole east wing. You must never go there."

"You did not restore it?"

"With my wife dead, I saw no need."

"What caused the fire?"

Miles shrugged. "I assume a fallen night candle."

His answer surprised her. "You never investigated?"

"An investigation would not have returned my wife to me."

"I understand."

Amber did *not* understand. If her love had been killed in a fire, she would have wanted to know how the fire started.

"May I walk outside?" she asked.

"You are not my prisoner, Princess."

"Will you join me?"

"I think not." Miles glanced toward the library. "My ledgers demand my attention."

"Thank you for the tour," Amber said, hiding her disappointment.

Leaving him there, Amber walked downstairs to the foyer. She decided to start at the front courtyard and work her way around the manor.

Amber stepped into bright sunshine. There was nary a passing cloud in the sky. Exotic flower fragrances perfumed the air, and masses of greenery bordered the stately brick drive.

Circling the manor to the left, Amber entered the west-facing garden. Lilacs grew against the mansion beneath her bedchamber window. Everywhere she looked was a profusion of color—purple irises, asters in a variety of hues, and roses.

Amber saw a gardener inspecting a sad-looking rosebush. "Good morning," she called.

The man turned at the sound of her voice and instantly doffed his cap. "Good morning, Your Highness."

His greeting surprised her. "You know who I am?"

"Everyone at Arden Hall knows who you are," the man said. "We've been waiting years for you. Now you're here, even if a bit tardy."

Amber blushed at his words, her complexion pinkening to the color of her gown. The earl's retainers seemed to regard her as a cure for what ailed him. She could never fulfill their expectations.

"What is wrong with this rosebush?" she asked, giving it her attention.

"Failure to thrive," the gardener said. "I'll need to remove it."

"Leave the rosebush to me," she told him. "I can cure it."

"How will you do that, Your Highness?"

"My love will coax it back to health."

The man grinned. "You're a true gardener, then?"

"I am that." Amber gave him her sunshine smile. Then she touched the rosebush and said, "Tomorrow I will bring my mandolin and revive your spirit with my music."

"A pleasure to meet you, Your Highness," the gardener said and then walked away.

Amber thought the south-facing grounds looked like paradise. Purple irises abounded in the flower garden. In the foreground on a terraced slope was a sunken garden with an octagonal pool surrounded by yew topiary.

Two rectangular pools edged in solid blocks of yew appeared in the distance. Beyond that stood a small stone building encompassed by a cobblestone wall.

Amber strolled in that direction and found the family chapel and graveyard. She opened the wooden gate and walked down a few stone stairs into the graveyard. How peaceful eternity would prove if she could lie beneath the sod in this secluded place.

Amber wandered the graveyard and read the names of the earl's ancestors. Her heart ached for him when she read his wife's: *Brenna Montgomery, 15th Countess Stratford. August 1793–November 1816. And her unborn child.*

His wife had been pregnant. What a double tragedy for the earl, who, in all probability, had not been in attendance at the funeral due to his own injury.

"I am sorry for your loss, Lady Brenna," Amber whispered to the dead woman, "but I need him now. Rest in peace, for Miles will always love you."

"Get away from my wife!"

Amber whirled around at the sound of the earl's shout. She could see the fury etched across his features.

"Go away." Miles towered over her, his dark gaze cold. "You don't belong here."

"I am sorry."

"Get out."

Frightened and hurt, Amber bolted past him and raced up the stone steps. She looked over her shoulder once and saw the earl with his head bowed and his hands covering his face.

Gulping back tears, Amber ran around the manor to the front drive and through the front door. She burst into the foyer, surprising the majordomo, and dashed for the stairs.

"Your Highness, may I help you?" the majordomo called, hurrying after her.

"No."

Her cry of refusal held all the anguish she had felt during her twenty years. A lifetime of being alone, unwanted, shunned.

Miles stood at his wife's grave, angry with himself for upsetting the princess, angry with the princess for charming him, angry with his wife for dying and putting him in this position.

"My love, you lie in an early grave," he whispered, touching the stone marker, "but I am a flesh-and-blood man." He dropped his hand to his side. "I am sorry, Brenna."

Turning away, Miles walked back to the house. He should never have shouted at the princess. His wife's death wasn't her fault. He would apologize to her later.

Miles went directly to the study to work on his business ledgers. Sometime later, he looked up when the majordomo walked into the room.

"Shall I serve you lunch here, my lord?"

"I'll eat with the princess."

"Her Highness sends her regrets," Pebbles told him, giving him a meaningful look. "She suffers with a headache and is resting in her chamber."

"Serve me here, then."

Apparently, Pebbles had witnessed the princess's return to the house. Her Highness was sulking in her chamber. Well, he had no intention of apologizing to a sulking woman. Brenna had never sulked, and he would not tolerate it in his home.

After lunch Miles started on the estate ledgers. The household ledgers followed that. The next time he looked up, Pebbles was setting the tea tray on the table in front of the settee.

Miles stood and stretched, his muscles protesting the long hours at his desk. He saw the solitary cup and saucer and realized how lonely his life was.

Until the princess arrived.

"Her Highness will not be joining me?"

"Her Highness is taking tea in her chamber."

Later, Miles walked upstairs to dress for dinner. Living in seclusion, he had dispensed with changing his clothes in the evening but, with the princess in residence, had resumed the custom.

Miles glanced at the connecting door and wondered if he should apologize now. After a moment's indecision, he crossed to the door and raised his hand to knock.

Losing his nerve, Miles dropped his hand to his side. He had never been very good with apologies, instead, he would pretend that nothing unpleasant had passed between them.

When he walked into the dining room, Pebbles handed Miles a glass of sherry. He crossed to the windows and looked outside at the night.

Five minutes passed and then another five. Ten minutes became fifteen.

Finally, Miles heard the sound of the princess and turned around, but only a footman had entered and now gestured to the majordomo. He whispered something to Pebbles, who nodded.

"My lord, Her Highness sends her regrets," Pebbles told him.

The princess wasn't sulking. She was avoiding him.

He had hurt her feelings, and now she preferred to remain in her chamber. Did she believe they could marry and produce children with her hiding in her chamber?

And then Miles knew. The princess would be leaving him.

That was what he wanted, wasn't it?

No. He did not want her to leave.

He did not want to pass his days alone.

He did not want his life reduced to a solitary cup and saucer.

"Hold dinner." Leaving the dining room, Miles walked upstairs but paused in the corridor outside her chamber. He had not apologized to anyone in years and felt uncertain about comforting a young woman.

Before he could talk himself out of it, Miles knocked on the door. He heard her call, touched his mask, and stepped inside.

Amber registered momentary surprise and then, like a true aristocrat, schooled her features into an expressionless mask. "Good evening, my lord." She looked away. "I apologize for not joining you, but my headache is no cause for alarm."

Miles sauntered across the bedchamber and stood in front of her chair where she could not avoid his gaze. He almost laughed out loud when she evaded him by returning her attention to the handkerchief she had been embroidering.

"I would never have guessed you were a coward."

Amber faltered for a moment but recovered her composure quickly. "Bravery is the child of desperation," she said, without looking up.

"How philosophical of you." Miles watched her jab the needle into the delicate cloth. "I thought you sewed poorly."

"I do." Amber attacked the handkerchief with the needle and yanked the thread through the cloth.

"I hope you aren't pretending the handkerchief is me."

That made her smile. "My lord—"

"Miles," he corrected her.

She ignored his correction. "I have decided to return to London. Sooner rather than later."

"Are you leaving because I shouted at you?"

"I am intruding on your privacy."

Miles stared at her. She was saying what he had been thinking yesterday. Only now—

"I bluster at people around me," he told her. "You really ought to bluster back."

"Blustering would be unseemly for a princess," Amber said, refusing to look at him. "Especially a princess in my position."

"What position is that?"

Amber looked up, her startling violet gaze meeting his. "A penniless, unacknowledged bastard."

His expression softened on her. "You are too hard on yourself."

"I see myself as the world sees me." Amber returned to her mutilation of the handkerchief.

"I do not see you like that."

"You do not see me at all." Amber set the handkerchief down and looked at him. "You mourn for your wife. An arrangement between us can never work."

"I see you all too clearly," Miles said, his tone rueful. "Brenna has been dead four years."

"Nevertheless, you mourn for her. I have no wish to intrude."

"Forgive my temper," Miles apologized. "If you stay a few more days, I promise not to bluster at you again. I *do* want to become better acquainted."

Amber stared at him so long that Miles thought she would refuse. Finally, she gave him a tentative smile and inclined her head.

"Will you dine with me?"

"I have not changed for dinner."

Miles offered his hand. "Please dine with me."

"Will you eat or sip your wine?"

"I will eat with you."

"Will you remove your mask?"

"No."

Accepting this minor concession, Amber placed her hand in his. Together, they walked downstairs to the dining room.

"Have I told you about my family?" Miles asked conversationally, as a footman began to serve their meal.

Amber shook her head.

"My younger sister Isabelle married John Saint-Germain, the Duke of Avon," Miles told her. "Isabelle and John have been blessed with six children. By the way, John introduced me to Rudolf."

"I love children," Amber said. "I always wanted brothers and sisters."

"You lived with your cousins," Miles reminded her.

"Only Rudolf would play with me or take me places," Amber told him. "The others did not want a female listening to their conversations."

Miles smiled. "I can see that your presence would inhibit man-talk. Who else cared for you?"

A smile of remembrance touched her lips. "Hilda, my uncle's cook, taught me to bake. Ivan, my uncle's gardener, taught me everything he knew."

Hilda the cook? Ivan the gardener? What kind of companions were those for a princess?

"What about friends your own age?" Miles asked.

"I already explained the circumstances of my birth and my family history." Amber dropped her gaze to her plate. "In my society, I was not considered an appropriate companion."

"I did not intend to sadden you," Miles said, his hand covering hers.

"You did not sadden me." Amber lifted her gaze to his. "I was mostly happy. I suppose I did not know any better."

Miles flicked a wrist at Pebbles, who whispered to the footman. The two retainers left the dining room and closed the door behind them.

"What about the czar?" Miles asked.

"Every New Year, Czar Alexander sends me a letter and a gift," Amber said, her expression becoming ani-

mated. "When I was twelve, the czar sent me his miniature by way of an artist who painted *my* miniature. The
czar wanted to see what I looked like. I cherish his
miniature and his letters more than anything else."

That surprised Miles. "You never met him?"

"The czar is much too important and busy to grant
insignificant me an interview," Amber defended her father against his tone of surprised censure. Her smile faltered as she said, "I had hoped . . ." She shrugged,
leaving her thought unfinished.

"What had you hoped?"

"I thought the czar would send for me when I became marriageable at eighteen. He never did, though."

Miles suffered the urge to throttle the unfeeling
monster who had snubbed his own daughter. "If the
czar had sent for you," he said, "we would never have
met."

Amber blushed. "I have been talking too much."

"I like the sound of your voice."

Miles stared at her hauntingly beautiful face. He had
been alone four years. She had been alone forever.

"Why did you leave Russia?" he asked. "And why do
you need a husband?"

"I would prefer to discuss that another time," she
told him, her gaze pleading for understanding. "I
promise I am a virgin."

"I did not mean to imply otherwise." Miles let the
topic die. "I enjoyed our waltz this morning."

"I enjoyed it, too."

The remainder of their evening passed pleasantly.
Much later, when the household had settled down for
the night, Miles paced his bedchamber and wondered
what to do about Amber. He would always love Brenna,
but he could not let the princess go.

Unable to resist the image of her asleep, Miles
donned his mask and crossed to the connecting door.

After listening for a moment, he stepped inside her bedchamber and paused. Again, the princess slept with the bedcurtains open and a night candle burning.

On silent feet, Miles advanced on the bed and stared at the face of an angel framed by silvery hair. Temptation rode him hard. Trying not to awaken her, he drew the coverlet back, and his breath caught raggedly in his throat.

The same impudent breast with its pink nipple had escaped the nightgown's bodice. With one finger, he caressed the silken swell and glided his fingertip across the nipple, making her sigh in her sleep.

She was soft. Incredibly, exquisitely soft.

Miles noticed something in her hand and took a closer look. The princess was clutching the miniature of a handsome older man. Too old to be Sergei. And then he realized the man was Czar Alexander, the father she had never met.

For the first time in four years, Miles felt pity for someone other than himself. He drew the coverlet up and touched his lips to her forehead, inhaling deeply of her scent. Lilacs, sunshine, and woman.

Miles glanced at the burning candle. The princess feared the dark. He feared a fire in the night.

Miles snuffed the candle, throwing the bedchamber into darkness. He would leave his door ajar. If the princess awakened in the night, he would comfort her.

Chapter 4

Perfect pink-tipped peaks—tempting him, enticing him, beckoning him.

"Good God," Miles muttered, wishing he had never seen her naked breast.

Sitting at his desk, Miles tried to concentrate on the numbers in his business ledger but saw her breast in his mind's eye. He forced himself to focus on the ledger. Apparently, the lush roundness of the number eight had appealed to his senses. He had drawn dark nipples in the middle of each circle that formed the number.

How would he explain this artwork to his London clerks when they arrived at Arden Hall for their next quarterly meeting? What came next? Would his sevens and eights start fornicating? He would be bankrupt before the first snow fell.

Bedding the princess would solve his problem, but he could not do that unless they struck a bargain. A serious discussion between him and the princess seemed imminent.

Brought low by a teat, Miles thought, disgusted with himself, as he tossed the quill down. He should keep his distance from her. She had him dreaming about intimacies best forgotten.

He had loved his wife.

Completely. Exclusively. Forever.

The scent of sunshine and lilacs, the czar's miniature clutched in a small hand, and the burning night candle had conspired to soften his heart. He was becoming much too attached to the princess. Her beauty and her innocence were enchanting, weaving a web of hope and desire around him, entangling him in her life.

Concentrating on the ledger proved impossible. Miles surrendered to his restlessness and wandered to the window. A creature of shadows for four long years, he had the unexpected urge to feel the sun on his face.

Miles opened the window and inhaled deeply of the early summer day. A warm, dry breeze carried the mingling scents of roses and lavender and lilacs. His gardens were a paradise, lush shades of green adorning primary- and pastel-colored flowers.

The faintest of sounds wafted through the air to him. The soprano tone with a violin pitch meant the princess was playing the mandolin. Her song held a bewitching charm. The melody flowed smoothly into elemental sounds—falling water, rustling leaves, waltzing wildflowers.

Miles touched his mask and left his study. Pebbles, wearing a rapturous expression on his face, stood in the foyer with the door open, listening to the music.

"Where is the princess?" Miles asked.

"Her Highness is serenading the rosebush."

"What rosebush?"

"The sick one," Pebbles answered. "Her Highness told the gardener she could restore its health with her music and love."

Miles stared at his retainer a long moment and then, shaking his head, walked outside. His whole household had been behaving oddly since the princess arrived.

In the courtyard, Miles paused to savor the warmth of the sun on his face. He could not imagine why he had hidden in the shadows for so long. And then the princess beckoned him with her mandolin.

Miles walked around the mansion but paused to touch his mask before entering the rear garden. The music stopped abruptly, and then he heard the princess.

"You seem more relaxed," she said. "Do you feel better?"

To whom was she speaking?

Miles stepped into the garden.

Amber sat on a blanket near the rosebush. She leaned close to it and plucked a few leaves.

"That did *not* hurt. Tomorrow, I will sing you a song about a nightingale who loved a rose. You can imagine the problems involved in *that* relationship."

Miles smiled. The princess was speaking to his rosebush.

"I see another friend." Amber set the mandolin aside and approached a solitary flower beneath a nearby tree, saying in a soothing voice, "Shy pansy, have you no friends to keep you company? I know how lonely life is without friends."

I know loneliness, too, Miles thought. Had fate sent him a lady to ease the pain in his heart?

"Amber?" Miles started across the garden. When she looked at him, he felt his spirits lift as if an angel had touched him. An angel with the body of a goddess.

"Good day, my lord."

Amusement lit his dark eyes. "You were speaking to the rosebush."

"Like all of God's creatures," Amber told him, "plants thrive with love."

"Would you care to walk to the river?"

"I would love to walk anywhere with you."

Miles gestured to the woodland. "The path to the river lies through those trees."

Placing her hand in his, Amber walked beside him across the manicured lawn. She glanced sidelong at his chiseled profile. From this angle, the earl appeared uninjured. His nose was straight, his lips full, his chin strong.

They passed through a row of enormous oaks that separated park from woodland. The path was cool and shaded and perfumed. Wildflowers and moss scented the air.

Accompanied by broadleaved beechwoods and ash, long-lived oaks crowded the woodland. Silver-white birch trees marked their path to the river where graceful willows offered shade.

"What a peaceful spot," Amber said. "Do you come here often?"

"I haven't been here in a long time." Miles removed his jacket and placed it beneath the sweeping branches of a willow.

"Thank you, my lord." Amber sat on the jacket and then patted the spot beside her in invitation.

"Escaping the house feels good," Miles said, accepting her invitation.

Amber made no reply. She assumed he had been sitting in the dark for four years.

"Why is your home called Arden Hall?" she asked, opting for a safe topic. "Your name is Montgomery."

"Arden Hall belonged to my mother's family. She was an heiress. Since her children would be Montgomerys, my father decided the manor should remain Arden Hall, and the Arden family would never be forgotten."

"Your father sounds like a generous man."

"Yes, he was that." Miles stood and walked a few paces toward the river. He picked up a stone and skimmed it across the top of the water. "I haven't done that since my boyhood."

Amber heard the smile in his voice. She stood and

walked toward him. Purposely, she positioned herself on the injured side of his face.

"You have inherited your father's generosity."

"You believe I am generous?"

"You have offered me your hospitality."

Miles glanced at her. "Prince Rudolf can be quite persuasive."

"Do you regret opening your home to me?" Amber asked, and then wished to recall her words. One should never ask a question unless prepared to hear a truthful answer.

"On the contrary, I enjoy your company."

Relief swept through her. The earl had spoken the words she wanted to hear, but had he spoken truthfully or politely? She would think before speaking in the future.

"Tell me, Princess. If you could be granted one wish, what would it be?"

Amber dropped her gaze, undecided whether to speak honestly or not. She did not want to frighten him.

"No wishes?"

"I have always wished for love," she admitted, lifting her gaze to his. "I wanted to be loved for myself, not my so-called beauty."

"Most women would sell their souls for your face," Miles remarked, skimming another stone across the water.

"Then most women are fools to wish for something so fleeting," Amber said, her tone mirroring her bitterness. "My beauty burdens me."

Miles turned to look at her. Their gazes touched. With one long finger, he traced a path down the side of her cheek.

"I never realized that life could be as difficult for a beautiful woman as it is for a plain one," he said.

"Life can be difficult for everyone," she replied.

"Misery makes no distinction between prince and pauper."

Miles inclined his head, accepting her philosophy.

"For what would you wish?" Amber asked, already knowing his answer.

"I would turn back time and have Brenna with me again."

"If that wasn't possible?"

"Until three days ago, I would have wished for death."

Amber tilted her head back to gaze fully into his face. "And now?"

"Now I would wish for a woman to care for me despite my scars." Miles inched his face closer to hers. "I want an heir."

He was going to kiss her.

Amber trembled, her heart beating wildly. Excitement shot through her body and sparked to life in the pit of her stomach. The earl's dark gaze held hers captive, and an instant later their breaths mingled.

Firm and warm, his lips touched hers in a gentle kiss. He smelled fresh, like pine trees and mountain heather.

Miles slipped an arm around her, drawing her against his body. His free hand moved to the back of her head and held her steady. His masculine essence—strength, power, dominance—surrounded her without threatening.

His lips enticed her, persuading her to return his kiss. And when she did, the tempo of his kiss changed, becoming possessive and demanding. *Hungry.*

Amber slid the palms of her hands up his chest to loop around his neck. She followed his lead, pressing herself against him, returning his kiss in kind. And then some.

He captured her whole being, and the world ceased to exist for her. His lips, his hands, his body became her universe.

Surrendering herself, Amber parted her lips at the

first touch of his tongue. A throaty moan escaped her when he thrust his tongue inside her mouth, tasting her sweetness. A melting sensation in her lower regions fanned the spark of desire into a flame.

Miles held her tighter, the hand at the small of her back dropping to her buttocks, pressing her against his arousal. The hand at the back of her head slid down her body to caress the rounded side of her breast through the thin material of her gown.

And then the kiss ended.

Miles stared at her dazed expression. He drew her against his chest, holding her close, giving her a chance to recover. For long moments, they cast one shadow. Then he dropped a kiss on the crown of her head, tilted her chin up, and said, "Thank you for the gift of your first kiss."

Amber felt an embarrassed blush heating her cheeks. "Thank you for accepting my gift and making the giving so pleasurable."

"You do not regret giving your first kiss to a scarred beast?"

Amber read the anxiety couched in his expression and touched his uninjured cheek. "You are a man, not a beast," she told him. "Your scars mark you a hero. I know no other man with the courage to defy fire to save the woman he loved."

"Not even Sergei?"

She gave him a rueful smile. "Especially not Sergei."

Miles stared into her disarming violet eyes and wondered if her flattering words were sincere or designed to entice him to the altar. Even a scarred beast wanted to be desired for himself, not used exclusively for whatever reason she needed a husband. Reluctant to relinquish her, he put an arm around her shoulder and led her toward the woodland path.

"Your Highness, the time for negotiations has arrived," Miles said. "Tonight, we will discuss our future."

* * *

How will the princess react to my proposal? Miles wondered, sipping his sherry, waiting for her arrival in the
dining room.

Proposal? His offer smelled like a proposition.

But what else could he do to test her sincerity? No
man wanted to be used for what he could do for the
woman.

The princess wasn't searching for a fortune or a title,
but she did want his name. He had no wish for a wife
who pretended tenderness and passion. The bargain he
intended to negotiate would strip the pretense from
her behavior. He would know if she was developing a
fondness for him or playing a role to deceive him.

Her mother had lacked moral fiber. Could the princess
have inherited that flaw? Would her acceptance of his
proposal mean she lacked morals . . . or that she suffered from desperation?

"Good evening, Miles."

"Good evening, Amber."

With an appreciative eye, Miles gave her a quick pe-
rusal. She had dressed to please, to attract, to entice
him into a marriage proposal.

Her gown was violet silk, matching her eye color, and
its bodice was cut low to reveal the swell of her alabaster
breasts. She had brushed her fair hair back and fashioned it in a knot at the nape of her delicate neck. Her
lack of jewels enhanced her natural beauty.

"I understand you have been busy this afternoon,"
Miles said, assisting her into the chair beside his.

"I have been baking," Amber said, gifting him with
her sunshine smile.

"Baking what?"

"A surprise."

"I can hardly wait." Miles cast her a sidelong glance
and teased, "So, Princess, do you always talk to plants?"

"Plants love voices and music." Her eyes sparkled

with merriment when she added, "I make the plants healthy and happy, and then I eat them."

Miles laughed out loud, drawing surprised looks from his servants. He stared at the salad and asked, "Is this one of your friends?"

Amber gave him an ambiguous smile. "I will never reveal that, or you might not eat it."

"You are incorrigible."

"I do not understand *incorrigible*."

"Beyond correction," Miles told her. "Your humor proves your naughtiness."

Amber gave him her sunshine smile, as if he had just given her a remarkable compliment.

During dinner Miles spoke of inconsequential matters, trivial topics designed to relax her guard before their negotiations. Though he refused to reconsider his actions, Miles began to doubt the wisdom of such machinations. Princess Amber was unlike any society lady he had ever met, including Brenna. She enjoyed working in the kitchen and getting her hands dirty in the garden. If she cared about a rosebush, could she care for him?

When their plates had been cleared, Amber gestured to Pebbles, who left the dining room to fetch her special dessert. She hoped the earl enjoyed her offering enough to consider her a welcome addition to his family. Her uncle's cook had always told her that the road to a man's heart was through his stomach. She was putting that theory to the test.

Pebbles set her culinary masterpiece on the table between them. Puff pastry surrounded a warm pudding, rich with cream and an assortment of sugared fruit.

"*Guriev kasha* is the king of all Russian desserts," Amber said, serving him herself. She watched him take his first bite.

"This tastes delicious." Miles sounded surprised. "What are the ingredients?"

"Eye of newt and toe of frog," Amber teased him, quoting Shakespeare, "wool of bat and tongue of dog, adder's fork and blind-worm's sting, lizard's leg and howlet's wing."

"For a charm of powerful trouble," Miles continued the Shakespearean quote, "Like a hell-broth boil and bubble."

"Double, double toil and trouble . . ."

"Fire, burn; and cauldron, bubble."

Both burst into laughter. Amber glanced at the servants and noted their pleased expressions.

"What is it, really?"

Amber leaned close and whispered, "A secret."

Without thinking, Miles planted a chaste kiss on her lips. He surprised her, the servants, and himself.

"I shouldn't have done that," he apologized.

"You did not regret stealing a kiss this morning," she reminded him, making the servants smile.

Miles changed the subject. "Did you know that Stratford is Shakespeare's home?"

"Will you take me to see his haunts?"

"I would love to give you the grand tour. Tomorrow?"

"I would like that very much." Amber glanced at the shocked majordomo and knew their outing marked the earl's first public appearance since the fire.

How would the townspeople react to the masked earl? Would they be friendly or fear him? Amber banished the disturbing thought that their first public appearance together could prove a disaster. She would worry about that when it happened.

"Shall we retire to the drawing room?" Miles suggested.

Amber stood, wondering what sort of negotiations the earl had in mind. Their situation seemed straightforward. Either he would marry her or not.

And if not?

She would return to London and search for a husband, but she would miss the earl. He was a strong man who had known great pain. She had known great pain, too. Finding another man like him would prove impossible.

Pebbles served them from the porcelain coffee service. The majordomo left the drawing room, closing the door behind, giving them privacy.

Miles paced back and forth in front of the hearth, which Amber did not consider an encouraging sign. She noted in dismay that he moved to the high-backed armchair rather than sit beside her on the settee.

"Why do you fear the dark?" Miles asked, catching her off guard.

"I do not fear the dark," she lied. "I prefer the light."

He touched his mask. "Do you want to remain at Arden Hall permanently?"

"Is this an invitation?"

Miles inclined his head.

"You will not regret this," she said, her smile filled with sunshine.

"Your answer is *yes?*"

Amber inclined her head.

"I don't believe you have considered the consequences of remaining here," he told her.

"Are you trying to dissuade me?"

"I want you to make an informed decision. You will never replace my wife."

Amber felt like weeping, her dream of a loving family evaporating like fog beneath the noonday sun. Yet, what choice did she have? What the earl offered was better than what awaited her in Russia.

Amber fixed her gaze on the carpet lest he see her pain. She had learned long ago never to show weakness, and emotional pain was a weakness that could be used against her.

"You won't regret this decision in a year or five or ten?" Miles asked.

"I will be a devoted wife," she promised him.

"I have not asked you to marry me."

Amber shot to her feet. "What do you mean?"

"I want an heir," Miles answered, "but neither of us knows if you are fertile or barren. I will marry you when you carry my child."

"How dare you suggest such a contemptible, self-serving arrangement," Amber exploded, sounding every inch the royal.

His expression and manner remained mild. "Blustering won't help."

"Blustering, my arse. You want me to give you my virtue without guarantee. You risk nothing."

"That is my offer." Miles folded his arms across his chest. "Take it or leave it."

Now Amber paced back and forth in front of the hearth. She knew she had no choice. Returning to London was not a viable option. Rudolf could not protect her indefinitely. She needed a husband's name and a child growing inside her. Only then would she feel safe.

"I agree to your terms," Amber said, her tone frigid. "Tonight?"

The earl gave her a puzzled look.

Embarrassment stained her cheeks. *"You know."*

"Tonight is ill-favored. I will choose the time." Miles gave her a speculative look. "You are unusually beautiful and carry royal blood in your veins. Why do you agree to such terms?"

"Do you believe beauty is a blessing?" Amber asked, her tone bitter. "My so-called beauty is a cross I bear. I wish I looked like Macbeth's witches."

"Why?"

"Bastards have desires and wishes like those born properly."

"And yours are?"

"I wanted a husband and children and love," Amber

admitted. "Unfortunately, I was born with beauty instead of legitimacy and must settle for a husband and children and no love."

"Couldn't you have had the same in Russia?"

"No family would welcome the bastard daughter of an adulteress," Amber told him. "Uncle Fedor would have sold me to the wealthiest aristocrat who wanted a noble mistress."

The earl looked away as if ashamed to meet her gaze. "Is that the reason you need a husband? Surely, your uncle will not follow you to England. Why didn't you remain in London and seek marriage with a more suitable gentleman?"

"There is more to my story," Amber said, "but that is for the ears of my husband only."

"Perhaps you should tell me everything. You *do* need a husband, after all."

"I will keep my own counsel." The sunshine was missing from the smile she gave him. "You *do* need an heir, my lord."

Miles inclined his head.

"I feel tired." Amber needed to get away from him to compose herself. "You will excuse me, please."

"I have upset you." Miles stood and took a step toward her but stopped when she stepped back.

"I am not easily upset," she told him. "I have many years' experience with people who believe I am inferior and deserve no respect."

Like you was left unspoken.

Amber felt his gaze on her until she escaped the drawing room. She struggled against tears and won the battle, her anger keeping her sorrow at bay.

How dare the earl put her in the position of becoming his mistress. Did the man have no morals? No shame? What prevented him from tossing her aside once she had given herself to him? What if she swelled with his child and he refused to marry her?

In that event, Cousin Rudolf would force the earl to marry her, but their marriage would prove disastrous. She needed to make him love her.

Wishing bells. The silver and gold bells the czar had sent her on her tenth birthday.

Blessed with salt consecrated on Saint Stephan's Day, the bells would carry her wish to heaven. She had already written the words *true love* inside one of them but had feared hanging it lest the sound draw her uncle's attention.

She didn't know if she believed the legend. Surely, hanging the bell in the window would do no harm.

Amber chose a red ribbon, the color of love, and slipped it through the tiny bell's loop. Standing on a chair, she tied the ribbon to the rod and then opened the window.

A gentle breeze shook the bell. Its delicate tinkling made her smile.

Amber fell asleep listening to the bell's tinkling and imagining the love its magic would bring.

Meanwhile, the Earl of Stratford paced his bedchamber and worried. How could he have agreed to escort her on a tour of Stratford? He had not left Arden Hall since the fire. How would the townspeople react to the sight of his mask? Would they recoil in horror, or would they treat him with the respectful deference they had always shown him?

Miles knew he was trapped. To cancel the excursion meant admitting to cowardice.

Doubts about the bargain he had made with the princess crept into his troubled thoughts. He had behaved badly and hurt her feelings. Her acceptance of his unreasonable demand shamed him.

Why would the princess agree to his bargain? What secret was she keeping? Was she immoral or desperate?

How could he marry her? Scarred beast that he was, he could never make her happy. Still, Miles wanted an heir to carry the Montgomery name. His face was scarred, but his seed was healthy. Why shouldn't he desire an heir? Every man reached for immortality.

Judging enough time had passed to insure the princess slept, Miles slipped into her bedchamber. The bedcurtains were open and the night candle burned, as it had the previous nights.

Miles heard a tinkling sound. On silent feet, he crossed the chamber and saw the tiny bell dangling from the rod and wondered at its significance.

Approaching the bed, Miles stared at the princess. Her beauty demanded gowns and jewels and seasons in London. He could give her the gowns and the jewels, but the seasons in London would prove impossible.

Without thinking, Miles reached to draw the coverlet back. He stopped himself, though.

The princess had agreed to give herself to him but needed time to consider the enormity of what she had promised him. If he touched her now, he would be unable to control his desire to bed her. Once he had taken her into his bed, he would never let her go.

After dropping a chaste kiss on her forehead, Miles snuffed the night candle and returned to his bedchamber. He left the door ajar lest she awakened in the night and needed his comfort.

Chapter 5

Where is she?

Miles paced back and forth across the foyer, irritated to be kept waiting like an eager suitor. He paused to glance at his pocket watch, having instructed the princess to meet him in the foyer at eleven o'clock. Her Highness was five bloody minutes late.

"Don't you have anything to do?" Miles growled at his majordomo.

Pebbles grinned. "No, my lord."

"Find something."

"My lord, who will—?"

"I am capable of opening my own bloody door."

"Yes, my lord." Pebbles disappeared down the corridor, but the sound of his chuckles drifted back to the foyer.

Terminating the disrespectful old codger seemed like a good idea. On the other hand, Pebbles had served the Montgomery family his whole life and would have no place to go.

And then Miles realized the foolishness of his thoughts. He wasn't irritated with the princess or his majordomo.

Anxiety coiled like a snake inside him, inciting him

to strike those unfortunates who crossed his path. Why shouldn't he feel nervous? Four years had passed since his last visit to Stratford. Miles wondered how the townspeople would react to the forbidding sight of him. They had known him as an affable peer of the realm. That man had died with his wife in the inferno, vanishing forever into a scarred and bitter beast. Perhaps he should cancel their outing.

Hearing footsteps on the stairs, Miles turned to see Amber, and thoughts of canceling disappeared. He had never seen a woman lovelier than she.

The princess wore a high-waisted pale pink gown, embroidered with white roses at the neckline and hem. She carried a white bonnet with pale pink ribbons.

"Are you prepared for your tour of Shakespeare's Stratford?" Miles asked, with a smile of greeting.

Amber returned his smile. "Quite prepared, my lord."

Taking her hand in his, Miles escorted her outside to the courtyard, where the coach and driver awaited them. Normally, he would have driven himself, but having no idea how the townspeople would react, he had decided to remain hidden within the safety of the coach.

Miles helped Amber into the coach and then climbed inside. He faced a choice. Sit beside or opposite her? He sat beside her.

"Tell me about the bell hanging in your window," Miles said conversationally. "Are you practicing the black arts in my home?"

Amber laughed, the softly seductive sound he was beginning to love. "The bell is a Russian superstition," she explained. "The tinkling of the bell frightens evil spirits away and brings the household good luck."

"I thank you for thinking of my household's well-being," he teased her. "I cannot imagine how we survived before your arrival."

"I believe I arrived just in time," she said, responding to his lighthearted tone.

"In time to save us from what?"

Amber gave him an ambiguous smile but said nothing.

"Your smile reminds me of the *Mona Lisa*," he whispered against her ear.

"Thank you, Leonardo."

Traveling north on Shipston Road, their coach passed woodland and meadow and riverbank. Wildflowers bloomed in rioting colors against a green background. Along the dense roadside hedgerow grew wild arum and Queen Anne's lace. Pale pink and violet lady's smock colored the fringes of the woodland while yellow dandelions dotted the rolling meadows. Scarlet poppy, blue iris, and orange balsam kept company with the willows along the riverbank.

Their coach crossed the Clopton Bridge, bringing them into Stratford proper. They traveled Bridge Street until the road forked into Henley Street.

Miles noted the passersby pause to watch his coach. He flicked a worried glance at the princess, but she seemed oblivious to the attention they were receiving.

His driver stopped in front of a half-timbered, Tudor-style building. Miles climbed down and then assisted the princess, his hands lingering on her waist a moment longer than necessary.

He stared into her eyes. How would she handle a negative reaction from the townspeople?

"Shakespeare entered the world in this house," Miles said, gesturing to the building. "The timber came from the Forest of Arden and the stone from Wilmcote. That attached building was his father's glove-making shop."

"Are we allowed inside?"

Miles inclined his head and opened the door. Inside, a man sat on a stool.

"Your Lordship," the man exclaimed in obvious surprise, bolting off the stool and doffing his cap.

Miles flicked another anxious glance at the princess

and then said to the man, "Good day, sir. I would like to show my guest the Bard's birthplace."

"Shall I show you around, my lord?"

"I can manage the tour."

"Very good, my lord." The man hesitated for a fraction of a second and then added, "Seeing you out and about is grand, my lord. The whole town has been praying for you."

"I appreciate your prayers." Miles turned to Amber and gestured to the room. "The kitchen and the common room comprise the house's first floor. This, of course, is the common room."

Miles watched her inspect the sparsely furnished room with its timber-framed walls. He hid a smile when he spied her sneaking touches as if to bring Shakespeare closer.

Letting his gaze drop from her face to her body, Miles admired her full breasts and slender waist. In his mind's eye, he saw her dusty pink nipples and the feminine curve of her hips. Good God, she probably had beautiful feet.

Her perfection gave him pause. He wondered again why such a beauty, who carried royal blood, would seek marriage with him. What secret was she keeping for her husband's ears only?

"Shall we?" Miles led the way out of the common room.

The kitchen had a large stone hearth and was equipped with utensils. Running from the floor to the ceiling timber, a wooden pole stood in the center of the stone floor. An iron loop had been attached to the lower part of the pole.

"What is it?" Amber asked.

"A poor person's nanny, a sixteenth-century babyminder," Miles answered and smiled at her surprised expression. "While performing her daily chores, mother locked the baby inside the loop to keep him safe."

"I never imagined Shakespeare as a child."

After inspecting the second-floor bedchamber where Shakespeare was born, they said farewell to the keeper and stepped outside the Henley Street house. Miles tensed when he saw the small crowd gathered near his coach. His moment of reckoning had arrived. He wanted neither their pity nor their fear.

An older woman stepped out of the crowd. "My lord, how wonderful to see you again *finally*," she said, drawing nods from the group behind her.

"Miss Kaitlyn Squelch, I simply could not wait another day to see you," Miles said, his lips twitching into a smile. "You are alone, Miss Squelch. Where are your sisters?"

"Gen and Laura decided to stay home today," Miss Squelch answered. "They will be sorry to have missed you." Her sharp gaze drifted to the princess.

"Your Highness, I present Miss Squelch, the chairwoman of our local historical society," Miles made the introduction. "Princess Amber is my"— *houseguest or fiancée?*—"my fiancée."

"Your Highness, I am honored to make your acquaintance," the woman said, dropping a curtsey. She looked at the earl, adding, "With all due respect, four years was long past time to leave Arden Hall and find a mate."

"I knew you would refuse my suit," Miles teased the woman, making everyone smile.

"Your husband-to-be has always been a flirtatious rascal," Miss Squelch told the princess.

"Once I am settled at Arden Hall, perhaps you and your sisters would care to take tea with me," Amber invited her.

Miles snapped his head around to look at the princess. Invite the gossipy Squelch sisters to tea? What was she planning?

"My sisters and I would be honored," Miss Squelch was saying to the princess.

"I am an admirer of Shakespeare and would like to help your historical society," Amber said. "I will look forward to our tea."

"We must be leaving now." Miles guided Amber to the coach and, after speaking to his driver, climbed inside to sit beside her.

"Why did you do that?" he demanded.

"Do what?"

"You invited the Squelch sisters to tea."

"And so they will come to tea."

"What will the people of Stratford think if we do not marry?"

"You should have considered that before you introduced me as your fiancée." Amber wondered if the earl was feeling trapped by his own words. "Besides, we *will* marry."

Miles gave her a long look. "You are very confident."

"Optimistic would be a more appropriate word," Amber corrected him. She glanced out the window. "We are not finishing our tour?"

"I can endure no more sentimental outpourings."

"The townspeople missed your smiling countenance and affable personality."

"Once upon a time, I *did* possess a smiling countenance and affable personality."

Feeling guilty about her remark, Amber touched his arm and waited for him to meet her gaze. "And so you shall possess those attributes again."

The earl made no reply but covered her hand with his own. She was forgiven for teasing him.

"We did not come this way," Amber remarked when their coach turned left after crossing Clopton Bridge.

"Very observant, Your Highness. We are going to Avon Park, my sister's home."

Amber wondered what his sister would think of her and their bargain. What if the duchess didn't like her? Would the earl marry her anyway?

"Relax, Princess." Miles slipped his arm around her shoulder. "I'm taking you to my sister's, not the gallows."

"Do I look presentable?"

Miles smiled at her feminine question. "Princess, you are the most beautiful woman I have ever seen."

"Yes, but do I look presentable?"

Miles laughed. "Your Highness, I have never seen a more presentable woman."

"Tell me about your sister," she said, trying to gauge her reception.

"Isabelle is not a typical society lady."

Amber decided she liked his sister already. Society ladies had always turned their noses up at her. She was the czar's daughter, but unless he acknowledged her, she had the wrong pedigree. Except for Sergei, she had never had a friend. Perhaps she would find a friend in the earl's sister.

"Isabelle fell in love with John when his younger brother and I traveled to New York," Miles told her. "I asked John to act as Belle's temporary guardian, and when I returned to England, they had already married."

"How romantic."

"As I recall, John was not thrilled to act as guardian for a young lady who everyone believed was unbalanced," Miles said. "Isabelle had an imaginary friend who, she insisted, was her guardian angel. Actually, John swears he saw and heard the angel speak, but temporary insanity could prove contagious."

"Is the angel still in residence with your sister?"

"She disappeared when my sister delivered her firstborn," Miles answered. "Isabelle insists her angel is lurking unseen in the shadows and waiting until her services are needed again."

"I like this story."

"Do you believe in angels?"

Amber shrugged. "I would like to think that angels exist."

"So would I, Princess."

"Good afternoon, Dobbs."

"Good afternoon, my lord. Miss Caroline will be especially pleased by your visit."

"I know the way." With his hand on the small of her back, Miles guided Amber across the foyer to the marble staircase.

Wearing smiles of greetings, the Duke and Duchess of Avon stood when they walked into the drawing room. Amber liked the earl's sister from the first moment her gaze touched the petite golden-haired woman.

"Your Highness, I present my sister and brother-in-law," Miles made the introduction. "John and Isabelle, Princess Amber is Prince Rudolf's cousin, recently arrived from Russia."

"I am pleased to make your acquaintances." Her smile wobbled from nerves. "Call me Amber."

"I am *very* happy to make your acquaintance," Isabelle said, and gave her brother a pointed look. "Call us Belle and John."

In that instant, Amber knew she had found a friend. She gave the earl's sister a smile filled with sunshine.

"Let's sit while Dobbs fetches the children," Isabelle said. "How do you like England, Amber?"

"I thought London was cramped and dirty, but your town of Stratford is lovely," she answered. "We have toured Shakespeare's birthplace this morning."

Both the duke and the duchess shifted surprised

gazes to the earl. Miles stretched his long legs out and remained silent.

"Tell us about yourself," John said.

I am the czar's unacknowledged bastard whom my uncle wants to sell into slavery. "I arrived in England several weeks ago," Amber told them, and flicked a blushing glance at the earl. "Rudolf thought Miles and I would suit."

"And do you?"

At a loss for words, Amber sent the earl a silent plea for help.

"We are becoming acquainted," Miles answered.

"Where is Prince Rudolf?" Isabelle asked, giving her brother a meaningful look. "The prince hasn't left his cousin unchaperoned, has he?"

"A business matter demanded his return to London," Miles said, the lie slipping easily from his lips. "Rudolf will return in a few days."

The duchess looked from her brother to his guest, who shifted uncomfortably on the settee, and then returned her gaze to the earl. "Perhaps Amber should remain with us until Rudolf returns."

"No." Miles sounded emphatic.

"Here are the children," Isabelle said, letting the matter drop.

Amber turned to see a group of children, two boys and four girls, ranging in age from five to ten, walk into the drawing room. Behind them followed two nannies, one holding a toddler's hand.

Amber smiled when she saw the children. The duke and the duchess were fortunate to have a large family. No one would ever feel lonely in this group.

"Uncle Miles is here," the older boy called.

A dark-haired girl broke from the group and dashed across the drawing room, calling, "Daddy!"

Amber dropped her mouth open in surprise when the girl threw herself into the earl's arms. *A daughter?*

Miles scooped the girl onto his lap. She wrapped her arms around his neck, gave him a smacking kiss on the lips, and held him as if she would never let go.

"You did not mention your daughter," Amber said, managing a smile when the girl looked at her.

"Caroline has lived with my sister since the fire," Miles told her.

"I love you, Daddy," Caroline said, demanding her father's attention.

"I love you more."

With her dark hair and blue eyes, the girl was the image of her mother, the woman in the portraits. That the earl loved his daughter was obvious. She had never seen him like this—happy, smiling, relaxed. He seemed a different man. Why did the girl live with her aunt instead of her father?

"Did you bring me a gift?" Caroline was asking her father.

"Yes, my greedy one." Miles pointed at Amber. "My gift is sitting there."

Caroline looked at Amber. "Is she my new mummy?"

"I brought you a princess," Miles told her. "Princess Amber, I present Caroline Montgomery, my daughter."

"I am very pleased to meet you," Amber said. "How old are you?"

"Five." Caroline held her hand up and wiggled her fingers for emphasis. "Are you a *real* princess?"

"Yes, I am."

"Where is your prince?"

"There he is." Amber pointed at the earl.

Caroline giggled. "That's Daddy, not a prince."

"How do you know your daddy is not a prince?"

"He doesn't wear a crown."

"Princes do not always wear crowns," Amber told her. "Princely is as princely does."

Caroline scrambled off her father's lap and sat beside Amber. "I like you."

"I like you, too."

"Are you going to marry Daddy?"

Amber felt a blush rising on her cheeks. "Your daddy has not asked me to marry him."

Caroline looked at her father. "Are you going to marry the princess?"

Miles appeared decidedly uncomfortable. "You will be the first to know if I do."

After greeting their uncle, the duke's children returned to their lessons. Only Caroline was allowed to stay.

"What shall we play today?" Miles asked his daughter.

"Let's go outside," Caroline said. "We'll drink tea in the playhouse."

"Let's meet for luncheon in an hour or so," Isabelle said, rising from her chair. "Amber, would you care to walk in the gardens?"

Amber smiled and inclined her head. She assumed the earl would want private time with his daughter.

Following the duchess out of the drawing room, Amber fell into step beside her when they walked down the corridor. Isabelle paused in front of a portrait of a distinguished-looking gentleman and his wife.

"These are my husband's parents," Isabelle said.

"I do believe His Grace resembles his handsome father," Amber replied. "Have both his parents passed away?"

"The dowager duchess is still living," Isabelle answered. "She is a remarkable woman. She taught me how to load and shoot a pistol."

"A pistol?" Amber echoed in surprise.

Isabelle nodded. "Whenever you see my mother-in-law and her sister carrying large reticules, they are armed and dangerous."

"Knowledge of pistols could be a useful talent," Amber said. "Perhaps, you could teach me sometime."

Suddenly an ungodly cacaphony of screeching sounds

came from the opposite end of the corridor. Amber whirled around, asking, "What is that noise?"

"Those are the dulcet sounds of my three oldest, untalented daughters having their music lesson," Isabelle answered. She looped her arm through Amber's, saying, "Let's look in on them."

The women started down the corridor toward the music room. Nearing it, they heard the long-suffering teacher, saying, "No, girls. Let's try this again."

Isabelle and Amber walked into the room. "I hear a definite improvement," the duchess praised her daughters. "Princess Amber, I present Mr. Barton, Stratford's music teacher. You have met Lily, Elizabeth, and Giselle."

"A pleasure to make your acquaintance," Amber told the teacher, who bowed over her hand. She looked at the girls, adding, "I play the mandolin and the piano."

"I play the flute," the duchess said. "Shall we give them a duet?"

"I would enjoy that."

Ten-year-old Lily rose from the piano bench so the princess could sit. Eight-year-old Elizabeth passed her mother the flute.

Amber looked at the duchess. "Play something, and I will follow your tune."

Isabelle lifted the flute to her lips. Recognizing the composition, Amber began her accompaniment. Their melody possessed a jaunty air that conjured elemental sounds: dancing sunbeams, chuckling brooks, wildflowers frolicking in a meadow.

"Bravo," Mr. Barton called. The three girls applauded.

The princess and the duchess curtsied to their audience of four and then left the music room. The off-key, screeching sounds began again before they had taken ten steps.

"Let's escape outside," Isabelle suggested. "Do you have any other talents?"

"I bake and garden."

"Do you sew, too?"

Amber nodded. "I sew whenever anger incites me to mutilation."

Isabelle laughed. "One cannot hang for attacking a piece of cloth."

Amber and Isabelle walked outside. The duchess was not what she would have expected. The earl's sister was cheerful and friendly.

"I'm glad my brother and you are becoming acquainted," Isabelle said, as they strolled through the formal gardens. "Do you like children?"

"I adore children and hope to have a large family," Amber answered. "I was an only child."

"Tell me about your family."

"After the deaths of my parents, I lived with Rudolf's father. Tell me about the earl."

"Before the fire, Miles devoted himself to his family," Isabelle answered, then paused to look into Amber's eyes. "You must possess magical powers to have persuaded him to venture into Stratford."

"Miracles happen every day."

"His scars do not bother you?"

"What do you mean by *bother?*"

"Frighten or disgust."

Amber smiled at the duchess. "There are worse things in life than scars."

"I am relieved to hear you say that," Isabelle said. "Miles nearly died from his burns and then relapsed when he realized Brenna had not survived. I don't want my brother hurt again."

"I will be a devoted wife if he will have me," Amber promised.

Before the duchess could reply, the sound of a little girl laughing reached them. Amber saw the earl and his daughter in the distance, disappearing into an enormous playhouse.

"Let's join them," Isabelle said.

Nearing the playhouse, Amber heard the earl saying, "I would love another cup of tea, Lady Caroline." She smiled at the thought that he enjoyed fatherhood. This was a side to the earl she had not seen.

"Princess Amber, do you think Lady Caroline is home?" Isabelle asked in a loud voice.

"I do not think anyone is home."

"I'm here," Caroline called, opening the door. "Princess, will you drink tea with me?"

"I would love a cup of tea." Amber turned to the duchess. "Your Grace, will you join us?"

"I must consult with Dobbs about our luncheon," Isabelle refused. "Another time, perhaps."

Amber stepped into the playhouse and laughed. More than six feet tall, the earl looked exceedingly silly sitting at a child's table.

"Sit here, Princess," Caroline said.

Amber lifted the cup to sip the make-believe brew. "What delicious tea."

"I didn't pour yours yet," Caroline said, and grinned when her father laughed. "Did you hear the gossip about Lady Begood?"

"No," Miles and Amber said simultaneously.

"Lady Begood let Lord Naughty get familiar with her," Caroline said in a loud whisper.

Again Miles and Amber laughed. "Do you know what *get familiar with* means?" the earl asked.

"I know Lord Naughty is a bad boy," Caroline told him. "Oh dear, we'll need more cakes. Excuse me while I go outside to get them."

"Hurry back, Caro." Miles lost his smile as soon as his daughter stepped outside. "If you don't mind, I would like to be alone with my daughter."

Amber ached at his words. She had always been left out as a child, which made his statement hurt more than it should.

"I did not intend to intrude." Amber stood to leave.

"Princess, where are you going," Caroline asked, walking into the playhouse. "I brought you cake."

"I need to visit the water closet."

The girl looked surprised. "Princesses do *that?*"

"Everyone does that."

Caroline looked at her father. "Even the king?"

"The king visits the water closet, too," Miles verified.

Amber left the playhouse and strolled across the lawn in the direction of the mansion. She understood the earl wanted private time with his daughter, but that did not lessen the hurt of his rejection.

"Princess."

Amber stopped walking and turned around. The earl waved at her to come back. Instead of returning to the playhouse, she resumed walking toward the mansion.

"Wait a minute," Miles called, jogging across the lawn. "Please come back. I didn't mean what I said."

Amber looked him straight in the eye. "You are feeling guilty because you think you hurt my feelings."

"Didn't I?"

"No, why should I—?"

"Your Highness, you are the most imcompetent liar I have ever met," Miles interrupted. "Forgive my unkindness. I couldn't help thinking that Brenna should have been sitting there, and my pain incited me to lash out at you."

"I understand." She touched his hand. "You do need time with your daughter, though. I will see you inside."

Without another word, Amber walked back to the mansion. She could feel the earl's gaze on her but refused to look over her shoulder.

She needed the earl to want her for herself. Guilt or pity or desire to possess her beauty was unacceptable.

Two hours later, after their luncheon, Amber sat between the five-year-old cousins, Caroline and Giselle, on the settee in the drawing room. Both girls wanted to cling to her simply because she was a *real* princess.

"I heard some wonderful music earlier," the duke remarked, looking at his daughters. "Either you are improving, or your mother was giving a command performance."

"Princess Amber and Mother played a duet," Lily told him.

The duchess looked at each of her daughters in turn. "Princess Amber plays two instruments, the piano and the mandolin. I am certain each of you is capable of mastering one."

"Princess, do you know any stories?" Caroline asked, clutching her arm.

Amber glanced at the earl, who sat nearby in a high-backed chair. "I know many stories."

"Will you tell us one?"

"Bedtime is better for stories," Amber hedged.

Sitting on her left, Giselle touched on her arm. "You won't be here at bedtime."

"Tell us a story about a princess," Miles said, and winked at her.

The two little girls clapped their hands.

"Once upon a time there lived an unhappy, orphaned princess," Amber began her story. "That means her mummy and her daddy had died."

"The king and the queen?"

Amber nodded at Caroline. "The poor little princess went to live with her uncle, Lord Dragon."

"Her uncle was a dragon?"

Amber turned to Giselle. "I am afraid so."

"What happened to this princess?" Miles asked.

"The princess ran away," Amber said. "She came to a dark forest where monsters lived. A ferocious dog leaped out at her from behind a tree. He barked and growled and snapped at her, but the princess refused to budge. She was more afraid of her uncle than anything else.

The dog walked toward her, growling low in his throat, and the princess noticed the dog's limp. Cautiously, she lifted its paw, saw a thorn, and yanked it out. From that day—"

"What was the dog's name?" Caroline interrupted.

Amber thought a moment. "Prince."

"Does Prince bite?" Giselle asked.

"Prince wanted the princess to believe he would bite," Amber said. "Prince did not want anyone to get too close to him."

"Why?" Caroline asked.

"Prince's previous owner had abandoned him," Amber answered, "and he did not want to feel bad again. From that day, Prince protected his princess. Then one day the princess hugged Prince and pressed a kiss on his muzzle. When she did that—"

"Did Prince drool?" Caroline asked.

Amber laughed. "Prince drooled globs and globs."

"Yuck, yuck, yuck," Caroline and Giselle exclaimed at the same time.

"When the princess kissed him," Amber continued, "Prince turned into a handsome prince, and they lived happily ever after."

Miles cocked a dark brow at her. "Is that Daniel and the lion or the princess and the frog?"

"Daddy, why don't you tell me a story?" Caroline asked.

"Only women tell stories," he answered.

"What do men do?"

"Gentlemen work hard to make money to purchase gowns and furs and jewels for their ladies."

Caroline clapped her hands and turned to Amber. "Boy, are we ever lucky to be girls, aren't we?"

Amber laughed. She could not remember the last time she had this much fun.

Later, Miles and Amber stood in the foyer and waited

for their carriage to be brought around. Caroline clung to her father as if she would never let him go.

"Don't leave me, Daddy," Caroline whined, her eyes filling with tears.

Miles lifted her into his arms and kissed her. "I will visit again soon. Give the princess a kiss."

Caroline leaned close and planted a kiss on her cheek. "I wish you were my mummy."

Amber blushed and returned the girl's kiss, saying, "I wish you were my little girl. You and Giselle must think of a story to tell me next time I visit."

"Little girls don't tell stories."

"What do they do?"

"Little girls listen."

Miles smiled at Amber. "Big girls would do well to adopt the good habit of listening, too."

Chapter 6

"Did I pass the test?" Amber asked, casting the earl a sidelong glance.

Miles cocked a dark brow at her. "What test?"

Amber knew that he knew to what she referred. Stalling for time to find the best words, she glanced out the coach's window as it wended its way down Avon Park's stately drive.

The sun had already set in the western sky. Its blazing red departure cooled into twilight's mauve and purple streaks.

"Why did you not tell me about your daughter?" Amber asked, fixing her gaze on his.

Now Miles looked away. "I didn't feel the need. Unlike others, I don't reveal my life story to anyone willing to listen."

"Are you referring to me?"

Instead of answering, Miles stretched his long legs out and rested his arm on the back of the black leather seat behind her. "Tell me the reason you need a husband."

"I do not feel the need to reveal that part of my life story."

The hint of a smile touched his lips. "I had begun to wonder if you were a royal doormat."

"You will *not* speak disrespectfully to me," Amber said, sounding every inch the royal.

"You seem amenable to whatever I say," Miles remarked, his lazy smile infuriating her.

"Do not confuse civility with a reluctance to argue." Amber turned away from him. "A doormat would have remained in Moscow, not disguised herself as a widow and traipsed across Europe to take refuge with her cousin."

Silence reigned for the remainder of the ride to Arden Hall. Amber realized he had evaded answering her question. She knew his relationship with his daughter was none of her business but doubted the earl realized how much he was hurting the little girl. A father should be a constant in his child's life, not a visitor. If the earl could feel what she had experienced as a child, he would understand the needless pain he was inflicting on his own daughter.

When the coach halted in Arden Hall's front courtyard, Amber summoned her courage and said, "Caroline needs to live with you."

Miles looked at her. "I beg your pardon?"

"Why have you banished your only child to live with relatives?"

"I want Caroline to live in a normal household."

"Living with relatives is abnormal," Amber said. "Caroline needs her father."

Miles opened the coach door, climbed out, and helped her down without speaking. "My daughter is none of your business," Miles said, his voice low, for her ears only. Turning his back on her, he walked toward the mansion, where Pebbles held the door open.

"Leaving Caroline there is hurting her," Amber argued, her tone almost pleading.

Miles stopped short and rounded on her. "Do you see yourself in my daughter?" he asked, heedless of the listening majordomo. "I assure you, Brenna was no adulteress, and Caroline is legitimate issue."

Amber stepped back as if she'd been struck, her complexion paling to a stark white. In an instant, her royal pride surfaced and forced her to retaliate.

"You miserable son of a bitch," Amber said in a scathing voice, surprising the earl and the majordomo. "Like a hog in swill, you wallow in your own misery and want everyone else to wallow in misery, too. Facing an uncertain, possibly unkind future takes courage—which you, my lord, are lacking."

Lifting her nose into the air, Amber brushed past him and started to climb the stairs. She paused when she heard the earl speak.

"Are you running away again, Your Highness? That scarcely speaks of courage."

"I refuse to listen to your insults." Amber started up the stairs again. She knew he walked behind her but refused to acknowledge his presence.

"I'm sorry," Miles said, and reached for her hand before she disappeared inside her bedchamber. "I didn't mean what I said."

Amber rounded on him. "You should think *before* speaking, my lord, or your voice will grow hoarse with all those apologies."

"My sister took Caroline while I recovered from my burns," Miles told her. "I thought leaving her with her cousins was for the best."

"You owe me no explanation."

"I *want* to explain. I love my daughter and want what is best for her, but I am unused to anyone's critical comments about raising my daughter. I did what I felt was right at the time."

Amber softened her gaze on him. "Household circumstances do not matter to Caroline. Your daughter loves you, even with your face scarred and your spirits low." Surprising him, she placed the palm of her hand against his masked cheek. "What lies in your heart defines your worth. You are more than a man hiding his scars beneath a mask. So much more."

Miles touched the hand she had placed on his scarred cheek. "Thank you for your concern for Caroline and me."

"Will you visit my chamber tonight?" Amber asked in invitation, responding to the yearning couched in his gaze.

The earl hesitated and then shuttered his expression. "Another time, perhaps."

Amber inclined her head and walked into her bedchamber. The day had been tiring, both physically and emotionally. She wanted to climb into bed and lose her troubles in sleep.

She crossed the chamber and opened the window. Instantly, the wishing bell moved in the evening's breeze, and the delicate tinkling, like the laughter of fairies, echoed in the room.

Miles Montgomery confused her. One moment he behaved amiably, even lovingly, but the next he snapped at her like Prince the dog. Did that mean *he* was confused about his feelings for her?

Why did the earl refuse her invitation? She had agreed to his outrageous demand. How could she conceive a child if they never actually——? All would be lost if Fedor found her before the earl and she wed.

Amber paced her chamber and tried to think of how she could hasten the earl's courtship. Apparently, she needed to seduce him but had no idea how to do that.

Following her instincts, Amber changed into a sheerer-than-gossamer nightgown. She padded on bare feet across the chamber to the connecting door and knocked before she lost her nerve.

A moment later, Miles opened the door. He still wore his mask but had changed into a black silk bedrobe.

Amber watched him slide his gaze from her face to her body. An expression of hunger appeared on his face. The earl seemed mesmerized by the gossamer silk covering her nakedness, playing a teasing game of peekaboo with his gaze.

"May I come inside?"

"Why?" He sounded suspicious.

"I would like to visit you before retiring."

Miles cocked a dark brow at her. "Why?"

I want to seduce you. "I cannot get—" Her complexion flamed with her embarrassment. "I cannot become pregnant if—We made a bargain, did we not?"

"I'm giving you a chance to change your mind."

Amber looked him straight in the eye. "I will not change my mind."

"Then perhaps I will. Go to bed, Princess."

"What is wrong with me?" she cried in embarrassed frustration.

"You aren't Brenna," he answered, anguish choking his voice.

With pain etched across her face, Amber stared at him for a long moment. All was lost. She could never be another woman, nor could she compete with the memory of his cherished wife. She reached to close the door.

Miles regretted the hurt he had put on her sweet expression. "Give me time, Princess."

"I do not have time to give you."

His gaze narrowed on her. "What do you mean?"

"The answer to that question is meant only for my husband." She closed the connecting door.

Feeling guilty, Miles stared at the door. Besides his daughter, the princess was the only person who had touched his mask, indirectly touching his scars, directly touching his heart. Why was he shutting her out?

Virgins were notoriously skittish about their first experience with a man. Why was she rushing him into bed? What was she hiding? Why didn't she have time to wait until he was ready?

Why, for God's sake, wasn't he ready?

Miles knew his wife's memory was not his only problem. He feared the princess's reaction when she saw his scars. Not only was his face burned but also the whole left side of his body—arm, trunk, leg. He could not bear seeing horrified rejection on her face, one reason he had hidden inside Arden Hall for years.

Sitting in the chair near the hearth, Miles waited until he judged she'd had enough time to fall asleep. He rose wearily, crossed to the connecting door, and listened to the silence. Entering her chamber, he approached the bed and stared at the sleeping princess. She was everything a man could want in a wife. He needed to set aside his fear and make her his own. Delay could mean losing his only chance to resume living.

Miles snuffed the night candle and returned to his own chamber. He left the door ajar and his mask on the bedside table lest she need him during the night.

Windswept rain changed day into twilight. Accompanying the rhythmic drumming on the windows, the soprano notes of a mandolin wafted through the air into the library. Princess Amber had changed the earl's life in only a few short days. He had felt sunshine warming his face; he had appeared in public; he had laughed out loud.

Long-dead desire had sprung to new life like the mythical phoenix. Her angel's face, her silver-blond hair, and her tempting breasts had conspired to persuade him to live again.

For some unknown reason, Princess Amber accepted him in spite of his scars while disdaining her own exquisite beauty. She loved children, as evidenced by her enjoyment of his daughter's company. Most importantly, the princess needed him as much as he needed her.

Life came without guarantees. The Lord had gifted each soul with instincts, not instructions. *Move now or forever lose your chance,* his instincts whispered.

And Miles listened.

Leaving the library, he followed the sound of the mandolin. He paused in the drawing room's entrance to admire an angel creating a heavenly melody.

Amber stopped playing, as if she felt watched. She looked around and, in spite of his harshness the previous evening, gave him her sunshine smile.

"Good evening, my lord." She set the mandolin aside.

Miles crossed the drawing room slowly in order to give himself time to summon the proper words. Standing in front of her, he stuck his hands in his trouser pockets and searched his mind for an opening statement. Good God, he hadn't felt this nervous with a woman since his university days.

"I missed you at lunch," the princess said, her tone coolly polite.

"I am swamped with yesterday's and today's paperwork," Miles lied.

"I see." Amber dropped her gaze to her lap.

She looked uncomfortable. Had he unknowingly lost his chance last night? He needed to do something. After his rejection of her the previous evening, the princess would not make the first move again.

Miles held his hand out as if asking her to dance. "Will you come upstairs with me?"

Her gaze mirrored her confusion. "Upstairs?"

"To bed."

Blood rushed to her cheeks in a ferocious blush. "You are certain?"

Miles gave her a rueful smile. "I believe *I* am supposed to ask that question."

"Is afternoon proper?" she whispered, placing her hand in his. "Should we not wait for night?"

"Any time is proper for lovemaking." Miles guided her out of the drawing room.

She is a virgin, he reminded himself as they climbed the stairs in silence. He must move slowly, lest he ruin her first experience and endanger their marriage before they had even spoken their vows.

Good God, what an unlikely pair they made.

He needed immediate release.

She needed a slow seduction.

Miles lifted her hand to his lips when they stood outside her bedchamber door. "Prepare yourself, and I will join you shortly."

"How do I prepare myself?" Amber asked, her expression panicked.

Miles struggled against a smile. "Change into your bedrobe."

After she disappeared into her chamber, Miles walked into his own chamber. He changed into his black silk bedrobe and then poured himself a shot of whisky. That went down in one gulp, burning a path to his stomach.

Judging enough time had passed, Miles touched his mask and knocked on the connecting door. He heard her call softly, walked into the bedchamber, and paused for a moment.

The princess had closed the drapes, casting the chamber into semidarkness. A night candle burned on the bedside table, and the bedcurtains were open.

"I shut the drapes," Amber said, her apprehension apparent in the movement of her hands.

"So I see." Miles sauntered toward her.

The princess's frightened expression reminded him of a fledgling warrior in the midst of a first battle. And so it was her first battle. With love.

"Is closing the drapes proper?" she asked, when he stood in front of her.

"No rules exist for lovemaking." Miles placed the palm of his hand against her cheek. "I promise there is nothing to fear."

Amber lifted her chin a notch, her violet gaze meeting his. "I feel no fear."

"It isn't too late to change to change your mind," Miles said, his face inching closer to hers. "You do not need to do this."

She made no reply. Her silence was his answer.

His lips touched hers in a tentative kiss, allowing her a moment to refuse his advances. She inched her body closer, her hands creeping up his chest to wrap around his neck, bringing her body in contact with his.

"So be it, Princess."

His kiss was long and slow and drugging. She sighed, savoring the sensation of his firm, warm lips on hers.

Miles flicked his tongue out and caressed the crease between her lips, which parted for him, allowing him entrance to her mouth. His passion heating her, she touched his tongue tentatively at first and then grew bolder until their tongues swirled together in an ancient mating dance.

Amber felt hot and cold all at the same time. She wanted him, needed him. His power and strength surrounded her, drew her irresistibly to him.

"I want to see you." Miles stepped back a pace and pulled one end of the sash holding her robe closed. With both hands, he reached up and pushed it off her shoulders, leaving her naked to his gaze. His breath caught raggedly at the sight of the exquisite beauty that would belong to him exclusively after today.

Amber stood motionless in front of him, her silver-blond hair cascading like a shimmering bride's veil to her waist. She watched his gaze drift from her face to linger on her breasts and then slip lower to her hips and legs.

Miles lifted her into his arms and placed her on the bed. He joined her there, kissing her thoroughly, stealing her breath away. And then his lips left hers to sprinkle kisses on her temples, eyelids, throat.

Acting on instinct, Amber entwined her arms around his neck and tried to draw him down on her. "I want to feel your flesh touching mine," she whispered.

"Soon, Princess." Miles captured her lips in a long, slow kiss. He slid his hands down her arms and then up the sensitive inner sides. His fingers traced the circle of her nipples, and then his lips followed his fingers. He flicked his tongue back and forth across the sensitive tips of her nipples, making her squirm with arousal.

Amber felt the stab of desire shoot from her nipples to the spot between her thighs. She had not known such pleasure existed, had never imagined the incredible feeling of a man's lips and hands on her. The spark of desire in her lower regions fanned into a flame growing hotter with each flick of his tongue, each roll of his fingertips around the bead of her nipple.

Arching her hips, Amber enticed him to take her. She wanted him inside her body. She wanted him to lose himself in her. She wanted him to mark her as his.

Miles knelt beside her, but before he could reach to remove his robe, she pulled at the belt. His passion-dulled mind cleared, and he remembered his scarred left side.

It was too late to stop.

Fright caught in his throat as he shrugged the robe off his shoulders, exposing his flaws to her gaze. Even the chamber's dimness could not hide the scars.

Dazed with desire, Amber traced her silken fingers across his chest and savored the feeling of his warm, muscled flesh. She sat up and dropped light kisses across his chest.

No flicker in her eyes.

No revulsion quickly masked.

As if my scars are invisible.

Miles groaned in mingling desire, relief, and awe. He pressed her back on the bed, lay on top of her, and captured her lips. He poured all his long-denied need into that single, stirring kiss.

For the first time in her young life, Amber felt a man's strength covering her, pressing her down. And she liked it.

"Make me yours," she whispered.

"As you wish, my princess."

After pulling a pillow beneath her bottom, Miles spread her thighs with his legs and poised himself to pierce. Slowly, he pushed the head of his manhood inside her moist entrance.

"Look at me, Princess."

Amber opened her eyes.

"Say *no* now," Miles warned, his voice husky with barely controlled need. "Or you will belong to me forever."

Amber arched her hips toward him, drawing him deeper inside her.

"Say the words, princess."

"I want you."

"Forever?"

"Forever."

"I am sorry, Princess." With one powerful thrust, Miles broke through her maidenhead and embedded his full length inside her, making her gasp.

After giving her a moment to accustom herself to him, Miles moved slowly and enticed her to move with him. Acting on instinct, Amber wrapped her legs around his waist and caught his rhythm. She met him thrust for thrust. He ground himself into her moist heat and, leaning down, sucked upon a nipple.

Amber cried out as throbbing waves of pleasure surged through her. Miles thrust deep and hard, shuddering as he poured his seed inside her.

For long moments, the only sound in the bedchamber was their labored breathing. Recovering himself, Miles rolled to the side and pulled her into his arms.

"The first time is difficult," he told her, dropping a kiss on the crown of her head. "The lovemaking will get better after today."

"Better than this?" She sounded surprised.

Miles tightened his embrace. "Much better."

"How many times will it take to get pregnant?" she asked, looking up at him.

"Only God knows the answer to that."

"Will we do this after I become pregnant?"

Miles gave her an indulgent smile. "We will do this whenever you want."

Good God, he had forgotten how inexperienced she actually was. "Close your eyes and sleep now." He stroked her back and, when her breathing evened, knew she slept.

I could love her.

Miles knew he could not endure losing another woman. How best to protect himself?

And then a plan formed in his mind. He would distance himself emotionally. He had loved Brenna too much not to be devastated by her loss and would not make the same mistake again.

Chapter 7

Amber awakened to the sound of rain hitting her window. The rhythmic pounding soothed her, filling her with security. She adored stormy days almost as much as she loved sunshine.

"Miles?" Amber rolled over. She was alone, the earl having slipped away while she slept.

She wished she could have awakened in his arms. Like lovers do. Or so she supposed.

Trying to recapture the moments shared with him, Amber yanked the coverlet over her head and closed her eyes. She could almost see his face inching closer, taste his lips, inhale his fresh scent, feel his strength pressing her down, hear his whispered words.

"Stop," Amber told herself, emerging from beneath the coverlet. Magical moments slipped away too quickly. Recapturing them would always prove impossible. She needed to make new moments in order to recapture the feeling.

Amber rose from the bed and looked down at her nudity, a reminder of the afternoon. She slipped into her robe and opened the window a crack to let the wind move her wishing bell.

Taking special care with her appearance, Amber chose a violet silk gown with scooped neckline. Then she brushed her light blond hair and wove it into a loose knot at the nape of her neck. On impulse, she searched one of the highboy's drawers. She withdrew a man's ring, a diamond-encrusted gold band with an enormous aquamarine stone. The royal insignia appeared on both sides of the ring that had once belonged to Czar Alexander.

The earl and she had come a long way in a very short time. Her gift of this ring, a cherished present from her father, would symbolize her hopes for their future.

Amber could hardly wait to see him. What would he say after the intimacies they had shared? She felt as naked emotionally as she had been physically a few hours earlier.

Humming a sprightly tune to buoy her courage, Amber walked downstairs to the dining room. Unfortunately, the earl wasn't there.

"Your Highness, let me escort you to the table," Pebbles said, rushing forward. "I will serve you myself tonight."

"Thank you. Where is His Lordship?"

"My lord sends his regrets." Pebbles set a bowl of spring soup in front of her. "He is working in his study."

"I see." Amber did not see at all. She had given the earl her virginity, and now he chose to ignore her.

Though she ached with disappointment, Amber kept her expression placid. She had displeased the earl. What other reason could there be for his making love and then ignoring her presence? Was he comparing her to his late wife? Perhaps she was only imagining the worst, and the earl's behavior was normal. She wished she could consult an older, more experienced woman.

Refusing to show her humiliation, Amber forced herself to sit alone at the dinner table for more than an hour, almost the same amount of time she would have sat if her host had been present. "Just-Pebbles, please convey my gratitude to Cook."

"Yes, Your Highness."

Amber climbed the main staircase to the second floor. Instead of continuing to the third floor, she walked in the direction of the library. If the earl was displeased, she would prefer to know now rather than worry all night.

She had always been like that. When her cousins had teased her about monsters living beneath her bed, she refused to worry all night. Instead, she lifted the coverlet and knelt down to confront whatever might be hiding. *Not the closet, though. Never the closet.*

Fingering the gold ring, Amber paused outside the library and debated whether to enter. She needed to face the earl as if she had not a worry in the world.

Pasting a sunny smile on her face, she stepped inside the library before she could retreat and, on shaking legs, crossed the enormous chamber to his study. She saw the earl look up at her entrance, and then he rose from his chair.

Amber felt the blush rising on her cheeks. She wondered if the earl was remembering their afternoon of passion.

"I apologize for interrupting," Amber said, gesturing for him to sit.

"Why are you blushing?" Amusement lit his dark eyes. "Lovemaking should never embarrass you."

"I wish we had dined together," she said, his words embarrassing her more. "I never did like dining alone."

"I apologize for deserting you," he said, his tone coolly polite. "I lost precious hours today."

"I do not want to keep you from your work." Amber felt uncertain. "I want to give you this." She set the ring on the desk in front of him.

Miles gave her a puzzled smile and dropped his gaze to the ring. He lifted it off the desk to inspect it.

"The stone is aquamarine, and the scrolled gold is encrusted with diamonds," Amber told him.

"This is a fine piece." Miles set it down on the desk instead of slipping it on his finger. "I thank you for thinking of me. Was there something else?"

He sounded like a stranger, not the man to whom she had given her virginity. "The ring belonged to my father," Amber said, hurt by his lack of enthusiasm. "You will see the royal insignia on both sides of the aquamarine."

Miles directed his gaze to hers. "Your father?"

"Czar Alexander."

"The czar sired you," Miles corrected her. "He chose not to father you. Good God, you never even met him."

His words crushed her heart. "If my father had been killed in a war before I was born," she argued, "he would still be my father."

"The czar was not killed in a war before you were born but lived within miles of you for part of the year," Miles said. "He chose never to invite you to meet him, publicly or not. Czar Alexander tossed you a crumb of affection which you gobbled like a starving woman."

"My father holds me in special regard," Amber cried. "I am the daughter he produced with the love of his life."

"Czar Alexander cared little for you or your mother," Miles said, hating himself for his cruelty.

Protect your heart. Protect your heart. Protect your heart.

"Your Highness," she corrected him.

"I beg your pardon?"

"Call me *Your Highness*. I revoke my permission to use my given name."

Miles snapped his brows together. "I do not say these things to hurt you."

"Czar Alexander loved my mother. What other reason could there be for his affair with her?"

"The czar desired your mother in his bed," he answered. "Unfortunately for them, their affair produced you."

"My father loves me," Amber insisted, her complexion stark white. "He never met me because of the scandal."

"That is precisely my point. If the czar truly loved you, he would have ignored the scandal and sent for you."

Tears welled up in her eyes. "You know nothing about the czar or my mother."

Miles opened his mouth to speak.

"I will *not* listen to your lies." She whirled away and ran out of the library.

Reaching the refuge of her chamber, Amber burst into tears. She had given her virginity to the earl, and now he had turned on her with his filthy lies. He had hurt her. Purposely. Why had he asked her to remain at Arden Hall if he felt that way about her origins? She had been packing to leave. He need not have kept her there.

All appeared lost.

No virginity. No husband. No prospects.

Amber sat on the chaise in front of the hearth. Almost reverently, she held the czar's miniature in her hand and stared at it. A sinking feeling settled around her heart.

The earl had spoken truthfully. The czar had desired her mother and sired her but did not choose to father her. A loving father would have sent for her and arranged a marriage when she became eighteen.

Amber recalled the evening at the opera, the only time she had ever seen the czar in person. On her sixteenth birthday she had attended the opera with Uncle Fedor, Sergei, and Sergei's mother. They had been standing in the theater's lobby when the czar and czarina entered with their entourage. The crowd parted for the czar's party, but he paused to stare at her for an excruciatingly long moment.

"Child, you have inherited your mother's beauty," Czar Alexander had said. "Felicitations on your birthday." Then he had moved on without another word. She never saw him again.

Wearied by her emotional outburst, Amber lay down on the chaise but kept the miniature clutched in her hand. She recalled the gossip the day after the opera. Sergei had told her that all of society was whispering about the czar speaking publicly to his by-blow. Perhaps the czar never acknowledged her in an effort to protect her from cruel tongues. She would like to think so.

One floor down in his study, Miles leaned over his desk and held his head in his hands. Self-loathing filled him. Guilt consumed him. He stared at the ring on the desk. He felt worse than if he had loved her and lost her.

He had hurt her. Purposely.

In order to survive, he needed to distance himself from her. Which was becoming increasingly difficult. How could he bear to love and lose another woman? He almost wished the princess had never come to Arden Hall.

Almost.

Miles lifted the ring off the desk. He wanted desperately to slip the ring on his finger but felt that action would bring him too close to the princess. Becoming emotionally involved with another woman would only lead to heartache. He pocketed the ring and rose from his chair.

Now he had the unenviable task of setting things right. He needed to apologize to the princess. He needed to hold her. He needed to possess her body, heart, soul.

Good God, he had been hurting four years. The princess had been hurting her whole life.

He had known happiness. She had known none.

Miles walked upstairs to his chamber. Setting the czar's ring on his dresser, he changed into his bedrobe and paced back and forth while he summoned the courage to face her.

Finally he opened the connecting door and stepped inside her chamber. As usual, the night candle burned on the bedside table. The bedcurtains remained open, but she was not in the bed.

Miles looked around and saw her, still fully clothed, sleeping on the chaise. He saw the czar's miniature clutched in her hand and felt his heart wrench. Lifting it out of her hand, he placed it on a nearby table.

"Miles?" She sounded more asleep than awake.

He knelt beside the chaise. "I am sorry, Princess."

"You were right. The czar never loved me."

"No, Princess, I was wrong. Your father loves you, but his position prevented him from acting upon his love."

"Do you truly think so?"

"How could he not love a daughter as sweet as you?" His mouth covered hers in a slow, healing kiss. That melted into another. And then another.

"Come, Princess," Miles said, standing. He offered her his hand. "I will help you to bed."

Amber placed her hand in his and rose from the chaise.

Miles unfastened the buttons on her gown and pushed it off her shoulders, letting it pool at her feet. He pressed his lips on the delicate nape of her neck and pulled the pins from her hair. A curtain of pale hair cascaded to her waist.

Gently, Miles turned her around, scooped her into his arms, and carried her across the chamber to the bed. He undressed her slowly—chemise, shoes, stockings, garters.

Amber reached to unfasten his robe, but he stayed her hand.

"I want to pleasure you," Miles said in a husky voice.

Joining her on the bed, Miles kissed each foot in turn and ran his tongue up the sensitive insides of her thighs. He tongued her navel and continued burning a sensuous path to her breasts, pausing to suck each nipple into arousal.

Her breath came in shallow gasps. She held him tightly against her breast, savoring the feeling of his lips tugging on her nipples.

His lips drifted lower to her belly and beyond. He pressed his face against the moist softness between her thighs.

Miles flicked his tongue up and down in a relentless but gentle assault on her womanhood. He licked and nipped her tiny nub while his fingers squeezed and taunted her aroused nipples into tight buds.

Surrendering herself, Amber melted against his tongue. She cried out as waves of throbbing pleasure washed over her.

When her love spasms ended, Miles lay beside her and pulled her against his body. Almost shyly, Amber dropped her hand to his groin. Miles stopped her. "For tonight, I only want to hold you."

Awakening alone the next morning, Amber wondered if she had dreamed the earl comforting her in the night. She rolled over, saw the indentation in the pillow, and slid her hand across it. There was nothing as intimate as pillows with indentations where a couple had lain together.

Filled with optimism, Amber began her morning ablutions. After changing into a white morning gown with petal pink embroidery at neckline and hem, she looked out the window at a sunny morning—she hoped a harbinger of a bright future.

The earl seemed to care for her at certain moments, and then he would distance himself. Why did the idea of caring for her disturb him?

He had hurt her feelings the previous evening and then tried to make amends. She needed to be patient with him. If only she knew an experienced woman who could counsel her. She didn't think the earl's sister would be a good choice, nor could she ask one of the servants. She would need to follow her instincts, but their whole relationship confused her.

Amber walked downstairs to the dining room. The earl wasn't there.

"Good morning, Your Highness," Pebbles greeted her.

"Good morning, Just-Pebbles." Amber managed a smile for the majordomo though her spirits had slipped a notch. "I will serve myself this morning."

Crossing to the sideboard, Amber selected a slice of ham and two baked eggs. Then she sat at the table, and the majordomo served her a cup of coffee along with the *Times*.

"This newspaper is dated yesterday."

"His Lordship has it delivered from London," Pebbles explained.

"Where is His Lordship?"

"He rode out earlier to inspect drainage problems on the estate."

Amber felt relieved that the earl was attending to business instead of avoiding her. She glanced at the portrait of the earl's late wife and then looked toward the sideboard. Only the majordomo was in the dining room.

Amber beckoned to him. "Just-Pebbles, I know I am breaching proper etiquette, but would you please sit here with me?"

The majordomo appeared surprised but did as she requested.

Amber chewed on her bottom lip for a moment and then asked, "Why does His Lordship have the late countess's portrait in every chamber?"

The majordomo smiled at her. "I have known His Lordship since his boyhood. Before his marriage, the earl was quite the lady's man who, I dare say, believed he would never fall in love. Then he met Lady Brenna.

"Once the earl recovered from his near-fatal injury, he ordered portraits of his late wife to be brought from his London town mansion. I think he feels guilty to be alive while she lies in an early grave. Also, the burn scars on his face prevented his emotional recovery. Had he never been injured, the earl would have resumed living before now. Please, Your Highness, be patient with His Lordship. He is a good man."

"Yes, His Lordship *is* a good man." Amber smiled at the majordomo. "Thank you for your insights, Just-Pebbles."

"You are welcome, Your Highness." Pebbles returned to his station near the sideboard.

Turning her attention to the *Times*, Amber read while she ate. The society gossip column on page three caught her eye.

> *. . . and the latest on the Kazanov princes. Prince Rudolf and Princess Samantha attended the opera with the princess's sister and her husband, the Earl and Countess of Winchester . . . . Prince Viktor and Princess Adele were seen enjoying a heated discussion in Hyde Park . . . . Prince Stepan supped privately with a certain opera singer, London's latest rage, also rumored to be a certain duke's by-blow . . . . Prince Mikhail and his young daughter inspected ponies at Smithfield in the company of the child's governess, rumored to be the sister of the aforementioned opera singer . . . Hmmmm.*

Amber had not known Viktor and Mikhail had married. Nor would she have imagined her cousins becoming entrenched in London society. She decided to read the newspaper every morning. If Fedor arrived in England, the reporter would certainly remark upon his arrival.

After breakfast Amber wandered outside. She tended the rosebush, all the while wondering if the earl had returned from his business.

Miles was still missing at lunch. Amber went upstairs to rest, wondering what was delaying him. As she passed the second floor, she stopped to stare down the corridor leading to the mansion's east wing, burned in the fire. Perhaps if she sneaked into that wing and found the cause of the fire, the earl could lay his wife to rest, leaving a piece of his heart for her.

Amber looked around to make certain no servants were loitering in the vicinity. With determination etched across her delicate features, she started down the corridor slowly. Very slowly. Filled with trepediation, she forced herself to move forward. With each step, the oppressive darkness pressed heavily against her, surrounding her like a tangible thing.

Were ghosts lurking in the east wing? Were monsters hiding in the dark? No matter. She would brave anything to bring the earl closer. Her future depended on her courage to face what she feared most, the darkness.

Passing a soot-coated window, Amber spied the earl riding up the stately brick drive. She would need to postpone her investigation lest he discover she was disobeying his command to stay away from the east wing. Retracing her steps, she hurried to her bedchamber, where she remained until the evening meal.

When she walked into the dining room for dinner, Amber felt her heart sink to her stomach. The earl had deserted her again.

Pebbles rushed forward. "Your Highness, allow me

to escort you to the table. His Lordship sends his regrets. The estate ledgers need his attention."

So do I, she thought, but managed a smile for the majordomo. "Did the drainage problem require his attention all day?"

"Yes, Your Highness."

"You will deliver a tray to His Lordship?"

"Yes, Your Highness."

Amber sat at the table for more than an hour, as she had done the previous evening. Deeming enough time had passed, she left the dining room and walked upstairs.

Amber paused outside the library to compose her rioting nerves. She needed to assume a casual attitude lest she frighten him with her eagerness.

After taking a fortifying breath, Amber stepped inside the library. The earl looked up and then stood as she walked toward him.

"I do hope the drainage problem is not too severe," she said, a smile pasted on her face, gesturing him to sit.

"Nothing that cannot be corrected," Miles said, sitting down again.

"I instructed Just-Pebbles to prepare you a tray. He will be along shortly."

"Thank you for thinking of me."

Amber hesitated, searching for something to say. "If you do not mind, I would like to borrow a book."

"Help yourself."

Amber crossed the library, feeling his gaze on her the whole way. She browsed the bookshelves without actually reading the titles and searched her mind for a reason to delay leaving. Finding none, she grabbed one of the volumes, cast the earl a blushing smile, and went to her bedchamber.

The earl is not avoiding me, she told herself, tossing the book on the bedside table. *Tomorrow the drainage problem will be solved, and he will spend time with me. At least take his meals with me.*

Much later, Amber awakened when Miles climbed into bed and drew her against his body. She wrapped her arms around his neck and pressed her lips and her body to his. She felt him lift her nightshift over her head, and then his hands were caressing her breasts, teasing her nipples.

"I want you," he whispered against her lips.

"And I want you," she said on a sigh.

Amber spread her legs as he moved over her. His body joined hers, and together they found a shared paradise.

Awakening alone in the morning, Amber wondered again if she had dreamed the earl in bed with her. Their lovemaking had seemed real, but that day proved to be a replica of the previous one.

And so did the day after that.

Ignored by day and possessed by night, Amber felt her irritation growing with each passing moment. She knew one thing for certain. She had no wish for a phantom lover. She refused to marry and live alone.

After breakfasting and lunching alone for the fourth day, Amber decided she would not dine alone again. If the earl refused to take his meals with her, there was little chance for a married life together.

Amber walked into the dining room that evening and looked at the majordomo. His face was red with embarrassment. Apparently, the earl had given his man another poor excuse for not dining with her, but this time she was ready.

"Is the earl tied to his desk this evening?"

"I'm afraid so, Your Highness."

"My poor lord is forced to eat a lonely dinner every evening," Amber said, feigning concern. "Fill two plates with whatever Cook has prepared and serve us in His Lordship's study."

"With pleasure, Your Highness."

Amber led the way into the library and watched the earl stand when she entered. Surprise registered on his face when he spied the majordomo, tray in hand, following in her wake.

"I have become as weary of dining alone as you must be," Amber said, reaching his desk. "Pebbles will serve us here. I am positive you can spare me thirty minutes of your time."

Miles acquiesced with a nod of his head. He cleared his desk of papers so the majordomo could set the tray down.

Amber sat in the chair on the other side of the desk and gave him her sunshine smile. "I believe Cook has outdone herself tonight," she said, looking at the roast beef.

"That will be all," Miles instructed his man.

"Yes, my lord." Pebbles grinned, indicating his awareness that the princess had outsmarted his master.

"Thirty minutes," Miles called before the majordomo disappeared out the door.

They ate in silence. Amber could not think of a single topic to discuss, the tone of his voice saying "thirty minutes" having stolen all coherent thoughts.

Finally he said, "Are you enjoying *Studies in Aristocratic Finances in the Sixteenth and Seventeenth Centuries?*"

Amber stared at him blankly. "I beg your pardon?"

"Are you enjoying the book you borrowed?" Miles repeated. "You know, *Studies in Aristocratic Finances in the Sixteenth and Seventeenth Centuries.*"

Amber felt the blood rushing to her face. She did not want him to ask questions about a book that had served as a pretext to see him. "I am finding the subject difficult to understand," she hedged, setting her napkin on the desk. "The topic is rather dry."

The earl would not allow her to retreat gracefully. "Why haven't you returned it and chosen another?"

"I did not want to disturb you."

"You disturbed me tonight."

Amber stood to leave. "I grew tired of living alone."

Miles relaxed back in his chair and studied her for a long moment. "Are you feeling neglected? I come to you every night."

"You come *inside* me, not to me," Amber snapped, surprising him and herself. "I am not merely a body to be used as a receptacle for your seed and will not tolerate being ignored or treated with disrespect."

"I said you could never replace my wife," Miles countered, rising from his chair. "The reality of that does indeed make you a body to nurture my heir."

Amber stepped back as if she had been struck, her complexion paling to a deathly white. The space between them loomed larger than his desk.

"You are no better than my uncle."

"What do you mean?"

In answer, Amber showed him her back and walked away.

"If you don't like this arrangement, Your Highness, find another gentleman in London," Miles called. "Better still, return to Russia."

Amber stopped short. The reality of Count Gromeko mating her with his stud came rushing back to her. No matter how contemptibly the earl behaved, what awaited her in Russia was worse.

"You are right," Amber amended herself, without turning to face him. "We made a bargain. I gain the protection of your name, and you gain an heir. I apologize for interrupting and promise not to do so again."

"Stop," Miles ordered, when she started for the door.

Amber turned around and saw him crossing the library toward her. Would he refuse to accept her apology? Would he return her to her cousin? What would she do if that happened? Uncle Fedor was no fool and had probably guessed her destination.

"Why do you accept harsh treatment from me?" Miles demanded, towering over her. "I want to know the reason you left Russia."

Overwhelmed by the fear of Fedor in London, Amber could not face another moment keeping her secret hidden inside. She hung her head, covered her face with her hands, and began to weep.

And then she felt the earl wrapping his arms around her. He guided her to the settee in front of the hearth. He sat beside her and drew her into his embrace. "Tell me what frightens you."

"I overheard a conversation between Uncle Fedor and Count Gromeko," Amber began, looking at him with violet eyes swimming with tears. "Gromeko is a slave dealer and purchased me from my uncle. He owns a male slave with the same coloring as I, which is highly prized in the eastern markets. He bought me to mate with this stud. When sold, our children would bring him and my uncle great wealth."

"Good God, nobody owns slaves."

"Perhaps nobody in England owns slaves," Amber corrected him. "The world is not England. Uncle Fedor is a smart man and most likely guessed my destination. He and Gromeko will be searching for me."

"I will protect you with my life," Miles promised her. "They will need to kill me before getting their hands on you."

"Do you understand the reason I need a husband?" Amber asked, touching his masked cheek.

Miles turned his head and kissed the palm of her hand. "I understand everything."

Chapter 8

There are worse things in life than being scarred by fire. Miles realized how foolishly he had lived for the past four years. The death of his wife was a heartwrenching loss, but many men lost their wives in a variety of ways from childbirth to illness to accident. The princess had faced the prospect of a lifetime of sexual slavery, a future so horrifyingly repugnant, his mind almost failed to grasp its reality.

He had made love to the princess and taken her virginity. She belonged to him, and he would kill the man who tried to steal her away.

Amber was more than a beautiful woman. Brave and nurturing, she deserved the happiness she had never known.

God had taken his wife and his face. In return, He had sent him an angel. Salvation had appeared in the form of a Russian princess.

"Come," Miles held his hand out to her.

They left the library and walked upstairs to her bedchamber. He unfastened her gown and reached for the sheerer-than-gossamer nightgown lying across the bed.

"You do not need to baby me."

"I *want* to baby you."

Amber let her gown drop to the floor. She stood in front of him, clad only in her lacy chemise, silk stockings, garters, and shoes. Reaching out, she stayed the hand that held her nightgown.

He met her gaze. "You don't need to do this tonight."

"I *want* to do this."

Amber pressed herself against his body, entwining her arms around his neck. She drew his head down, her lips capturing his in a smoldering kiss. Her gesture surprised Miles. She wanted him. There was no mistaking the passion in her kiss.

Amber lifted her lips from his and stepped back a pace. Holding his gaze captive to hers, she slipped the straps of her chemise off her shoulders, letting the garment pool at her feet. And then she stood only in her silk stockings, garters, and shoes.

The princess could not possibly know how arousing she looked. When she caressed the bulge in his breeches, he snaked his hands out and yanked her against him, where she belonged.

Their kiss was long and languorous.

"I want no barriers between us," Amber whispered, her eyes glazed with desire. "Remove your mask and make love to me."

Miles froze. "I cannot—"

"We will snuff the candle."

"You fear the dark."

"I fear nothing with you."

Miles kissed her again and then removed his jacket, waistcoat, and shirt. His breath caught in his throat when she glided her silken fingers across his chest.

Gently setting her on the edge of the bed, Miles slowly rolled her garter and stocking down her leg. His lips followed his hands, his tongue tracing a path up the sensitive inside of her thigh. "So soft." He pressed his face against the valley between her thighs. "So sweet."

Miles lavished his attention on her other leg, rolling the silk stocking down and tickling the inside of her thigh with his tongue. He dipped his head and kissed the secret spot between her thighs, savoring the sound of her throaty moan.

Standing, Miles paused for long moments just to look at her. The princess was everything a man could want in a woman, but she wanted too much in return—she wanted him to bare his scars, his heart, his soul to her.

If he removed the mask, would he lose her and forever regret the action? How could any woman care for a man as scarred as he? Miles sat on the edge of the bed to remove his shoes, hose, and breeches. Unable to resist, he ran his fingers lightly across her belly.

Amber read the emotions warring across his face. *Indecision. Anxiety. Yearning.* She opened her arms in invitation, welcoming him without conditions.

His expression cleared. He snuffed the candle, casting the chamber into darkness. Then he removed his mask and set it on the bedside table, taking them one step closer to complete intimacy.

Miles stretched out on the bed, his muscular body lying across hers. Taking her face in both hands, he kissed her thoroughly, pouring all of his need into that stirring kiss.

Amber returned his kiss in kind. She flicked her tongue across the crease of his lips, making him groan. He parted his lips for her, and she slipped her tongue inside, exploring his mouth, teasing him.

Miles glided his lips across her face, planting kisses on her cheeks, temples, eyelids. He kissed a path down the column of her throat, and she arched her body toward him, offering herself.

Lower, his lips drifted, burning a path to her breasts. He sucked upon one and then the other, his tongue flicking across the sensitive tip.

"Yes," she whispered, pleasure shooting through her, making her yearn for his possession.

Miles knelt between her legs. He flicked his tongue down the sensitive inside of her thigh and then teased her other leg the same way. With both hands, he grasped her hips and lifted her, pressing his face between her thighs, savoring the essence of her womanhood.

Amber surrendered completely. With a soft cry, she melted against his mouth as heat surged through her.

Lowering her hips, Miles pulled a pillow beneath her bottom. He slid inside her and buried himself deep until their groins touched. Moving slowly at first, he enticed her to move with him, and when she did, he quickened their tempo.

Amber wrapped her legs around his waist and met him thrust for thrust. When he ground himself against her, she entwined her arms around his neck and pulled his face closer.

"Miles," she sighed, and pressed her lips on the scarred cheek.

That one kiss sent him reeling over the edge.

Miles lost control, shuddering and spilling his seed inside her. He captured her lips in one last, lingering kiss and rolled to the side, keeping her imprisoned within his embrace.

They spoke no words.

None were needed.

He would never let her go.

Never.

Miles kissed the crown of her head. She had made him feel like a whole man again. Yes, his injured cheek was actually smooth to the touch and looked worse than it felt, but she had kissed his scars without hesitation.

"Sleep in peace," he whispered, "for you need never worry about your uncle again."

"They will search for me," she said.

"I will kill them," Miles promised, his tone deadly.

"Thank you for protecting me." Amber fell asleep in his arms, her head against his chest.

I love her, Miles thought. The princess had brought him back from the depths of despair, a walking dead man. What if she left him once the danger had passed? She would never have chosen him if she had not needed protection.

He had loved Brenna, but his wife would never have been attracted to him if he had been scarred before they met. As much as he had loved her, Miles knew she would never have been as nurturing as the princess.

How strange were fate's twists and turns. He had thought his life was over. Now he would marry a princess, enjoy a family again, sire more children. He would give his princess gowns and jewels and—someday perhaps—seasons in London as befitting her beauty.

Her inner beauty far surpassed her uncommon physical beauty. She was a treasure to cherish.

He would begin courting her in earnest. They would wed before the end of the month.

I love him, Amber thought, awakening alone the following morning. Too bad, the earl still loved and mourned his wife. She would not think about that now but concentrate on the positive.

Amber closed her eyes and conjured the earl's image in her mind's eye. Despite his injury, Miles was a handsome man and masterful lover. Again she saw his face inching closer, felt his body covering hers, inhaled his fresh scent.

Strange, how love sneaked up on people and caught them unaware. She would keep the words of love inside lest her boldness frighten him, but she would demonstrate her love in whatever way she could. Perhaps the earl would love her, a tiny bit, once she delivered their firstborn.

A horrifying thought occurred to her. What if the earl postponed marriage until she bore him a son? Would she bear a bastard like herself?

There would be no way of knowing if she carried a boy or a girl. The earl would never chance his son being born out of wedlock.

Carrying a tray, Miles walked into her bedchamber without knocking. "You have awakened."

Amber smiled at him, a blush heating her cheeks. "You tired me last night."

"Are you complaining?"

"Reminiscing."

Miles sat on the edge of the bed. He gestured for her to sit up and, when she did, placed the tray on her lap.

"Breakfast is served, Princess."

Amber tucked the blanket beneath her arms, covering her breasts. "Did you cook this for me?" she teased him.

"I would never do that unless I wished to make you ill. Tell me about your reminiscing."

"I was daydreaming about . . . *you know*."

"Sweetheart, I told you never to feel embarrassed by what we do in bed." Miles leaned back against the headboard and put his arm around her shoulder.

Amber cast him a sidelong glance. He had sat beside her with the masked side of his face turned to her. She smiled inwardly to think how much trust they had managed to build between them. When she first arrived, he would not let her walk on that side of his body.

"The doing does not embarrass me," she told him. "Discussing the doing embarrasses me."

Miles laughed at that. "Very well, Princess, I will guess your secret thoughts. Were you, perchance, daydreaming about this?" He kissed her. "Your lips are deliciously greasy from the butter."

"Yes, my lord, I was reminiscing about our kisses."

"Were you thinking about this?" Miles slipped his

hand beneath the blanket to cup a breast as if judging its weight and gently squeezed her nipple between his thumb and forefinger.

Amber sighed. She turned her head toward him and welcomed his kiss.

"We will finish this later," Miles said, lifting his lips from hers. "If you weren't a lazy lugabed, you would know how glorious the day is. I must finish paperwork this morning, but would you care to share a picnic lunch with me?"

Happiness shone from her eyes. "I would love to share anything with you."

"Darling, a lady should never wear her heart on her sleeve."

"My heart lies inside my chest," she said with a puzzled smile.

"And what a lovely chest it is," Miles said, and then stood. "Meet me in the foyer at noon. Cook is preparing a basket for us." He winked at her and quit the chamber.

Five minutes before noon, Amber hurried downstairs. She wore a white morning gown and had woven her silver-blond hair into one thick braid.

With a wicker food basket in hand and a folded blanket draped over his arm, Miles waited in the foyer and spoke to Pebbles. When he looked in her direction, Amber gave him her sunshine smile.

The majordomo opened the door for them, saying, "Enjoy the afternoon."

"Thank you, Just-Pebbles." Amber cast the earl a puzzled look when he laughed out loud.

Miles and Amber walked across the manicured lawn toward the giant oaks that separated park from woodland. Amber felt lighthearted and, without thinking, gave a little skip of joy.

"Carry this," Miles ordered, passing her the blanket.

"Oh, what a glorious day for a picnic," she said.

They walked into the woodland and followed the cool, shaded path to the river. Oaks, beechwoods, ash, and silver-white birch crowded together here like old friends. Newmown hay and wild rose scented the air.

"Look what the rain brought." Amber pointed at a cluster of mushrooms. "Do you think any fairies are watching us pass by?"

"The only sprite I see is carrying a blanket."

Amber smiled at him. The earl was in an exceptional mood. She didn't know what had brought the change in him but was thankful to Whomever.

At the river, Miles unfolded the blanket beneath the sweeping branches of a willow and placed the wicker food basket on top of it. "Your seat, my lady," he said, gesturing to the blanket.

Amber plopped down and patted the spot beside her. Miles sat down and, unable to resist, tugged on her braid.

"You look like a young girl."

"I am a young girl when compared to your advanced age."

"Thirty-two years scarcely qualifies as ancient."

"You may believe that if it makes you feel better."

Miles laughed, a sound that was music to her ears. Amber recalled how angry he had been the first few days she had been in residence.

"You frightened me at first," she admitted, casting him a flirtatious smile.

"Frightening you was my plan," he told her. "I mistakenly believed you would go away."

"I am more tenacious than I appear."

"For that, I am grateful."

"Wait a minute." Amber stood and walked over to a patch of grass where dandelions grew. After plucking one, she returned to sit beside him again and held the dandelion beneath his chin. "You adore butter."

"I adore butter and your company." Miles leaned close to plant a kiss on her lips.

"I adore your company, too."

"Let's wade in the shallows," he said, removing his shoes and hose.

Amber followed his lead. Barefoot, she walked to the edge of the river and, hiking up the skirt of her gown, dipped her toes in the river.

"The cool water feels good," she said.

"Shall we swim?"

"Swim? What if someone—?"

"The land belongs to me. No one will see us if we disrobe."

"I do not know how to swim."

"Then I will teach you." Miles took her hand in his and led her back to the blanket. He doffed his shirt and tossed it down and then paused to unfasten her gown.

"Are you certain no one will see us?"

"I promise." He tossed his breeches aside.

Amber dropped her chemise on top of her gown. She looked at him but kept her gaze on his face, which made him smile.

"I feel very wicked," Amber said, holding his hand.

"I feel like Adam and Eve." Miles led her into the river. "They shared an idyllic existence before the serpent slithered into their paradise."

"I hope no serpent slithers into our paradise," she said, her voice barely louder than a whisper, as if she was speaking to herself.

"I will teach you the doggie paddle." Miles took both of her hands in his. "Let your legs float behind you off the riverbed and kick your feet." She complied. "That is correct." For the next ten minutes, he pulled her around in the water while she practiced kicking her feet.

"Now I will hold you beneath your belly while you kick your legs and paddle your arms like a dog." Miles demonstrated for her.

"You will not let go?"

"I will never let you go."

With the palms of his hands beneath her belly, Amber kicked her feet and paddled like a dog. She glided back and forth across the water and, after fifteen minutes, realized the earl had dropped his hands.

"I was swimming," she exclaimed, a smile of accomplishment lighting her face.

Miles grinned and held his hand out. "Come, Princess. We'll dry off while we eat lunch."

"Can we swim again tomorrow?"

"We'll see."

Amber dashed from the river to the relative protection of the willow tree's sweeping branches. With decidedly less modesty, Miles followed at a slower gait.

"Put this on." He passed her his shirt and then donned his breeches.

"Swimming made me hungry." Amber opened the wicker food basket. "What do you want to eat?"

"You."

"Would you like cold roasted princess or a spicy egg, anchovy, and Amber sandwich?"

Miles grinned. "I prefer my Amber hot."

"Then you will need to make do with chicken. Do you want a leg, thigh, or—?" Amber giggled, unable to finish.

He gave her a knowing smile. "I'll take your breast."

Amber placed the roasted chicken breast and an egg and anchovy sandwich on a plate. Then she passed him the plate and a napkin. For herself, she chose a cucumber sandwich and a macaroon.

"The macaroons are for dessert."

Amber gave him an innocent look. "I thought *I* was dessert."

"You will be dessert if I see more of your leg."

"I did meet him once," Amber said, becoming serious.

"Whom did you meet?"

"My father. On my sixteenth birthday," Amber told him, "I attended the opera for the first time with Uncle Fedor, Sergei, and Sergei's mother. With their entourage, the czar and czarina entered the lobby. He paused beside me." She closed her eyes, picturing the scene in her mind. "Czar Alexander said I had inherited my mother's beauty. Then he wished me a happy birthday."

Miles lifted her hand to his lips. "You see, Princess, the czar does love you. He even knows your birthday."

After they had eaten and packed the remains away, Miles lay down on his back and closed his eyes. Amber plucked a blade of grass, leaned over him, and glided it across his unmasked cheek.

When his lips twitched into a smile, an imp entered her soul. She tickled his nipple with the blade of grass.

"You are going to keep me awake, aren't you?"

"Probably."

Miles put his arms around her and pulled her down across his chest. "Tell me the reason you fear the dark."

Amber planted a kiss on his lips. "Uncle Fedor knew that I feared monsters living in closets," she began, her eyes filling with remembered pain. "He always disciplined me by locking me in a closet."

"I don't believe an angel like you ever required discipline," Miles said, his anger rising at the idea of her being locked in a closet. "Why didn't your cousins protect you?"

"Rudolf attended the university. My other cousins were too young to offer much protection." Amber smiled when a long-lost memory surfaced. "Rudolf arrived home once when I was crying in the closet. He chopped the door down with an axe and then went after Fedor. Only his brothers prevented him from murdering my uncle. Fedor feared Rudolf, who always championed me."

Miles moved his hand behind her head and gently

drew her face toward his. He kissed her lingeringly and then asked, "Princess Amber, will you do me the honor of becoming my wife?"

"I do not know if I am with child."

"I *want* to marry you. God willing, we will have a dozen children."

Amber gave him a smile filled with sunshine. "Yes, I will marry you."

"Let's get dressed and go home," Miles said. "We'll send notes to my sister and your cousin explaining that we have decided to marry as soon as possible."

"I would like to invite the Squelch sisters. They will represent your villagers."

Miles burst out laughing. "Darling, the citizens of Stratford are not *my* villagers."

"Whose villagers are they? Your brother-in-law's?"

"The citizens of Stratford belong to themselves," Miles explained. "They are free men and women."

"I see." Amber did not understand at all. "Still, I would like to invite those Squelch sisters."

"If you want the Squelch sisters, darling, then you will have them."

"Will your daughter live with us?"

"Do you want Caroline?"

"She belongs with us."

"I knew you would say that. We'll write those notes after dinner and post them in the morning."

Later, wearing only her chemise, Amber rested in her chamber before dressing for dinner. She lay on the bed but found napping impossible, too excited by the prospect of marrying the earl.

Today had proven a milestone in her life. The earl had proposed marriage and taught her to swim. The reason he had softened his attitude eluded her, but she felt grateful to Whomever for instigating the change.

I love him. At least, she thought she loved him. How could one be certain of true love? She had been fond of

Sergei but had never harbored these intense feelings for him. Perhaps she had known a love between Sergei and herself would be doomed. Still, she had always believed each woman had one great love in her life. For her mother, she supposed, the czar had been that man. For her, the earl would be her love.

What about his love for her? Shouldn't the woman be the man's greatest love? She thought of Brenna Montgomery. Would she always place second behind the earl's first wife? If only she knew a woman who could advise her.

Amber knew one thing for sure. The final barrier between the earl and her was that mask. Removing his mask in her presence was of utmost importance to their future. She needed to see his scars in the light of day. Accepting his scars would prove her love. Once the mask came off, no barriers would lie between them. Only then would they share true intimacy.

The sound of the door opening drew her attention. She smiled when she saw the object of her thoughts crossing the chamber.

"For you." Miles offered her a single red rose. "I didn't hurt your rosebush. At least, I heard no *ouch* cries."

"Thank you." Amber leaned against the headboard.

"Is the rosebush a boy or a girl?" Miles asked, leaning close to press a kiss on her lips.

"Both." Amber entwined her arms around his neck.

That made Miles smile. He gave her a lingering kiss. "Tell me the story about the nightingale and the rose," he said, leaning beside her against the headboard.

"How do you know about that story?"

"I overheard your conversation with the rosebush."

"Once upon a time, there lived only white roses," Amber began. "One night a perfect white rose awakened to the song of a nightingale who whispered *I love you*. When the rose blushed, pink roses bloomed all over the world."

Miles nuzzled her neck, his lips and his tongue sending delicious shivers coursing through her body. She sighed at the sensation but heard him whisper, "Finish your story."

"The nightingale moved closer, and when the rose opened her petals, he stole her virginity," Amber said, her breathing ragged as he slipped his hand down the top of her chemise to tease her nipples. "The rose colored red with shame, and red roses bloomed all over the world. Since that long-ago evening, the nightingale serenades the rose and begs for her favors, but the rose keeps her petals closed."

"How sad." Miles captured her lips in a slow, soul-stealing kiss.

They fell back on the bed. He pulled the top of her chemise down, freeing her breasts, and then caught a nipple between his lips.

"Yes," she whispered, clutching his head to her breast.

Miles slid a hand between her legs. "Open your petals for me," he whispered, his voice husky.

She spread her legs, and he pushed the bottom of her chemise up to her waist. Then he freed his erect manhood from his breeches.

Amber wrapped her legs around his waist and pulled him close. Miles groaned, gliding slowly inside her until their groins touched, and they began to move together.

"I knew you would not leave her a virgin," said a voice beside the bed.

Miles froze. Amber opened her eyes to see a pistol pointed at the side of the earl's head.

"You will need to marry her."

"I plan to marry her."

Prince Rudolf lowered the pistol. "In that case, you may finish what you were doing." Laughter lurked in his voice. "We will wait in the drawing room."

We? How many damn people were standing in his bedchamber?

Miles turned his head to see the prince leaving. He sat up and adjusted his clothing.

Amber touched his hand. "You do not need to marry me if you feel—"

He silenced her with a kiss. "I *want* to marry you."

Chapter 9

"Your cousins won't do me bodily harm, will they?" Miles joked, pausing outside the drawing room.

His question made Amber smile. "I doubt Rudolf will make me a widow before the wedding."

Unable to resist, Miles planted a kiss on her lips. "Why are you blushing?"

"Being caught like *that* embarrasses me," she admitted, dropping her gaze to his chest.

Miles tilted her chin up to gaze into her violet eyes. "Never feel embarrassed by our lovemaking." He took her hand in his and drew her forward into the drawing room.

"Lo, the groom and his bride cometh," Prince Rudolf announced when they appeared.

Five Kazanov gazes turned in their direction. Miles glanced at Amber, noted her blush deepening into scarlet, and knew she hoped her cousin had not told the others how he had found them. Her modesty pleased him, especially since she discarded it at the bedchamber door.

"Help yourselves to my whisky," Miles said, noting the glasses in their hands.

Prince Rudolf grinned. "I assumed we would be waiting hours, but that was rather quick," he said, eliciting smothered chuckles from his three brothers. He looked at the princess, asking, "Are you certain you want to marry him?"

"Interruption promotes shriveling," Miles said.

"I do not understand," Amber said, confused by the words and the smiles.

"May the Lord keep you from learning its meaning," Princess Samantha said.

"Welcome to Arden Hall," Amber greeted her cousin's wife.

"Seeing you again is a pleasure, Your Highness," Miles said, bowing over her hand.

"Too many years have passed," Samantha said.

"Come, Miles." Amber drew him toward the three young men who resembled Rudolf. "Meet my cousins."

Miles shook hands with Princes Viktor, Mikhail, and Stepan. With their black hair and dark eyes, the four Kazanov princes resembled each other but were as different from the princess as night and day. Then he remembered she was no true Kazanov, but the by-product of her mother's affair with the czar.

After giving each of her cousins a hug, Amber sat beside Samantha on the settee. "I am pleased that you came along with Rudolf. I have been wishing for a lady who can advise me on certain issues."

Miles perched on the side of the settee. "What issues?"

"Female issues," Amber answered, making her cousins smile.

Samantha patted her hand. "I will be happy to answer your questions."

"What questions?" Miles asked, looking confused.

"Female questions," Amber said. This time the cousins laughed out loud. "My lord, there are some topics that ladies can only discuss with other ladies."

"Like what?"

"Private, female topics."

Even Miles laughed this time. He looked at Rudolf, saying, "You will stay at Arden Hall, of course."

"Pebbles has already sent maids to freshen chambers," Rudolf told him.

"Your Highness, you have acquired a nasty habit of taking control of other people's lives."

"Montgomery, someone needed to take control of your life and set it straight," the prince told him. "By the way, I will send you a case of vodka upon my return to London."

"Real men drink vodka," Prince Viktor said.

"Save the whisky for the ladies," Prince Mikhail agreed.

"I do not care what we drink as long as you protect our precious cousin," Prince Stepan said.

Amber hid her face in her hands. "Rudolf, you shared my secret?"

"I needed to warn them about Fedor," Rudolf defended himself. "I presume you have told the earl."

"I know everything," Miles said. "I will protect her with my life."

"The shame belongs to Fedor," Prince Viktor told Amber.

"We should have dispatched him before leaving Moscow," Stepan said.

"Murdering one's father is bad business," Mikhail reminded his brothers. "Besides, Vladimir is almost as bad as Fedor. Thankfully, our father's diabolical thinking never infected us."

"Who is Vladimir?" Miles asked.

"Vladimir is Viktor's older twin brother," Amber answered.

"Fedor's heir," Rudolf added.

Miles looked confused. "You are the oldest, aren't you?"

"Fedor is only my legal father." Rudolf smiled at the

earl. "My brothers and I share a mother, but my natural sire is an English nobleman."

Prince Viktor changed the subject, saying, "We have secured a special marriage license."

"The minister will arrive in the morning," Mikhail added.

Miles spoke up. "I would like—"

"We have already sent a message to the Duke and the Duchess of Avon," Rudolf interrupted.

"We instructed your cook to prepare a wedding breakfast," Stepan said.

"Rudolf and I purchased a wedding ring," Samantha said. "We hope you don't mind."

"You have thought of everything." Amber laughed with delight and glanced at the earl, who appeared uncomfortable with her family's presumptions. "What if Miles had refused?"

Prince Rudolf grinned. "There was no chance of that happening."

"What about the Squelch sisters?" Amber asked.

"Inviting them at the last minute is unseemly," Miles answered. "We'll invite them to tea at a later date."

"Who are the Squelch sisters?" Samantha asked.

"His villagers."

Miles laughed out loud. "Darling, I told you the villagers belong to themselves."

"I do not understand," Amber said, shaking her head. She turned to her cousins, adding," "I have been reading about you in the *Times*." To Viktor, she said, "I had no idea you were married. Where is your princess?"

"Adele had other plans," Viktor answered, his lips curling in distaste.

"You are not in accord?"

"We are never in accord."

"I told you not to marry her," Rudolf reminded him.

"I wish I had listened."

Amber looked at Stepan. "What will you do with this

opera singer?" she asked, eliciting ribald laughter from the men.

Prince Stepan cast his brothers a quelling look. "Miss Fancy Flambeau is perfection. I intend to marry her, no matter the scandal our union will create."

"Rumor says that Miss Flambeau wants nothing to do with you or any other nobleman," Prince Mikhail said.

"I will change her mind."

Amber looked at Mikhail. "I was sorry to learn that you had been widowed, but I would love to meet your daughter."

"I can arrange that."

"Will the opera singer's sister accompany her?" Amber asked, making her cousins laugh.

In an obvious attempt to turn the conversation away from his governess, Prince Mikhail gestured to the portrait above the hearth. "Is that your late wife?" he asked the earl.

Amber felt her heart lurch when the earl answered, his love apparent in his voice. "Yes, that is my Brenna."

"What a lovely woman," Viktor was saying.

"Brenna Montgomery was a sweet woman, too," Samantha added.

"How did the fire start?" Stepan asked.

Miles shrugged. "I never investigated."

Amber watched her cousins turn surprised gazes on the earl. "Miles was badly injured and gravely ill for a long time," she said in his defense.

"If you do not understand what caused the fire," Rudolf said, "you cannot protect yourself from another."

"I have nothing to wear to my own wedding," Amber said, diverting attention from the fire. She refused to sit there and allow her cousins to criticize her intended husband. After the wedding, she would investigate the cause of the fire and hoped its origin had not vanished over the years.

"I brought you my own wedding gown," Samantha told her.

Amber smiled. "You have thought of everything."

"Dinner is served," Pebbles announced, stepping into the drawing room. "Come and get it."

"Thank you, Just-Pebbles."

The four Russian princes looked at each other and burst into laughter. "I told you his majordomo was an Original," Rudolf said.

"I can hardly wait to see the wedding gown," Amber said, looping her hand through Samantha's arm. She walked out of the drawing room with her. "I thank Rudolf and you for all you have done for me."

Samantha patted her hand. "We couldn't be happier for you. With Miles for a husband, you need fear nothing."

Pebbles was in his glory, supervising the serving of so many dinner guests. They dined on oyster soup, celery crab salad, potatoes in a mustard vinaigrette, and roasted quails.

"Good evening," Isabelle Saint-Germain called, walking into the dining room with her husband. "We came as soon as we received the good news."

The Kazanov princes and the earl stood at her entrance, but the duchess gestured for them to sit. Pebbles rushed forward to set places for the Duke and Duchess of Avon.

Before taking her seat at the table, Isabelle hurried across the room. She kissed her brother's uninjured cheek first and then Amber's. "I am so happy for you," she said. "We will need a special license, a wedding ring, and a gown for the princess."

"My cousins have taken care of the details," Amber told her future sister-in-law.

Dinner progressed pleasantly. Amber had never felt so much a part of a family as she did now. This was all she had ever wanted from life. Except love and children.

"Caroline will live with us," Amber told the duchess.

Isabelle smiled. "I will give you a week alone and then send Caroline home."

"Cousin Terrence will be terribly disappointed," John Saint-Germain remarked. "Terrence was depending on you leaving no male heirs."

"Who is this Terrence?" Amber asked.

"Terrence Pines, my closest cousin, inherits the title and the land if I die without heirs," Miles answered. "I assure you that my cousin will be happy for us, especially when we are blessed with sons."

Amber flicked a glance at the duke. She noted his doubtful expression. Could the earl be blinded by family loyalty? That worried her.

"How do I recognize true love?" Amber asked her cousin's wife. With her marriage only moments away, she worried about the earl's feelings for her. Was she about to trap herself in a loveless marriage? She desperately wanted to believe the earl would grow to love her.

"Your heart will recognize if a love is true," Samantha answered. "Are you worried that you cannot love the earl?"

"No, I worry about the earl not loving me," Amber answered, making the other woman smile. "How do I compete with his wife's memory?"

"Brenna Montgomery is gone," Samantha told her. "Miles will always have a special place for her in his heart, but he will love you, too. Come, look at yourself in the mirror."

Amber followed her across the bedchamber to the cheval mirror. Studying her appearance, Amber decided that she looked like a true princess.

The wedding gown had been created in white satin overlaid with lace and adorned with tiny seed pearls. Its bodice had a squared neckline, dropped waist, and long, flowing sleeves shaped like bells. A jeweled tiara served as her headdress.

A knock on the door drew their attention. It swung open, admitting the earl's sister.

"Welcome to the family," Isabelle said, kissing her cheek. "You are exquisitely lovely and, I hope, will become the sister I never had."

"Do you think Miles will ever care for me?"

"Do you love him?"

"With all of my heart."

"Be patient with my brother," Isabelle said. "He needs you."

Another knock sounded on the door. Wearing a broad smile, Prince Rudolf walked into the bedchamber. Samantha and Isabelle slipped out of the room, leaving her alone with her cousin.

"Thank you for finding me a husband."

"You are certain about marrying the earl?" Rudolf asked, guiding her toward the door.

"Miles is a special man, more special than I deserve," Amber answered. "I wish he could love me."

"How could he not love you?" Rudolf said, looping her hand through the crook of his arm. "You are the most lovable woman I know."

"Is there any news of Uncle Fedor?"

"He is not in England," Rudolf assured her. "Do not let thoughts of him ruin your wedding day."

"I cannot help feeling that Fedor and Gromeko will search for me," Amber said. "Fedor knows I will run to you for protection."

"If Fedor threatens you," Rudolf said, sounding like the earl, "I will kill him. Come, your groom awaits his bride."

Prince Rudolf escorted Amber down one flight of stairs to the library. Everyone turned when they crossed the chamber to the hearth where Miles and the minister waited.

Amber noted the portrait of Brenna Montgomery hanging over the hearth. Again, she wondered if she would always walk in the shadow cast by the earl's first wife.

Rudolf placed her hand in the earl's and stepped back. Miles surprised her by raising her hand to his lips. Together, they turned to face the minister.

The ceremony was surprisingly short. Her only blunder came when the earl placed the wedding ring on her finger.

"With this ring I thee wed," Miles vowed, slipping the ring on her finger. "With my body I thee worship, and with all my worldly goods I thee endow . . ."

Amber dropped her gaze to the ring he was sliding onto the third finger of her left hand, a simple band of gold topped by an enormous diamond, but it was the earl's ring that captured her attention. He was wearing her gift, the ring that had once belonged to the czar.

Her heart filled with joy. Amber threw herself into his arms, pulling his head toward her. She kissed him with passion, eliciting chuckles from her cousins.

"Child, you need to wait until the end of the ceremony for that," the minister said.

Amber blushed and released the earl. "Please continue."

"Those whom God hath joined together let no man put asunder," the clergyman said. Finally, he ended with the words, "I pronounce that they be man and wife together . . ."

Miles drew her into his arms. His lips covered hers in a lingering kiss.

Their wedding breakfast was a simple affair. There were

grilled salmon steaks, baked eggs au gratin, stuffed mushrooms, hot buttered biscuits, assorted cheeses and fruits, and wedding cake.

Miles and Amber sat together along one of the long sides of the rectangular dining table. The others sat on either side of them and along the opposite length of the table.

The Duke of Avon stood and raised his flute of champagne. "To the bride."

Amber blushed as everyone lifted champagne flutes in a toast to her. She looked at her husband, who surprised her when he stood to speak.

"I would like to thank Rudolf for interfering in my life," Miles said, slanting an amused glance at the prince.

Everyone laughed. Even the servants wore smiles.

"If not for Amber," he continued, raising his champagne flute in salute to her, "I would still be sitting in the dark."

"What are we celebrating?" asked a voice from the doorway, drawing their attention. Expensively garbed in the latest fashion, the man was short and slender. His light brown hair and mustache combined with deep-set eyes to give him a weasel's appearance.

"We are celebrating Miles's marriage," the Duke of Avon answered, finding his voice first, drawing a surprised look from the newcomer.

"Sit down, Terrence, and join us," Miles invited him. "Amber, I present my cousin, Terrence Pines. Princess Amber is a Kazanov cousin."

"Best wishes, Your Highness," Pines said, sitting at the end of the table where the majordomo set a place for him. "With your reclusive life, Miles, I'm surprised you found a wife."

Amber looked at the man sharply. The weasel's smile did not reach his eyes. In fact, hatred leaped at her husband from the man. She had long experience with hatred and recognized that emotion when she saw it.

"Perhaps my luck is changing," Miles was saying.

"Miles and Amber will soon produce an heir for Arden Hall," the Duke of Avon remarked. "That means you won't inherit."

Pines shrugged. "Inheriting Arden Hall means nothing as long as Cousin Miles finds happiness."

Amber could barely control herself from making a protective sign of the cross. She glanced at her oldest cousin, who shifted his gaze from Pines to her and nodded almost imperceptibly. Thankfully, she realized her cousin recognized the man's hatred for her husband.

"On the night of the fire," Pines was saying, "I would have been hard-pressed to see any good days on your horizon. Happily, life has proven me wrong."

Amber stared at the weasel. She had not known that he had been visiting Arden Hall on that fateful night. Her husband had never spoken of what happened. How convenient for the cousin that the countess, who could have been carrying an heir, passed away that night.

Too convenient.

Conditioned to be suspicious of others' motives, Amber decided that fate would never have shown a favorable face to this man. Every nerve in her body screamed *danger.*

"I have seen so little of my dear cousins in recent years," Amber said, determined to protect her husband and the child she could be carrying. "I beg you, cousins, visit with us a few more days to renew our acquaintances." She turned to her husband, asking, "You do not mind, do you?"

"I welcome the prospect of guests," Miles answered, his hand covering hers. "Arden Hall has been empty for too long."

"Our shared businesses require our attention," the Duke of Avon said. "Isabelle and I will stay through tomorrow."

"My cousin's new-found happiness has put me in a festive mood," Pines said. "I will stay a few days, too."

When breakfast ended, Amber kissed her husband and left the dining room with Samantha and Isabelle. The two women would help her change out of the wedding gown.

"Lady Montgomery," Rudolf called, as the women reached the foyer.

Amber paused at the base of the stairs. She smiled at her cousin's use of her married name.

"We'll meet you in your bedchamber," Samantha said, continuing up the stairs with the duchess.

"Why do you want us to remain here?" Rudolf asked, his voice low so none but she could hear.

"Pines hates Miles," Amber answered, concern etched across her face. "I saw it in his eyes."

Rudolf nodded. "I saw it, too."

"No one else noticed."

"We two have experience with hatred."

"Pines was visiting the night of the fire," Amber said. "I do not trust him."

"We will stay to protect you until Pines rides north," Rudolf promised.

"What will prevent him from riding north and then returning when you and the others have gone?"

"Lady Montgomery, you worry too much," Rudolf said. "Trust me to protect you."

Amber inclined her head and then walked upstairs. She let Samantha and Isabelle help her out of the wedding gown and then dressed in a pink silk gown.

"I need to speak to you about an important matter," Amber told them.

Neither woman spoke. They exchanged glances and looked at her.

"I do not trust Terrence Pines."

Isabelle laughed. "Terrence can be obnoxious company but hardly untrustworthy. The man is a buffoon."

"I saw the hatred in his eyes directed at Miles," Amber told them.

"How could you see what no one else noticed?" Samantha asked.

"Rudolf recognized the man's hatred, too. He and I have experience with hateful looks," Amber said. "Pines may have had something to do with the fire. Will you help me?"

"What do you want us to do?" Isabelle asked, her expression troubled.

"When the men go out tomorrow, I want to search the east wing," Amber said. "Pines was visiting on the night of the fire. Miles never inspected the east wing, and there could be proof concerning the fire's origin."

"What if Pines did leave something and sneaks in there tonight?" Samantha asked.

"Terrence won't go there during the night," Isabelle said. "He wouldn't be able to see anything."

The remainder of the day passed at a snail's pace for Amber. After dinner, coffee and tea were served in the drawing room before she could finally escape to her bedchamber.

Wearing a transparent nightgown, Amber stood in front of the cheval mirror and brushed her silver-blond hair. She could hardly wait for Miles to come to her so they could make love as husband and wife.

In the mirror, Amber saw him walk into the bedchamber and cross the room to stand behind her. Miles pushed the thick blond mane aside and nuzzled her neck. Then he slipped his arms under hers to cup her breasts over the gossamer silk, his fingertips caressing her nipples.

Amber sighed and leaned against him, allowing his hands to roam wherever they would. He pushed the straps of her nightgown off her shoulders and let it fall to the floor in a pool of silk.

Miles slid one hand down the soft skin of her belly. At the same time, he gently squeezed a nipple between his thumb and forefinger.

"I want to see my son sucking on this nipple," he whispered against her ear.

"I want to carry your son inside my body," she said, his touch making her yearn for his possession.

Amber felt a melting sensation in her lower regions. She closed her eyes and savored the feeling of his arousal.

"Open your eyes," Miles whispered. "I want you to watch your husband touching you."

Amber opened her eyes and watched him in the mirror. He caressed each breast, finally squeezing her nipples into arousal. Then he slid one hand down the silkiness of her belly to stroke the secret place between her thighs.

"Oh, Miles," she moaned. The sight and the feeling of his hands on her body was almost too much to endure.

"Surrender, my love," he said hoarsely. "Let youself go."

His whispered words and his masterful touch sent her crashing over pleasure's precipice. Amber cried out, surrendering to the throbbing pleasure.

Miles turned her around in his arms and captured her lips in a lingering kiss. She unfastened his black silk bedrobe and pushed it off his shoulders.

"I am your wife and want to see your face," Amber whispered, needing to break down the final barrier. "Will you remove your mask for me?"

"Don't ask me to do that."

Amber placed the palm of her hand against his masked cheek. "Whenever you are ready, my husband, so will I be ready, too."

She had time to tear his defenses down, a lifetime of proving her love. She could afford to be generous.

Entwining her arms around his neck, Amber pressed her body against his, savoring the sensation of her flesh touching his, and surrendered to his kiss. Miles scooped her into his arms and carried her to the bed. After snuffing out the candle, he removed his mask and joined her.

Amber knew in her heart that her husband would trust in her love and one day reveal his scars. Only then would they truly be husband and wife, their hearts entwined as one.

Chapter 10

Windswept rain. Which meant the men would not be fishing or riding that day.

Amber sighed and stared out her bedchamber window at the pelting rain. She had slept through breakfast, her husband having worn her out the night before. The hour was closing on lunch, and she had not given Pebbles his special instructions.

Since the men would be staying home, searching the east wing for incriminating evidence would be postponed. She could not chance her husband discovering her plans.

And then there was the problem of what to do with Terrence Pines. The longer he remained inside Arden Hall, the bigger the risk of his sneaking into the east wind and removing what he did not want found.

"Molly," Amber called, turning away from the window.

The maid appeared in the dressing room doorway. "Yes, Your Highness?"

"I want you to tell Princess Samantha and Lady Isabelle to attend me here as soon as possible," Amber instructed the girl. "Then instruct Just-Pebbles to come here, but not to mention anything to my husband."

The maid gave her a puzzled smile and left the chamber.

Amber paced back and forth while she waited. Someone knocked on the door and then opened it.

Both Samantha and Isabelle walked into the bedchamber.

"Look at this rain," Amber said, gesturing toward the window. "The men will not leave the house today."

"We will search the east wing tomorrow or the day after that," Isabelle said.

"I promise Rudolf and I will stay until we are sure about Pines, one way or the other," Samantha said.

"The rain is not the only problem," Amber told them. "We will need to watch Terrence. I will try to keep him busy under the guise of getting acquainted with my husband's cousin, but you will need to help me. I do not want Miles to become suspicious."

"I will help," Samantha said.

"So will I," Isabelle agreed.

A knock on the door drew their attention. Amber called, "Enter."

Pebbles walked into the bedchamber, a confused look appearing on his face when he saw the three of them. "Is something wrong, Your Highness?"

"I need your help, Just-Pebbles," Amber said, walking toward the majordomo. When the duchess laughed, she flicked her a questioning glance.

"How may I serve you?" the majordomo asked.

"Where is my husband?"

"His Lordship and the others are meeting in his office."

"Is Terrence Pines with them?"

"I believe so."

"Good." Amber gave the older man the sunniest

smile she could summon. "I want two footmen stationed near the entrance to the east wing."

"Very good, Your Highness. What shall I tell His Lordship?"

"Do *not* tell His Lordship anything," Amber said. "Do *not* mention this conversation."

"Her Highness believes Terrence may sneak into the east wing," Isabelle explained. "We think he may have set the fire that killed Lady Brenna."

"When the men go out tomorrow," Samantha added, "the three of us will search the east wing for incriminating evidence."

"Why don't you tell His Lordship what you suspect?" Pebbles asked.

"That would be too easy," Isabelle answered, and winked at the older man.

"You know my husband, probably better than I," Amber said. "He would never believe ill of a family member."

Pebbles nodded. "Do not worry, Your Highness. I will instruct a footman—"

"*Two* footmen," Amber interrupted. "If Pines sends one on an errand, the other will stand guard. He cannot send two men on the same errand. One footman should stay out of sight lest Pines think of an errand that requires two."

"Your Highness, you are a remarkable woman," the majordomo said.

"Thank you, Just-Pebbles."

Isabelle Saint-Germain laughed again. "His name is just Pebbles."

Amber looked at her. "Yes, I know."

"Macbeth's witches have arrived for lunch," Miles teased, when the three women walked into the dining room.

Amber laughed at her husband's joke and sat near Terrence Pines at the opposite end of the table. Samantha sat between her husband and his brother Mikhail.

"That remark is insulting," Isabelle told her brother, sitting between her husband and the princess.

Prince Rudolf, seated beside Miles, looked down the length of the table and said, "I do not mind moving if the bride would care to—"

"I am fine where I am," Amber said, gesturing her cousin to stay where he was. "I will use this time to become acquainted with my cousin-by-marriage."

Pebbles supervised the serving of lunch. There were spicy vegetable soup and a medley of potted dishes—chicken, shrimp, ham, mushrooms—as well as filet of sole and salad.

"Where is Joseph?" Miles asked the majordomo. "Doesn't he usually serve?"

"Joseph is completing a task for Her Highness," Pebbles informed him.

Miles gazed at his wife down the length of the table. "What task?"

Amber gave him an ambiguous smile. "A surprise."

"I can hardly wait." Miles looked at Rudolf but spoke loud enough for all to hear. "My wife baked me a special Russian dessert one day, and when I asked her its ingredients, she spouted Shakespeare at me. You know, "eye of newt" and the rest of the witches' ingredients for their infernal cauldron. I still have not managed to discover what I was eating."

Everyone laughed. Amber warmed to the sound of the earl referring to her as his wife. If lucky, she would hold her own child within a year. Hopefully, his love would follow that.

"Tell me about yourself, Terrence," Amber said, giving him her sunniest smile.

"There is not much to tell," Pines said. "I travel to

London once or twice a year and sometimes stop to visit Miles when I do."

"Do you have a wife and children?" she asked.

"I am a bachelor."

"It is never too late to marry and father some children." Amber dropped her gaze for a moment and then gave him a flirtatious smile. "What activities do you enjoy on rainy days?"

Her question elicited ribald laughter from her cousins. Amber cast a quelling look in their direction and then glanced at her husband, catching his speculative expression. "Would you care to play chess with me after lunch?" she asked Terrence.

Pines appeared flattered. "I would love a game of chess."

An hour later, Amber sat across a table from Terrence Pines in front of the hearth in the drawing room. Isabelle and Samantha sat on the settee near them to watch the chess game. Princes Viktor, Mikhail, and Stepan sat at another table and played hazard. Miles, Rudolf, and John sat together on the opposite of the room and spoke in quiet tones.

"I will take the black chessmen," Amber said to Pines, "and you may take the first move."

"As you wish, Your Highness."

Terrence started the game by moving his king's pawn two squares forward. This allowed his queen and one bishop to get into the action.

Amber decided to play recklessly and lose the game. If he won, Pines would want to play again or give her instructions that would keep him busy for hours. She did not believe he would venture into the east wing after sunset, the darkness arriving early because of the storm.

Smiling sweetly at her opponent, Amber brought her queen's knight out. He leaped over the pawns, ready for action.

"That was a bold move," Terrence said.

"I enjoy taking risks."

Terrence advanced his queen's pawn two squares, giving his queen more scope and unblocking his second bishop.

Amber countered by moving her king's pawn two squares, attacking the white queen's pawn with both knight and pawn.

"You need to learn restraint," Terrence said, advancing his queen's pawn one square forward, threatening her black knight.

"You could be correct," Amber said, and moved her knight out of harm's way.

Amber flicked a quick glance across the room. Though her husband was involved in a conversation, his gaze was fixed on her. She suffered the sudden feeling that he suspected what she was doing.

Pines moved his king's bishop's pawn two squares forward to attack her pawn one square. If he took her pawn, she would take him on the next move.

Bringing his king's knight into play, Pines threatened her king's pawn. Amber moved her bishop, effectively pinning his knight down. If he moved his knight, his queen would be unprotected.

"That was an excellent move," Terrence complimented her. "I see you have some experience with the game."

"Thank you, sir," Amber said, "but I consider myself a fair player only."

Pines brought his second knight into play. Amber moved her knight to attack his king's bishop's pawn.

He moved his king's rook's pawn one square forward to threaten her bishop. She drew first blood by capturing his knight with her bishop.

Terrence smiled at her and moved his bishop to attack her king, calling, "Check."

His cunning caught her by surprise. Amber advanced her queen's bishop's pawn one square, interposing it between her king and his attacking bishop.

He captured her pawn with his queen's pawn. She retaliated by capturing his all-powerful queen with her bishop.

"You think you have the advantage, Your Highness," Terrence said, "but you are destined to lose."

Pines captured her queen's knight with his pawn, which left her king open to his bishop's attack. "Check."

Amber moved her king, saving him from the bishop.

Now Pines moved his knight, calling, "Check."

Amber realized her husband's cousin was no fool, though he chose to dress and act like one. That made him particularly dangerous. One would never suspect a buffoon to attack.

She moved her king one square forward to save him. He countered by moving his king's bishop's pawn one square. "Checkmate," he announced.

Amber stared in surprise at the board. He had won the game—and in doing so had showed his cunning mind to her.

"You failed to consider the safety of your king," Terrence told her. "On your seventh move, you should have retreated your bishop to the square in front of the queen to protect your king from danger."

"So I will win if I remember to protect my king from danger," Amber said.

"That is correct."

"I will never leave my king unprotected again," Amber said, thinking of her husband. Then she gave Samantha and Isabelle a meaningful look.

"Will you play chess with me?" Samantha asked. "I would appreciate your giving me pointers on my game."

"Yes, of course." Terrence stood to stretch his legs. "I need a break for a few minutes, though."

"Where are you going?" Amber asked, her voice sounding overly loud in the quiet chamber.

"I need to visit the water closet."

Amber bolted out of her chair. "I will go with you."

Terrence Pines looked at her, a shocked expression on his face. Samantha and Isabelle giggled. Amber glanced at the other men, including her husband, who were staring at her.

Blushing with embarrassment, Amber laughed nervously and then amended herself. "I meant, I will walk with you. I forgot my embroidery in my chamber. I like to sew while I sit here."

Amber glanced at her husband. Miles wore a doubtful expression. He knew she was lying.

Leaving the drawing room with Pines, Amber felt her husband's gaze on her back. She hurried upstairs and grabbed her embroidery. Returning to the second floor, she paused to speak with Joseph and Albert, the footmen guarding the east wing's entrance.

"Pines tried to get past us once," Joseph reported.

"He sent Joseph on an errand before he realized there were two of us," Albert added.

That proved Pines had lost something incriminating in the fire. Amber wondered why he had not tried to retrieve it before now. Perhaps he felt secure as long as Miles lived a reclusive existence but feared exposure if her husband decided to renovate because of acquiring a wife.

"I thank you for your loyalty to His Lordship," Amber said to the footmen. "You may leave at dark but return at first light."

Terrence Pines had already returned to the drawing room and was giving chess instruction to Samantha and Isabelle. Ignoring her husband, Amber sat on the settee and started to embroider a handkerchief.

"I want to speak with you," Miles whispered against her ear, surprising her. "Privately."

Amber turned her head to look at him and managed a smile. She followed him out of the drawing room, down the corridor, and into the library.

"What are you doing?" Miles asked, rounding on her.

Amber decided to play dumb. "I am speaking with you."

His expression told Amber that her answer did not make him especially happy. "Why are you women fawning over Terrence?" he asked. "What are you planning?"

"I am merely becoming acquainted with your cousin."

"What about Samantha and Isabelle?"

Amber shrugged. "I cannot speak for them."

Miles stared at her for an excruciatingly long moment. "Keep your secrets, then." He chuckled. "I almost feel sorry for Terrence."

Standing on tiptoes, Amber entwined her arms around his neck and pulled him toward her. She planted a kiss on his lips.

"Trust me, husband. I would never keep any dark secrets from you." *Unless necessary to protect my king's safety.*

"The men are leaving," Amber said, standing at the window in the drawing room the following afternoon.

Isabelle and Samantha hurried across the room. The men were crossing the lawn in the direction of the woodland, their destination the Avon River and their planned activity fishing. Which, Amber calculated, would allow two or three hours for searching the east wing.

"You could be wrong about Terrence," Isabelle said. "He seems more like a coward than a murderer."

"Lighting a fire while others sleep proves his cowardice," Amber said. "Why are you carrying a reticule?"

"If we find something," Isabelle answered, "I can hide it in my reticule."

The three women left the drawing room and headed

toward the east wing. They paused outside the door that led into the manor's burned wing. Though four years had passed, the stagnant air still held the scent of smoke, and a melancholy atmosphere pervaded the soot-coated area.

"Watch your step," Amber warned, leading the way into the destruction.

"What are we looking for?" Samantha asked, picking her way through the debris.

"Tinder and flint would prove the fire had been set," Isabelle answered.

After more than an hour of searching, Amber was becoming increasingly frustrated. She knew she wasn't wrong about Pines. The proof of his guilt hid somewhere beneath the soot and destruction. No one committed a perfect murder.

Amber leaned against a windowsill. Absently, she lifted a finger to wipe soot from the glass, allowing light into the room. A sunbeam glinted on an object lying on the floor near the window. It was a rectangular metal box. Amber lifted it up and opened the lid. Several Lucifer matches and a piece of sandpaper lay inside. A gentleman's accoutrement. "Come here," she called to the other women as she wiped the box to reveal silver.

All three stared at the box. The initials TP had been engraved on its cover.

"My God, Terrence murdered for my brother's title and lands," Isabelle said in a horrified whisper.

"Where did you find this?" Samantha asked.

"I wiped the soot from this," Amber answered, turning to the window. "Look, Pines is returning alone. What should we do?"

"Pebbles," Isabelle called out. "Send a footman to fetch the men. And hurry."

"Yes, Your Grace," they heard the majordomo answer from the corridor.

"Pebbles loves eavesdropping," Isabelle said. "Amber,

you stand here and confront Terrence when he arrives."
She lifted a pistol out of her reticule, adding, "Samantha
and I will hide."

"Don't worry," Samantha said, lifting her skirt to
draw a small but deadly-looking dagger from a sheath
strapped to her leg.

Isabelle and Samantha hurried across the chamber
to hide along the wall behind the door. Shaking in
fright, Amber held the silver matchbox and faced the
door. Droplets of perspiration rolled down the crevice
between her breasts. A noise in the corridor made her
heartbeat quicken. The trembling in her hands picked
up speed, her knees shook, her breath came in shallow
gasps.

And then the door opened.

"What are you doing here?" Pines demanded, surprised.

"Are you looking for this?" Amber asked, holding the
matchbox up, keeping her gaze on him lest he realize
the other two women were advancing on him.

"I lost that in the fire."

Amber stepped back as he moved toward her. "You
set the fire to kill my husband."

"What a pity that an exquisite piece of womanflesh
should suffer a fatal accident," Pines said, an unholy
gleam in his eyes. "You will fall from the window behind
you."

"I don't think so." Isabelle touched the back of his
head with the pistol.

Samantha touched his cheek with the tip of the dagger. "I don't think so, either."

"Slowly lift your hands into the air and turn around,"
Isabelle ordered. "Walk to the library. I'll shoot if you
try anything."

"Cousin Isabelle—"

"*Move.*"

With their prisoner in the lead, the three women followed him to the library. Pebbles met them there. Amber lifted a length of rope from the majordomo's hands.

"Tie his wrists together," Isabelle instructed her.

Amber stepped closer.

In a flash of movement, Pines grabbed the rope out of her hand, wrapped it around her neck, and pulled hard. "Drop the pistol or I'll strangle her," Terrence threatened.

Isabelle started to lower the pistol. At the same moment, Samantha leaped close and flicked the blade down his cheek.

"You sliced me," Pines screamed, blood spurting from his wound, releasing his captive to clutch his face.

"How dare you touch a princess of Russia," Amber gasped, rounding on him. Spying an old broadsword mounted on the wall, she grabbed it and nearly toppled over from its weight. She intended to cleave the man in half for what he had done to her and her husband.

"Prepare to burn in hell," Amber said, struggling to lift the broadsword.

"Stop." Her husband stood in the doorway.

Amber stopped, but the broadsword threatened to topple her backward. Miles reached her in time and easily lifted the sword out of her hands.

"What the bloody hell is happening?" Miles demanded, as the other men crossed the room toward them.

"Those bitches are trying to kill me," Pines cried. "Look at my face."

"Samantha, my love, did you slice this man?" Prince Rudolf asked, laughter lurking in his voice.

"He needed slicing."

The Duke of Avon lifted the pistol out of his wife's hand, asking, "Sweetheart, were you planning to shoot Cousin Terrence?"

"I warned him not to move," Isabelle explained, "but he wrapped the rope around the princess's neck and strangled her."

"Look what we found in the east wing," Amber said, when her husband turned to her.

Miles lifted her chin and inspected the bruising around her neck. Rounding on his cousin, he asked, "You did this to my wife?" There was no mistaking the deadly anger in his voice and expression.

"You don't understand," Pines whined. "These bitches ambushed me."

"Look," Amber cried, and shoved the silver matchbox into her husband's hands. "This proves your cousin set the fire."

"She's lying," Pines insisted.

Miles stared at the matchbox with the initials TP engraved on its cover. Lifting the lid, he saw the Lucifer matches and sandpaper.

"Where did you get this?"

Amber glared at his cousin before answering, "I found it in the east wing."

"You went into the east wing after I forbade you to go there?" Miles said, passing the matchbox to his brother-in-law.

Amber dropped her mouth open in surprise. "You are not grateful that we discovered a murderer?"

"Miles, you aren't being fair," Isabelle spoke up. "The princess worried—"

"Stay out of my marriage," Miles interrupted, silencing her. He looked at his wife. "My gratitude does not alter the fact that you disobeyed me."

For a few seconds Amber was at a loss for words. Then she appealed to her cousin. "Rudolf—"

"Do not complain to me," the prince interrupted her. "Only yesterday you vowed obedience to your husband, and today you broke that vow."

Amber could not believe what she had heard. Rudolf always sided with her, no matter the circumstance.

"We will discuss this later," Miles said, with a glance at his cousin. "I have a more pressing problem than your disobedience."

"What will you do to him? He deserves to die."

"You may leave now. Take the other ladies with you."

"Leave?"

"Practice your stitches, or bake a cake," Miles said. "We men will handle this now."

Amber narrowed her gaze on him but retreated when he cocked a brow at her. She turned on her heels and followed Isabelle and Samantha.

After his wife had disappeared, Miles gave his cousin his full attention. Nobody said a word, for which he was thankful, knowing in his heart that his cousin had started the fire that killed Brenna. With the least bit of encouragement, Miles would finish the job the ladies had begun.

"What do you say about this?" Miles asked, holding the matchbox up.

"My face is bleeding," his cousin whined.

Miles stepped closer. Dangerously closer.

"I know nothing about the fire," Pines said hastily.

"Liar," Prince Rudolf growled.

"I swear I am innocent of any wrongdoing."

Miles could not suppress his anguish. "You killed Brenna."

"Let us take him into the woods and shoot him," Rudolf suggested. His three brothers nodded in agreement.

"Disposing of his body will not be difficult," Prince Viktor said.

Miles stared at his cousin, trying to squelch the temptation to kill him. He whirled away and stared into the hearth.

"You can't seriously be considering this," Pines wailed.

Miles felt his brother-in-law's hand on his shoulder. "No one would blame you."

"I cannot condone murder," Miles said. "No matter how much he deserves to die."

"Execution is not murder," Prince Stepan said.

"Nevertheless, we will deliver Terrence to the magistrate in the morning." Miles needed to get away from his cousin before he changed his mind.

"The matchbox may not be enough for a conviction," Prince Rudolf said.

"A man needs to live with his own conscience," Prince Mikhail said. "Let the earl decide for himself."

Miles turned to the prince. "Thank you for that."

"His existence threatens Amber and the child she could be carrying," Rudolf argued.

"Pebbles," Miles called.

Obviously having been eavesdropping, the majordomo immediately rushed into the library. "Yes, my lord?"

"Do we have a key for any of the top-floor chambers?"

"Yes, my lord."

"I can't bear to look at him," Miles said, turning to Rudolf. "Will you and your brothers take him upstairs and lock him inside?"

"I had nothing to do with the fire," Pines defended himself as Viktor and Stepan yanked him out of the chair. "For God's sake, I saved your life."

"*I* pulled the earl from the flames," Pebbles corrected him. "You came to my aid after I had saved him."

With the majordomo leading the way, the four Russian princes dragged his protesting cousin out of the library. Once they had disappeared, Miles poured himself a whisky and downed it in one gulp.

Wandering to the window, Miles stared out at the summer afternoon. The world looked the same as it had a few minutes earlier—shining sun, blooming flowers, chirping birds. All seemed different somehow, the past's heartache rushing back to him in a wave of emotion.

He almost wished his bride had stayed out of the east wing. *Almost.*

"Your wounds are bleeding again," the Duke of Avon said, grasping his shoulder.

Miles reached up and touched his brother-in-law's hand. "I cannot believe Terrence killed Brenna to inherit a title."

"All men are not honorable," John said. "Don't judge your wife too harshly. She was thinking of your welfare."

"If we had delayed a few minutes," Miles said, a grudging smile touching the corners of his lips, "the ladies would have saved us the trouble of a trial. I could hardly believe my eyes when I saw Amber trying to lift that old broadsword. By the way, I didn't know my sister carried a pistol."

"My mother taught her that little trick," John admitted. "Carrying a large reticule means my mother is armed and dangerous."

"Can she or my sister shoot?"

"Very well, thank you."

"Do you think Rudolf knew Samantha carried a dagger?"

"The prince appeared more amused than surprised."

"I need to make peace with my wife," Miles said. Without another word, he left the library.

Amber paced back and forth in front of the hearth in the drawing room and fumed about her husband's attitude. Instead of reprimanding her for disobedience, he should have praised her for ferreting out a murderer. *The ingrate.*

"Is Pines dead?" she asked when her husband appeared. "He deserves to die."

Miles ignored her question. "Come with me."

Was that amusement in his eyes? Or anger at her disobedience?

Amber gave him a disgruntled look. "Are you still angry?"

Miles shuttered his expression. "We will discuss this behind closed doors."

Amber inclined her head and marched beside him down the corridor toward the stairs. Her husband was tall, his long-legged gait forcing her to take three steps for every one of his, conveying the unspoken message that he was in charge, not she.

Miles ushered her inside her bedchamber. Amber rounded on him, her hands on her hips.

"What do you have to say to me?" she challenged him.

Miles snaked his hands out to grasp her upper arms and yanked her against his unyielding frame. Surprised, Amber stared at him through enormous violet eyes.

Dipping his head, he captured her lips in an urgent kiss as if he feared losing her. She slid her hands up his chest, looped her arms around his neck, and returned his kiss with equal passion.

Their kiss ended as abruptly as it began.

"If you ever pull another stunt like that," Miles warned her, "I'll take you across my knee."

"What does *stunt* mean?" Amber asked, confused. "Why would you take me across your knee? Is that a new—you know—position?"

Miles closed his eyes and swallowed his laughter. So much for husbandly discipline.

"Sit here," he said, guiding her to the bed.

Amber sat on the edge of the bed and looked at him expectantly. Miles sat beside her and put his arm around her, drawing her close.

"Darling, you did a very foolish thing today," he told her. "Terrence could have murdered you, too. You should have voiced your concerns and allowed me to investigate."

Trying to appear contrite, Amber touched her bruised neck in an unspoken reminder that she had been injured on his behalf. "I promise never to do anything like this again."

Miles studied her for a long moment as if doubting her words. "Why did you suspect Terrence? You never met him before yesterday."

Amber shrugged. "He would have gained by your death. His presence on the night of the fire combined with the expression in his eyes shouted his guilt."

"What expression?"

"I recognized his hatred."

Miles gave her an indulgent smile. "Sweetheart, how could you see what no one else saw?"

"Rudolf saw it, too."

Miles appeared confused. "I don't understand."

"Rudolf and I have experience with hate," Amber tried to explain.

"How could anyone possibly dislike you?" Miles asked, holding her close. "You are an angel."

"Thank you, my husband."

"You are welcome, my wife."

"I promise never to do anything so foolish again."

Unless absolutely necessary.

Chapter 11

A long, shrill scream pierced the night.

Amber opened her eyes, uncertain of what had awakened her. Miles sat on the edge of the bed and donned his mask.

"What is it?" she asked, placing the palm of her hand against his back.

Miles glanced over his shoulder at her. "I don't know." He pulled his breeches up and reached for his robe. "Go back to sleep."

"I am going with you," Amber said, scrambling off the bed. She donned her bedrobe and fastened it tightly around her waist.

Clutching the night candle, Miles headed for the door. Amber walked a step behind him. John and Isabelle, along with Rudolf and Samantha, stood at the top of the stairs.

"You heard that, too?" Miles asked, turning to walk up the stairs to the third floor. "Do you think it was Terrence?"

"The scream came from outside," John said.

The three couples hurried downstairs to the foyer and then outside to the courtyard. Following voices, they walked around the mansion to see a small crowd gathered. Pebbles and several footmen stood in a circle and stared at something on the ground.

New voices sounded behind them. Amber looked around to see her three cousins, wrapped in bedrobes, hurrying toward them.

The footmen stepped back so the earl could see what held their attention. On the ground lay the lifeless body of Terrence Pines.

Amber shifted her gaze to her husband, who turned toward her cousins. Before he could speak, the princes held their hands up in a gesture of innocence.

"His neck is broken," the Duke of Avon said, crouching down to inspect the body.

"Terrence must have been trying to escape," Rudolf said, staring at the top-floor window.

"God's will be done," Pebbles said.

"Amen," said Princes Viktor, Mikhail, and Stepan.

Amber peeked at Rudolf, who actually winked at her. And she knew. Her cousins had executed Pines by tossing him out the upper-floor window.

She touched her husband's arm. "The Lord punished his crime and saved us from scandal."

"Who are we to question God's wisdom?" Miles turned to the footmen, instructing, "Wrap the body in a sheet and place him in the chapel until morning."

Everyone except the footmen returned inside. No one spoke as they climbed the stairs to their bedchambers.

"Go to bed," Miles said, passing Amber the night candle. "I need a drink."

Reaching her husband's bedchamber, Amber removed her bedrobe and climbed into bed. What was her husband feeling about his cousin's death? She hoped he wasn't feeling guilty on the off-chance that Pines had been innocent.

Her husband was an honorable man and trusted

other men to be equally honorable. She prayed he would never suspect her cousins' guilt. That could cause trouble in her marriage.

A long time later Amber heard the door open. Through half-closed eyes, she watched Miles cross the chamber to the bed. He tossed his robe aside and sat on the edge of the bed to remove his breeches, then snuffed out the night candle.

Amber sensed his movement as he removed his mask. The bed creaked as he lay down and rolled toward her, drawing her into his arms.

"How do you feel?" she asked.

"Relieved."

"Terrence did not confess."

"Do you believe in his guilt?" he asked.

"Yes."

"So do I." Miles planted a kiss on her lips. "Your cousins do not fool me, though."

"What do you mean?"

"Do not tell your cousins this," Miles said, "but Terrence feared heights and would never have climbed out that window." He dropped his hand to her breast. "His execution has reminded me again how precarious life is." He rolled over, pinning her beneath him, his lips hovering above hers. "One should never lose the opportunity to affirm life, especially by making love. Do you agree, my sweet?"

Amber answered by wrapping her legs around his waist.

"The coach is coming up the drive."

Miles looked at Amber and tossed the quill aside. He rose from his desk and followed his wife downstairs to the courtyard.

Days earlier, the magistrate had ruled Terrence Pines's death accidental. All involved had returned to their own lives. After giving the newlyweds a week to settle into married life, the Duke and Duchess of Avon ordered their niece's belongings packed and sent her home to Arden Hall.

"Welcome home, Caroline," Amber called, when the coach halted in the courtyard.

Miles opened the door and laughed when his daughter leaped into his arms. "Welcome home, Caro."

"I heard you married my daddy," Caroline said, after kissing her father. "Do I call you Mummy?"

Amber hesitated. She had no problem with her stepdaughter calling her Mummy, but the earl might have a different opinion.

Miles shrugged and inclined his head. His gaze conveyed the message that he would leave the decision to her.

"Of course you may call me Mummy." Amber smiled at her stepdaughter. "Just-Pebbles is waiting to serve us lunch. Are you hungry?"

Caroline clapped her hands together. "I'm so damn happy," she said.

Both Miles and Amber stared in surprise at her. Recovering herself first, Amber said, "That is a bad word."

"You mean *damn?*"

"Where did you hear that?" Miles asked.

Caroline gave him an innocent smile. "Lord Naughty says *damn* all the time."

Amber laughed, earning a frown from her husband.

"Do not encourage her," Miles said, walking toward the mansion. "And you, Miss Montgomery, do not use Lord Naughty's vocabulary."

"Welcome home, Miss Caroline," Pebbles greeted them at the door.

"Who is that man?"

"Just-Pebbles works for your father," Amber answered. "He has known you since you were a baby."

"I never saw him before," Caroline said, making them smile.

"Luncheon is served," Pebbles announced, and followed the three of them down the corridor to the dining room.

Miles sat at the head of the table. Amber sat beside him, her back to the hearth, and the little girl sat opposite her.

A roasted chicken with mushroom stuffing appeared on the table. Brown gravy, roasted potatoes, and roasted parsnips accompanied it.

Pebbles poured the earl a glass of wine and then looked at Amber, who refused with a shake of her head. Watching this byplay, Caroline said, "I prefer lemonade, Just-Pebbles."

Miles laughed, drawing his daughter's attention. "Are you certain you wouldn't like wine, Lady Caroline?"

"Lemonade makes me pucker like a fish." Caroline pursed her lips into a fishlike pucker.

Amber burst into delighted laughter. Between the two of them, she thought—his daughter and herself—the earl's heart would surely heal.

"What is the latest news about Lord Naughty and Lady Begood?" Amber asked.

Caroline shook her head sadly. "Lord Naughty *ruined* Lady Begood."

Miles shouted with laughter, earning a reproving look from his daughter. "I'm sorry," he apologized.

"Being ruined is no laughing matter," Caroline told him.

Amber giggled. "How exactly did Lord Naughty ruin Lady Begood?"

Caroline lowered her voice to a loud whisper, "Lady Begood danced with him *five* times at Lady Gossip's ball. What a scandalbroth." She pointed toward the hearth, asking, "Who is that lady?"

Amber didn't need to look over her shoulder to know the child was referring to the portrait of Brenna

Montgomery. She slid her gaze from the daughter to the father, who cleared his throat.

"That lady is your mother," the earl told her, obviously uncomfortable with the fact that his daughter didn't know her own mother.

"Oh." Caroline stared at the portrait a moment longer and then resumed eating. After a few minutes, she asked, "Mummy, what will we play after lunch?"

"I thought a nap would be a good idea."

Caroline looked horrified. "Only babies take naps."

"Why don't we walk in the garden instead," Amber suggested.

The remainder of their luncheon passed without event. When Miles headed for his office, Amber and Caroline walked outside.

"I want to introduce you to a special friend," Amber said, leading the girl around the mansion. She ushered her across the lawn and said, "This rosebush hurt. See how my love healed it. These blossoms are perfect."

"Daddy hurts, too," Caroline said. "Can you make him feel better?"

Amber assumed the girl was referring to the earl's face. How could she explain that physical scars could not be cured?

"Why do you think your daddy hurts?"

"Daddy hurt his heart," Caroline answered, placing her hand across her chest. "That's what Aunt Belle said. Can you fix him?"

Amber blinked back tears and swallowed the lump of emotion in her throat. "I will try my hardest to make him well."

"What's that?" Caroline asked, pointing at the stone building in the distance.

"That is your family's chapel."

"Can we look?"

Amber nodded and, taking the child's hand in hers,

led her across the garden to the graveyard. She opened the wooden gate and went down the stone steps first, explaining, "Your ancestors lie at rest here."

"What are *ancestors?*"

"Ancestors are relatives who have come and gone."

"Come and gone where?"

Amber smiled at her question. "Come to earth and gone to heaven."

Caroline nodded as if she understood. "Where is my first mummy?"

Amber walked in the direction of Brenna Montgomery's grave marker. She felt certain the girl had questions only her father could answer.

"Brenna was your mummy's name," Amber told her. "She loved you very much, more than life itself. Your daddy loved her so much he put her portrait in every room. No matter where he stands, your daddy can see her face. In fact, your daddy was injured trying to save her by running into the fire instead of away from it. Only special people receive that kind of love."

"Do you?"

Amber didn't know what to say. "Someday, if I am lucky . . ." Taking the girl's hand in hers, she turned to leave and gave a tiny gasp of surprise.

Miles stood there.

Amber wondered how much he had heard. She hoped he wouldn't shout at her.

"Caroline has questions," Amber said. "I will leave you to your privacy." She brushed past him, but he grasped her arm, preventing her from leaving.

"Please stay."

Her heart filled with hope.

When she inclined her head, Miles released her. He lifted his daughter into his arms, asking, "What do you want to know, sweet?"

"Does dying hurt?" Caroline asked, staring into his eyes.

"Sometimes dying does hurt," Miles answered.

Caroline looked worried. "Fire burns, and burns hurt."

"Your mother did not hurt," Miles assured her. "The smoke stole her breath. She went to sleep and never opened her eyes again."

Caroline digested this piece of information. "Why don't you have a picture of my new mummy?"

"I plan to make a picture of her and you," Miles said. "First I need to hire an artist. Can you wait until then?"

Caroline nodded.

"Do you have more questions?"

Caroline nodded. "Do you know any stories, Mummy?"

Amber gave her a sunshine smile. "I know hundreds of stories and promise to tell you one every night at bedtime."

Amber kept her promise every night for two months, the happiest sixty days of her entire life.

The summer solstice heralded the changing season, followed by the dog days. August waned, as did summer's heat. Splashes of goldenrod appeared here and there, foreshadowing autumn's rioting blaze. September gave birth to purple asters, color-tipped trees, and Michaelmas daisies.

"I love hedgehog pudding," Caroline said, standing at the work table in the center of the kitchen. "Daddy loves it, too."

"Have you ever eaten hedgehog pudding?" Amber asked, admiring their creation.

"No."

"How do you know you love it?"

"I love it because you made it."

"That makes sense to me," Mrs. Meade said, working at the butcher block near the stove.

Hedgehog pudding consisted of an oval-shaped

sponge cake saturated in sherry. Flaked almonds, packed in rows covering the cake, served as the hedgehog prickles. A baked custard moated the cake.

"Nanny Smart, does this look like a hog?" Caroline asked.

"*Hedge*hog," the older woman corrected her.

Caroline approached the cook. "What are you making?"

"Fried bloaters."

Mrs. Meade chopped the head and the tail off the fish. Then she opened the bloater's back and boned it.

Queasiness gripped Amber. Like the roll and pitch of a ship at sea, her stomach flip-flopped with nausea. She raised her hand to her throat and tried to quell the sickness.

"Take Caroline upstairs," Mrs. Meade ordered the nanny. Then she whisked Amber outside the kitchen door.

Amber retched in the herb garden. Her face ashen, she straightened when her spasms ended. Beads of perspiration beaded her upper lip and rolled down her neck to the valley between her breasts.

"I am sorry," Amber apologized. "I believe the bloaters got the better of me."

Mrs. Meade helped her sit on the door stoop. "Keep your head down until your strength returns."

"I cannot imagine what is wrong. One minute I was perfectly well and the next . . ."

"You're carrying His Lordship's heir."

Amber looked up in surprise. "How can that be?"

"The usual way, I suppose."

"Are you certain?"

"You have all the symptoms," Mrs. Meade told her. "Excuse my boldness, but have you had your menses lately?"

Amber started to shake her head but thought her

sickness would return. "I cannot remember the last time."

"Eat bread each morning before you rise," Mrs. Meade advised her. "Do not put yourself in the path of certain scents or even sights."

"Like bloaters having their heads chopped off?"

"You'll need to nap each afternoon," the older woman told her, helping her up. "Go along to your chamber and rest a while."

Amber left the kitchen. She was safe. Fedor could not force her to return to Russia now. She wore the earl's wedding band on her finger and carried his child inside her womb. Her husband would protect her with his life. If not for love of her, then desire for his heir.

Gaining her bedchamber, Amber removed her gown and lay on the bed. She could not help thinking that she would have what she had always wanted, a family.

While his wife climbed the stairs to her bedchamber, Miles sat in his study one floor down. Frowning, he read the letter from Prince Rudolf delivered by courier.

I received a letter from Fedor demanding Amber's return but believe this could be a ploy. I suspect Fedor is already in London.

We cannot protect Amber indefinitely. Bring her to London to ferret Fedor out of his hole. Do not tell Amber what we plan. . . .

The last thing Miles wanted to do was travel to London. He hadn't appeared in society since before the fire and had no idea what his reception would be. More importantly, he did not want to place his wife in danger by using her as bait.

On the other hand, Prince Rudolf did make sense. After all, how could they possibly guard her every moment of every day until Fedor or Gromeko died?

"My lord?"

Miles focused on his majordomo. "Yes, Pebbles?"

"Mrs. Meade said that Her Highness is ill."

"Thank you, Pebbles." Miles hurried out of his study and took the stairs two at a time.

With concern etched across his features, Miles perched on the edge of his wife's bed. "Meade said you were ill."

Amber put her arms around his neck, savoring the heat emanating from his body. She felt his strong arms holding her, rested her head against his shoulder, and met his gaze. Love shone from her eyes. "We are going to have a baby."

Miles looked momentarily surprised. Then he smiled, "Are you certain?"

"Meade says I have all the symptoms."

Miles lowered his lips to hers. His kiss was tender, gentle, almost reverent.

"I will not break."

In response, Miles deepened his kiss, drawing her onto his lap, holding her against his muscular frame. Finally he lifted his lips away and said, "Thank you."

Amber placed a finger across his mouth. "Do not thank me until I deliver our child."

"All will be well," he assured her. "Or are you planning to worry the whole nine months?"

"Probably longer."

"How long?"

"I will worry about our children until the day I die."

That made him smile. He crushed her against his chest and said, "That means you will make an excellent mother."

"Make love to me?"

"I can never refuse you that."

Miles put her off his lap and, a moment later, stood naked in front of her. Amber rose from the bed, her eyes gleaming with a mixture of love and desire. With silken fingers, she caressed her husband's erection and smiled when he moaned.

"Enough." Miles slid the straps of her chemise off her shoulders, and the garment pooled at her feet. He drew her nakedness against his own, their hot flesh touching from breast to thigh, and kissed her lingeringly.

"I want no barriers between us." Amber placed the palm of her hand against his masked cheek. "Remove your mask. *Please*."

Reluctance appeared in his eyes. "You don't know what you are asking."

"I am asking for your trust."

"We have been content these past two months."

"We will continue to be content," Amber assured him. "Please, Miles, bare yourself to me as I have bared myself to you."

"I can't," he said in a choked voice.

She had lost.

"You remove the mask for me." Miles closed his eyes against seeing her reaction.

Seeing the tense expression on her husband's face, Amber felt fear coiling inside her. She steeled herself for what she would see. Slowly, she raised her hands to the mask and then hesitated. Summoning her courage, she lifted it off and set it down.

Yes, his facial scars were ugly. Pretty scars did not exist. And yet—

Amber saw only Miles. Her husband. Her lover. Her protector. No scars. "Open your eyes." When he did, she pressed a gentle kiss on his scarred cheek and whispered, "I love you."

Miles groaned in relief and pulled her into his arms. His lips captured hers in a kiss that lasted forever.

Scooping her into his arms, he placed her on the bed and then lay beside her. "I don't want to hurt you or—"

"You will not hurt us," she told him, caressing his scarred cheek.

Miles gathered her into his embrace. With one large hand on the back of her head and the other clasping her buttocks, he held her steady as he kissed her.

Amber loved the strength of his arms surrounding her, the heat emanating from his body, the hard planes of his muscles touching her softness. She melted against him, offering herself.

A primitive possessiveness surged through Miles. This woman was his mate, nurturing his seed inside her womb. She had accepted him unconditionally, seeing past the scars to the man beneath.

Miles kissed her, his tongue slipping into her mouth, tasting her sweetness. His thrusting tongue mirrored the movement of his hips. Rolling onto his back, he pulled her on top of him. Amber pushed her tongue past his lips, controlling their kiss.

With a soft smile on her lips, Amber lowered herself onto his erection. Slowly. Very slowly.

Miles cupped her breasts and traced his thumb across her sensitive nipples. Amber moaned at the sensation. She reveled in their joining, his body hot and hard inside her. She circled his nipples with her fingers, making them hard.

"Ride me, wife."

And Amber rode him.

Slowly at first, Amber increased the tempo of her undulations. Staring into his eyes, she felt the melting in her lower regions ready to explode.

"Surrender to me," Miles whispered. He held her hips in a firm grasp and thrust upward.

Amber flew over pleasure's precipice. She threw her head back, mewling low in her throat, her moist heat contracting around her husband. He shuddered as his seed flooded her.

Miles held her against his body as they floated back

to earth from their shared paradise. His hands stroked her back and buttocks as aftershocks shook her body. He tightened his grip when he felt her kiss the side of his throat and again murmur her love. He wanted to say the words, return her emotion, but stopped himself.

Saying those three words could jinx them. He knew she needed to hear them, but it was too soon. A piece of his heart believed he would be betraying Brenna's memory.

For the first time in four long years, Miles felt his spirits soaring. His wife's love and acceptance had broken the melancholy chains he had wrapped around his heart.

He dropped a kiss on the crown of her head. "We are going to London," he told her. When she looked at him in surprise, he added, "I own a town mansion and will give you the funds to decorate to your heart's content."

"My heart is content to remain in Stratford."

"Come the spring, you will have grown too big to travel," Miles said. "I plan to take you to the opera, balls, whist parties, riding in Hyde Park—"

"Can Caroline come, too?"

"Yes, of course."

"And we will not stay long?"

"No."

Amber searched his eyes for the truth, asking, "Are you ready for society?"

"With you beside me, I am ready for anything."

"What if Fedor—?"

"You need never fear your uncle again," Miles promised her. "If he comes to England, I will kill him."

Chapter 12

They arrived at the Berkeley Square mansion on the evening of October's first day. All four of Amber's cousins and Miles's sister and brother-in-law planned to remain in London for the duration of their visit.

"Good morning, Just-Pebbles." Amber stood at the sideboard and helped herself to breakfast the next morning.

"Good morning, Your Highness," the majordomo greeted her. "Would you prefer coffee or tea?"

"Tea, I think."

Amber joined Miles and Caroline at the table. Her husband was reading the morning *Times* while her stepdaughter pushed scrambled eggs around on her plate.

Visiting London made Amber nervous, but she decided to make the best of it for her husband's sake. She would never go anywhere alone, she decided, and would read the *Times* each morning for news of Fedor.

Miles looked up from the newspaper. "What will my two favorite ladies do this morning?"

"Caroline and I will inspect the health of your garden," Amber answered. She looked at her stepdaughter. "Is that all right with you?"

The little girl nodded.

"Later, Caroline and I will bake a happiness cake," Amber added, and winked at the girl.

Miles smiled. "How does one bake a happiness cake?"

"Mix a cup of good deeds with forgiveness and joy," Caroline told her father, returning her stepmother's wink.

"Bake with love," Amber prompted her.

"Serve with a blessing and a smile," Caroline finished.

"I can't wait to taste it," Miles said.

"What are your plans?" Amber asked.

"Rudolf is meeting with me here."

Amber dropped her gaze to the *Times*, asking, "Is there anything interesting?"

Miles turned to the society gossip column on page three and read, "Injured while fighting the fire that claimed his wife, the Earl of Stratford has emerged from his four-year seclusion. The earl will introduce his recent bride, Princess Amber Kazanov, to London society."

"The *Times* mentioned us?" Amber blanched, her stomach flip-flopped, and her hands trembled at the thought that Fedor and Gromeko were in London and knew her whereabouts. "Who told the reporter we were here?"

Miles turned to his daughter. "Will you do Daddy a favor? Tell Nanny Smart to fetch shawls for Mummy and you."

Caroline nodded and left the dining room.

"Rudolf told the reporter about our arrival," Miles said. "The marriage of a princess and my return to society are newsworthy."

"I did not want our presence in London printed in a newspaper. Uncle Fedor will know where to find me."

"That is precisely what we thought, too."

His statement surprised and confused her. "I do not understand."

"I will not let anything bad happen to you," Miles assured her, reaching to cover her hand. "We cannot hide in Stratford forever."

Amber yanked her hand back. "*You* hid in Stratford when doing so suited you."

"That is not to the point."

"What is to the point?" Amber asked, standing. "What threatens me is unimportant?"

"Wouldn't you rather live knowing that Fedor posed no threat?"

"The risk is too great," she cried.

"Amber . . ." Miles rubbed the uninjured side of his face in frustration.

"I trusted you to protect me," she said, "but you and my cousin have placed me in danger." Amber started for the door. Miles stood to go after her, but Caroline appeared with the shawls.

Accompanied by Nanny Smart, Amber and Caroline walked outside to the garden. The trees were depressingly barren, having shed their orange, red, and gold leaves in a recent wind and rainstorm.

Watching her stepdaughter leap into a pile of dead leaves, Amber wished she could recapture her own youthful exuberance—except that she had never enjoyed such innocent joy. Her mother's murder had aged her prematurely into adulthood, and living in her uncle's home had produced little joy.

Amber wandered around the garden, inspecting shrubs and plants. A solitary rosebush appeared doomed from neglect, in urgent need of her ministrations. To that end, she picked its dead leaves but decided to prune it the following day. At the moment, she worried about taking her anger at her husband out on the rosebush.

* * *

Miles stood at the window in his study and watched his wife and daughter. "Amber would have preferred to hide in Stratford," he told the prince. "Using her as bait is a betrayal of her trust."

"We cannot protect her indefinitely," Rudolf said, relaxing in a chair. "We need to force Fedor's hand, assuming he is in England. She will forgive you when her safety is assured."

Miles raised his brows at his cousin-in-law. "That is easy for you to say. You aren't living with an angry pregnant wife."

"You will survive. Did you hear what happened at King's Bench the other day?"

"No."

"A newly appointed judge found a woman guilty of prostitution but forgot what the punishment was," Rudolf said, his expression solemn. "He stopped the proceedings and left the courtroom to consult the Chief Justice, asking how much he should give a prostitute. The Chief Justice shrugged and told him *a few shillings*."

Miles threw back his head and shouted with laughter.

"Excuse me, my lord."

"Yes, Pebbles?"

"A gentleman in the foyer is demanding to speak with the princess."

"Damn, I forgot about Pushkin when I slipped the reporter that information about your marriage," Rudolf said.

Count Sergei Pushkin. His wife's former suitor. "Tell him the Countess of Stratford is unavailable."

Pebbles left the study. Miles and Rudolf sat in silence, neither believing the Russian nobleman would go quietly.

Pebbles returned. "He refuses to leave."

Miles glanced at Rudolf. "Escort him here," he instructed the majordomo.

Count Sergei Pushkin was tall and broad-shouldered and as handsome as he was big. Piercing gray eyes topped by black brows. A thick mane of black hair on his head. *No scars.*

Miles stood when the other man walked into his study but did not offer his hand. He couldn't help thinking that the count's dark good looks were the perfect foil for Amber's petite blondeness. They would have made an extremely attractive couple.

"I would invite you to sit," Miles said, "but you won't be staying."

With those words, the gauntlet dropped. Sergei rounded on the prince first. "You swore you had no idea where she was," he accused him.

Rudolf smiled. "I lied."

"I demand to speak with Princess Amber," Pushkin said, turning to Miles.

"What do you wish to say to my wife?" Miles asked, his expression placid but the hands at his sides clenched into fists.

"Your marriage cannot be legal."

"I assure you it is."

"I can vouch for its legality," Rudolf interjected.

Pushkin ignored him. "Amber loves me," he said. "I intend to marry her."

"English law prevents my wife from having two husbands."

"I want to see her."

Miles stared at his rival for a long moment and, like his wife, wished they had remained in Stratford. No matter what he did to prevent their meeting, Pushkin would somehow find a way to speak to her. Amber would be furious when she discovered he had sent the man away.

"Pebbles."

Obviously eavesdropping again, the majordomo rushed into the study. "Yes, my lord?"

"Send my wife to me."

Pebbles inclined his head, cast the count a murderous glare, and left the study.

Her husband wanted to apologize, Amber thought, climbing the stairs to answer his summons. She might have approved of his and her cousin's plan to draw Fedor out. If she wasn't the bait. Now she sympathized with the plight of the poor worm dangling on the end of the hook.

Amber walked into the study and stopped short when she saw Sergei. She dropped her mouth open in surprise and then recovered herself. "Sergei," she cried, and rushed across the room to give him a welcoming hug.

And then Amber noticed that no one else was smiling. Her husband, her cousin, and her childhood friend appeared ready for battle.

"Tell me you have not married this"—Sergei glanced at Miles—"this English beast."

Amber flinched at the insult. She could understand his surprise and even his anger at her sudden marriage, but those were no good reasons for insulting her husband. "Why have you come to England?" she asked, stepping away from him.

"Why? I have come to take you home."

Amber regretted hurting her old friend. He must have cared deeply for her, or he would never have left Moscow to look for her.

"My home is with my husband."

Sergei ignored her statement. "Why did you leave Moscow?"

Amber would not even consider telling him the truth. That would be too humiliating.

"Fedor threatened me."

"I would have protected you," Sergei said. "Princess,

we have loved each other forever and will annul this hasty marriage. The earl took advantage of you."

"I took advantage of the earl." Amber flicked a glance at her husband. Her *angry* husband. "Long before I left Moscow, I told you to find another woman to marry. Your mother would never—"

"My mother *will* accept our marriage," Sergei interrupted her.

Amber looked at her husband and then her cousin. No help there. They were watching her, waiting for her to get rid of Sergei.

Guilt and regret filled her. As the Pushkin heir, Sergei had been pampered his whole life and was unused to having his wishes thwarted. She did not believe he would respond to kindness and go quietly.

On the other hand, Sergei had always been kind to her. Amber could not force herself to the necessary cruelty. He had been her friend—her only friend—since childhood. Yes, he had spoken of marriage, but she had never taken his words of love seriously and had never considered the possibility of a future with him.

Why was Miles watching this without coming to her aid? For that matter, her cousin was unusually silent.

"I will not leave," Amber said, taking his hands in hers, "but you will always hold a special place in my heart."

"I want a place in your bed," Sergei snapped. "Look at him. You cannot possibly love him."

Amber dropped his hands and stepped back as if he had struck her. His pain did not give him license to lash out at others. Especially her wonderful husband. "You dare enter my home and insult my husband and me," she said, full-bodied anger sweeping through her.

"I am upset and do not know what I am saying," Sergei retreated from his outraged position. "I carry a letter from your father."

"My father?" she echoed in confusion.

Sergei produced a sealed missive and passed it to her. "From Czar Alexander."

Amber sat down and, with badly shaking hands, opened the letter:

> *Amber, daughter of my heart.*
> *Running away was wrong. My feelings are hurt that you did not trust me with your problems. If you will return home with Count Pushkin, I will acknowledge you and give my permission for your marriage to the count.*
> *Your father, Czar Alexander*

Amber bowed her head and wept quietly. She made no protest when her cousin lifted the letter from her hand, read it, and passed it to her husband.

"This could be a forgery," Rudolf said.

"That letter is no forgery." Sergei knelt beside Amber's chair and took her hands in his. "Come with me now, Princess, and we will marry."

Amber raised her head and looked at him through eyes that mirrored her misery. "The czar had twenty years to acknowledge me," she said, hurt that the offer had come too late. "You have always been a good friend, but I have spoken solemn vows before God."

Sergei stared at her for a long moment. Finally, he nodded and stood. "I will remain in London for a time. You will change your mind. If not, we will part as friends."

Amber dropped her gaze to her lap and made no reply.

"You have said what you came to say," Rudolf broke the sudden silence.

"I will see you again before I go home," Sergei told her. He looked at Miles, adding, "If you hurt her, I will make you wish for death."

Sergei quit the chamber. Rudolf followed him out, leaving the Earl and Countess of Stratford alone.

"I apologize for Sergei," Amber said, staring at her hands folded in her lap.

No reply.

Amber lifted her gaze to her husband. "What are you thinking?"

Miles stared at her, his dark eyes cold. "I think you left Moscow too soon."

Hurt by his words, Amber rose from her chair and quit the study. She walked upstairs to her bedchamber, needing a few private moments to compose herself.

How had she managed to hurt two men she cared for the most in the world? Sergei had been her childhood friend. Refusing his offer of marriage had hurt him.

She loved her husband and cherished his child growing inside her. Why was he angry that she had remained steadfast and chosen him?

He should never have married her. Miles had seen the way his wife looked at Sergei, recognizing the regret in her gaze. Her reason for rejecting the Russian was less than encouraging. She had spoken her vows before God. No mention of love there.

That omission positively screamed her true feelings. She had married him for protection. Her words of love rang false.

Lifting his hand, Miles stared at the ring she had given him. Why should he wear a gift given by a woman who loved another man?

Sliding the ring off his finger, he set it on his dresser. He hoped he could as easily set aside his love for her.

Grabbing his cravat, Miles crossed his bedchamber to the cheval mirror but paused when he saw his own reflection. He touched his scarred cheek. No beard grew on the scars, and one side of his mouth drooped slightly. Luckily, he had not lost an eye.

If only he had never removed his mask in her presence. If only she had never seen his scars.

Would he have had a chance to keep her love? Only God knew the answer to that. Miles knew one thing for certain. His scars prevented him from competing against the handsome Russian.

Amber had woven a magical spell around him. Her exquisite beauty, her unconditional acceptance, her sweet words of love had conspired to enslave him. To make him forget his scars. To make him miserable.

There were no happily-ever-afters in life. He should have known better.

After donning his mask, Miles walked downstairs alone instead of escorting Amber to dinner. The room was empty except for Pebbles and a footman.

"Your sherry, my lord."

Miles took the glass but said nothing.

"Will Her Highness be joining you for dinner?"

"Her Highness always dines with me, doesn't she?" His voice was sharp.

"I apologize," Pebbles drawled, narrowing his gaze on him. "I ask because Her Highness usually accompanies you."

Miles knew he was behaving unreasonably. "There is no need to apologize."

"Yes, I know," Pebbles said, his tone haughty. "I *am* the man who saved your life."

"Sometimes I wish you had let me burn," Miles snapped, shocking the majordomo and the footman.

Amber walked into the dining room at that moment. She nodded at the majordomo. Her expression said she had heard her husband.

"Your son and I are famished," Amber said, ignoring his failure to escort her to dinner.

Miles gave her a sidelong glance. "How do you know you carry a boy?"

"Woman's intuition."

That almost made him smile. *Almost.*

Dismissing the footman, Pebbles served them himself. After setting the deviled rump steaks and stuffed tomatoes on the table, he filled their glasses and retreated to the sideboard.

"Caroline isn't joining us?" Miles asked.

"She ate earlier."

"Why?"

Amber looked him straight in the eye. "We need to discuss what happened today."

Miles sat back in his chair and stared at her. *He* wanted to discuss the reason she could not tell the Russian she loved her husband.

He saw her hesitate. Searching for words? Or courage?

Amber dropped her gaze to his hand holding the wineglass. Miles knew the moment she realized he wasn't wearing the czar's ring. A little pain now would save them more pain later, he told himself.

Amber lifted her gaze to his. "You are not wearing the ring."

Steeling himself against the hurt in her expression, Miles glanced at his hand. "Ah, yes, I misplaced it," he lied, his tone indifferent.

Amber set her napkin on the stable and stood. "You will excuse me, please." Her tone was formal and much too polite.

"You haven't finished dinner. Where are you going?"

"I cherished that ring as a token of my father's love," Amber said, rounding on him. "And you cavalierly tell me it is missing?"

Miles dismissed her anger with a wave of his hand. "The ring is somewhere in my bedchamber."

"The important point is where the ring is not. *On your finger.*" Amber left the dining room.

In misery, Miles watched her go. He had not wanted

to hurt her feelings, but he would not beg for love from his own wife. The love he wanted from her belonged to another man. He gestured Pebbles to refill his wine glass.

In an instant the majordomo stood beside him. "Congratulations, my lord. You have just hurt the best thing that ever happened to you."

Miles turned his head to look at the older man. "You forget your place, Pebbles."

"I forget nothing."

"Since when does a majordomo question his employer's personal life?"

Pebbles cocked a brow at him. "Since the majordomo saved the employer's life, and the employer insists on behaving like an arse."

Miles couldn't argue with that. "If the countess asks," he said, standing to leave, "tell her I am meeting with the Duke of Avon."

Thinking about her husband, Amber climbed the stairs to her bedchamber. She wished Sergei had never come to England. What had she done to provoke her husband's anger? Hadn't she refused Sergei's invitation to return to Moscow and marry him? Now she faced the unenviable task of persuading her husband to believe in her love.

Amber had chosen her husband and rejected her father's offer of acknowledgement, something she had desired her whole life. She had done so without hesitation or regret. Couldn't Miles see how much she valued him? Why did he avoid discussing his feelings? How could she reassure him of her love if he refused to speak about it?

A knock sounded on the door, drawing her attention. "Enter," she called.

The majordomo appeared. "His Lordship asked me to tell you that he has gone to meet with the Duke of Avon."

"Thank you, Just-Pebbles."

The majordomo smiled. "You are welcome, Your Highness."

Amber paced the bedchamber and wondered what to do. Not for the first time, she wished she could speak with a more experienced woman. And then she thought of her sister-in-law's words to her on her wedding day. *Be patient with my brother. He needs you.*

Miles did not love her. That much was true. At least, he had never professed such feelings for her. He *had* behaved like a devoted husband, though. She had been content, believing their child would bring them closer.

Amber stood at the connecting door to her husband's chamber. Should she sleep in his bed or not? She saw no reason to change their custom of sleeping together. After all, he had not forbidden her to sleep in his bed.

How long could a man remain angry with the woman who carried his child and shared his bed? If the woman was nearly naked . . .

Amber changed into her sheerest nightgown and slipped into her husband's bed. She lay awake for hours, waiting for his return, but her courage failed her in the end.

Hearing the door open, Amber snapped her eyes shut and feigned sleep. In a moment her husband would undress and slip into bed. Then she would cuddle against him, seeking his body heat, and by sunrise his anger would have vanished.

Amber heard him crossing the chamber to the bed. Silence. Then she heard his footsteps retreating. She opened her eyes in time to see him disappear into her chamber.

Her husband did not want to sleep with her.

With her heart breaking, Amber hid her face against the pillow and wept quietly.

Awakening in the morning, Amber decided to speak to Miles that day. If she needed to force the issue, then so be it. She would not weep for him again, nor would the sun set without a discussion of what had transpired the previous day.

She hurried downstairs to the dining room, determined to settle what was between them. She hoped to catch Miles before he went riding or buried himself in his study.

Unfortunately, the dining room was deserted except for the majordomo. Which meant she would need to interrupt the earl if he had gone to his study.

"Is His Lordship riding or working?" she asked the majordomo.

"Working."

Finishing her breakfast, Amber read the society gossip column to see if it mentioned Fedor. Then she went to her husband's study.

She hesitated at the door, her insecurities surfacing like an old friend. Would Miles be in a receptive mood? Probably not.

She should have planned what to say. But if she left now, her courage might fail her later. She tapped on the door and then entered without invitation. Her husband and two of his clerks were conferring. All three men stood at her entrance.

"I apologize for intruding." Amber backed toward the door. "I will speak with you later."

Miles inclined his head.

Leaving Caroline with Nanny Smart in the garden, Amber returned to the study early in the afternoon. She had hoped to see Miles at lunch, but he never appeared.

Amber stared at the closed door a long time. Her courage failed her. She started back down the corridor but, hearing the door open, whirled around.

The majordomo hurried toward her and handed her a slip of paper. "From His Lordship."

Amber unfolded the note and read: *Opera tonight. Eight o'clock.*

Anger surged through her. How dare he speak to her through notes.

"Is there a reply?"

"I will deliver it myself."

Walking back to the study, Amber swung the door open with a crash and marched toward her husband's desk. She tossed the note at him, demanding, "What is the meaning of this?"

Miles stared at her for a moment. "I sent you a reminder of tonight's schedule."

"I am no idiot and can read the damn thing," Amber told him. "You have avoided me for two days."

"You misunderstand."

"I am your wife," Amber said, her voice rising in proportion to her anger. "You will *not* send me notes, you will *not* avoid speaking to me, and you will *not* treat me with disrespect. Do you understand?"

Smothered laughter erupted behind her.

Amber whirled around to see her oldest cousin sitting in a high-backed chair. "What do you find so amusing?" she challenged him.

Rudolf grinned. "You."

Amber did not know what to reply to that. Her cousin had defused her angry righteousness.

"Rudolf received this today," Miles said, drawing her attention.

Amber took the letter from him and sat in a chair. Prince Fedor Kazanov demanded that Rudolf send her home. Her uncle had made an excellent match for her, and Rudolf had no legal right to interfere.

"Does this mean Fedor is not in London?" she asked.

Miles shrugged. "Appearances can be deceptive."

"Though encouraged, we agree that caution is needed," Rudolf said, standing. He looked from Amber to Miles and then grinned. "I will leave you to your *discussion.*"

His face an expressionless mask, Miles looked at her and said, "I am listening to you now."

Amber folded her hands in her lap. "I want to know the reason you have been avoiding me. If this is because of Sergei—"

"I have been conducting business, not avoiding you."

Amber knew he was lying. "You did not sleep beside me last night."

"You looked too peaceful to disturb," Miles said, his gaze skittering away from hers.

If he thought she looked peaceful, her husband needed spectacles. "I want to know the *real* reason you no longer want to sleep beside me."

Miles ran a hand through his hair. "I *do* want to sleep beside you, but Pushkin's marriage proposal alters our situation."

"I do not know why it should," Amber said. "I chose *you,* not Sergei or my father's acknowledgement."

His gaze on her softened. "One day you may feel differently about refusing your father," Miles said. "Would you have chosen me if you weren't carrying my child?"

"Do you doubt me?"

"I believe you may be confused. I am giving you the opportunity to reconsider your feelings."

"I know my own feelings," Amber said, standing to leave. She paused at the door. *"Do you know yours?"*

Chapter 13

He loved her. Miles knew damn well what he felt, and loving the princess did not make him especially happy. No matter the emotional distance he had put between them, he had not prevented himself from falling in love. How could he protect himself from heartache?

Amber did not really love him, he was sure of that. It was completely impossible that she could love him. But what if she did?

Keeping his distance from her was proving much too difficult and in the end could cost him what he craved most. Amber was *his* wife and carried *his* baby. He would not give her up without a fight.

Miles slid his arms into his black dresscoat. He donned his mask and inspected himself in the cheval mirror. Tonight would be his first public appearance in more than four years. He wondered what society would think of his masked countenance.

Miles knocked on the connecting door to his wife's bedchamber and walked inside without waiting for permission. Gazing at her, he felt that he had never seen a more beautiful woman. Her silver-blond hair was woven into a knot at the nape of her neck, and she wore a violet silk gown, its neckline low and rounded, its shoulder sleeves puffed. Matching slippers, long evening gloves, and reticule completed her outfit.

Miles lifted her hand to his lips. "You are exquisite."

"Are you nervous?"

"No. Are you?"

"Yes."

"There is no reason for nervousness," Miles said, guiding her toward the door. "We make a handsome couple."

The coach ride to the Royal Opera House was short. They arrived in front of the theater at the same time as Rudolf and Samantha.

"Brace yourself," Miles whispered, noting his wife's anxious expression.

The two couples entered the theater. Almost instantly, those operagoers loitering in the lobby turned their interested gazes on them.

Miles sensed Amber inching closer. He gave her an intimate smile and slipped her hand through the crook of his arm. Though he nodded at several people, Miles kept moving toward the staircase leading to the opera boxes.

"Brace yourself again," he whispered.

Operagoers in the other boxes noted their entrance. All eyes turned in their direction. Ladies raised their lorgnettes for a better view.

And then someone clapped. Others joined in.

Damn idiots. Miles made a show of acknowledging their approval by bowing to them. He gestured to Amber, who smiled at their audience and inclined her head.

"I wish I had worn my crown," Amber whispered, making her husband smile.

"Montgomery, if your entertainment is finished," Rudolf drawled, "perhaps we could watch the opera."

Sitting between Miles and Samantha, Amber felt satisfied by the way their evening was proceeding. In spite of his denial, her husband had been nervous. That his peers not only accepted him and but also admired him for his sacrifice pleased her immensely.

Amber knew the evening was young, though. She tried not to think of the emotional consequences if something went wrong.

"How are you feeling, cousin?"

Amber turned in her chair. Prince Stepan had entered the opera box and sat behind her.

"Good evening, Stepan."

"Rudolf told me the happy news about the baby," Stepan said, and shook her husband's hand. "Miss Fancy Flambeau will be singing the part of Cherubino in tonight's opera. Watch for her."

"I would like to meet Miss Flambeau," Amber said. "She must be a special lady to have earned your admiration."

"Fancy will be performing later in the week at Samantha's uncle's ball," Stepan told her. "I believe you met the Duke of Inverary before going to Stratford."

"We will look forward to meeting Miss Flambeau," Miles said.

Amber had expected the object of her cousin's affection to be buxom like most other opera singers, but the opposite proved true. Miss Fancy Flambeau was a petite dark-haired woman with a startlingly strong voice.

Engrossed in the opera and the woman's near-perfect voice, Amber felt uncomfortable suddenly. Her skin prickled, and the fine hairs on the nape of her neck rose like hackles. An uncanny feeling of being watched surged through her, making her heart beat faster.

Amber glanced around. No one appeared to be paying her any particular attention. She would definitely scan the crowd at intermission, though.

Miles leaned close and whispered against her ear, "Are you ill?"

"I feel fine." Amber managed a smile for him.

"You seem uncomfortable."

"A little queasy, nothing more."

Princes Viktor and Mikhail appeared in the opera box the moment intermission began, drawing her attention from scanning the crowded theater. Both cousins kissed her cheek and shook her husband's hand.

"Congratulations on the baby," Prince Viktor said.

"Impending motherhood seems to agree with you," Prince Mikhail added.

Amber blushed. "I am happy and content. Where has Stepan gone?"

Mikhail rolled his eyes. "Stepan feared some other gallant would reach Miss Flambeau's dressing room first."

"Unfortunately for him, Miss Flambeau never sees anyone during intermission," Viktor added. "He is guarding a closed door."

"Where is Princess Adele?" Amber asked. "I had hoped to meet her."

"Adele had other plans for this evening," Viktor answered.

"Will she attend the Duke of Inverary's ball?"

Viktor shrugged. "I have absolutely no idea what Adele will do from one moment to the next."

"I advised you not to marry her," Rudolf spoke up.

"Rudolf," Samantha whispered, a warning note in her voice.

Viktor ignored his oldest brother. He turned to Mikhail, saying, "We should be off."

Two gentlemen walked into the opera box, passing the princes on their way out. One was Sergei Pushkin and the other a stranger.

Amber felt her heart sink. She wished her old friend would go away. Permanently. His presence in London was ruining her marriage. He must realize she would never leave her husband. Why did he not return to Moscow and move forward with his life?

Amber flicked a sidelong glance at Miles. He did not appear especially happy.

Sergei would have had to be dead to miss their displeasure. He ignored it. "Princess, may I make known to you Baron Igor Slominsky, a fellow countryman." The baron was an attractive man with angular features, black hair, and piercing blue eyes.

"A pleasure to make your acquaintance," Amber said, forcing a smile. "My husband, the Earl of Stratford."

"You look more beautiful than ever," Sergei said. "The color of your gown matches your eyes perfectly."

Amber made no reply. She willed Sergei to be gone. She disliked the thought of hurting her oldest friend, but she would do it if necessary.

"I wonder if we might ride together in Hyde Park one morning," Sergei said, ignoring her husband.

Was he intent on ruining her marriage? If so, then he was no friend of hers. "That will be impossible," Amber refused. "If I were to ride with anyone, I would choose my husband to ride with me."

Baron Slominsky made the supreme mistake of insinuating himself into the conversation. "Surely, your husband would not object to your spending an hour with an old friend?"

"My husband would never object to my having friends." Amber smiled sweetly, intending to shock her old friend into leaving her alone. "My husband does object to endangering our first child. My sojourns to Hyde Park will be done from within the safety of a coach in the company of women who can advise me about babies and childrearing."

Both Sergei and Baron Slominsky dropped their startled gazes to her body. Sergei appeared ready to explode, but the baron recovered his composure.

"Congratulations," Slominsky said, and shook her husband's hand.

Sergei said nothing. A moment later, he made a hasty retreat and took his friend with him.

Amber wished the intermission would end. No such luck.

The curtain parted again, this time revealing a gentleman and a lady. Both Miles and Rudolf stood at the woman's queenly entrance.

The dark-haired beauty was tall and curvaceous. She wore a red silk gown that displayed her generous cleavage, and her queenly poise spoke of sophistication.

The woman held out her hand to Miles, who kissed it. "You have kept yourself in Stratford too long," she said, her voice throaty and seductive. "You cannot imagine how pleased I am to see you."

"I cannot imagine you even realized I was missing from your circle of admirers." Miles looked at Amber. "I present Vanessa Stanton, the Countess of Tewksbury, and her cousin, Charles Bradford, the Earl of Langley."

Vanessa Stanton gave Amber the most insincere smile she had ever seen. "Princess Amber, you are a lovely child," the woman said. "I can see the reason Miles married you." Then she dismissed Amber completely, saying, "Miles, you must promise not to bury yourself in Stratford again."

Comparing her own assets to the English beauty, Amber found herself lacking. Vanessa Stanton was everything she wished to be. She shifted her gaze to the cousin, who was staring at her.

"Pay no attention to my cousin," Vanessa told her. "Charles adores blondes."

"Charles has a special fondness for blondes named Adele," Rudolf remarked, making the other man blanche.

Vanessa looked at Miles. "Is Caroline in London?"

"Yes."

"I would love to introduce my son to your daughter," she said. "Perhaps fate will accept a match between our families this time."

And Amber knew. Her husband and this woman had been more than friends. Full-bodied jealousy bloomed within her at the thought that Miles and this woman had shared intimacies.

Had Miles loved the woman? What had happened to separate them? Amber knew one thing for certain. Vanessa Stanton wanted to resume that relationship with Miles.

"What do you think, Your Highness?" Vanessa was asking. "Shall I bring my son around to meet Caroline?"

"My stepdaughter is entirely too young to consider matrimony," Amber answered. "Bring him around in a couple of decades."

Vanessa Stanton smiled, seemingly amused by her wit, but Amber knew better. She recognized the cold challenge in the other woman's eyes.

Lady Stanton and her cousin soon left, and the opera resumed.

Again, Amber suffered the feeling that someone was watching her. She tried to scan the crowd without alerting her husband to what she was doing.

And then Amber caught a glimpse of a familiar, dark-haired figure standing in the back of an opera box on the opposite side of the theater. Her breath caught in her throat, and she grabbed her husband's arm.

"The letter was a trick." Amber turned eyes filled with fright on her husband. "Uncle Fedor is in this theater."

"Where?"

"Over there." Amber gestured to the now empty opera box. "I swear Fedor was there a moment ago."

"You could be right," Miles said, watching the socialites leaving their seats at the opera's end.

"We will be on guard," Rudolf assured her. "Samantha and I are going to the Pembrokes' ball. Will we see you there?"

"Yes, unless——" Miles looked at his wife's anxious expression. "Shall we go home or to the Pembrokes'?"

"I will be fine." Amber knew the significance of the evening for Miles. If they delayed mingling with society, her husband would be even more nervous than he had been that night.

The ride from the Royal Opera House to Park Lane took less time than the wait to alight from their coach in front of the Pembrokes' front door.

Amber felt nervous, sensing the aristocratic crowd was waiting to speak with her husband after his four-year absence. Apparently, everyone wanted to boast of welcoming one of their own back into the fold.

With her less than respectable origins, Amber had never stepped into society before and did not know what to expect. What would these English people think of her? Would they accept her as they had accepted her cousins?

Amber decided to keep her head held proudly high at all times. She was a princess of Russia and an English countess by marriage to one of their own. Nobody knew she was an unacknowledged bastard whose very existence had destroyed her mother and her mother's husband.

Unless Sergei—No, that idea was too absurd. Her oldest friend would do nothing to hurt her, nor would he even consider betraying her trust.

"Are you well?" Miles asked, placing a comforting arm around her shoulders. "We can return to Berkeley Square if you are not ready for this."

Amber managed a smile for him. Her husband had more to make him nervous than she did, yet he thought of how she was feeling. Which was an encouraging sign.

"I am only a little nervous," she answered. "I dislike meeting new people but will survive the evening."

"Everyone will love you," he assured her.

Rudolf and Samantha waited for them in the foyer. Together, the four of them climbed the stairs to the ballroom.

"Prince Rudolf and Princess Samantha Kazanov," the Pembroke majordomo announced. Then, "The Earl of Stratford and Princess Amber, the Countess of Stratford."

All conversation in the ballroom ceased. A sea of curious gazes turned in their direction. Someone clapped his hands. Others joined him until the ballroom filled with thunderous applause.

Amber froze, unused to being the object of this much attention. She had always preferred hiding in the background lest someone remark on her disreputable origins.

"If you do not breathe," Miles whispered, leaning close, "you will never make it down these stairs. If I try to rescue another wife, I will need to listen to all that noise again."

Amber inclined her head. She took a deep, exaggerated breath, making her husband smile, slipped her hand through the crook of his arm, and started down the stairs.

In an instant, a throng of well-wishers surrounded them. Amber inched closer to Miles. He put his left arm around her waist and drew her protectively close.

The crowd parted for their host and hostess, the Earl and Countess of Pembroke.

"Welcome to London," the earl greeted them.

"How wonderful to see you again," his countess added, her voice warm. "Bringing a beautiful, young bride with you has certainly disappointed many of these ladies."

"Princess Amber, I present the Earl and Countess of Pembroke," Miles said, making the introduction.

"I am pleased to make your acquaintances," Amber said.

"We are *very* pleased to meet you," the countess returned. "John and Isabelle arrived earlier."

After a few minutes of exchanging pleasantries, Miles and Amber left the Pembrokes and crossed the ballroom to their group. Unfortunately, everyone wanted to speak with Miles and meet his royal bride. Twenty minutes passed before they reached the opposite side of the ballroom.

"I believe you have survived your first foray into London society," Isabelle said.

Amber gave her sister-in-law a nervous smile. "The evening is not finished yet."

"By tomorrow morning, you will be a huge success," Samantha said. "One and all will declare you an Original."

"And an Incomparable," Miles whispered against her ear.

Amber smiled at him. "Thank you, my lord."

Miles held out his hand. "Dance with me?"

"I would love to dance with you."

The orchestra was playing a waltz. Miles and Amber walked onto the dance floor, and she stepped into his arms. They moved with natural grace, as if they had waltzed together a thousand times.

"Do you realize this is our first public dance?" Amber asked.

"Imagine that," Miles teased her. "We have music, too, instead of off-key humming."

Amber laughed and gazed with love into his eyes. Miles appeared even more besotted than she.

Returning to their group, Amber found herself facing a ravishingly beautiful brunette. The woman was tall and generously endowed, her peacock blue gown matching her blue eyes.

"Miles, welcome home," the woman said, taking his hands in hers.

"You look as lovely as ever," Miles greeted her.

"Amber, I present Georgiana Devon, the Countess of Dorset."

"I am pleased to make your acquaintance," Amber greeted her.

"You seem a bit overwhelmed by the crowd," Georgiana said. "Everything will fall into place once you begin to know us." She gestured to the gentleman beside her. "I present Grover Dalrymple, the Earl of Street."

Amber smiled at the man who bowed over her hand.

"Princess, may I have the honor of your next dance?" the Earl of Street asked.

Amber had absolutely no idea how to refuse someone without being impolite. She had never been invited to any Moscow balls and had no experience to summon.

"That would be nice," she accepted.

Stepping onto the dance floor, Amber caught a glimpse of Sergei standing across the ballroom and watching her. A moment later, he stepped onto the dance floor with the lady beside him, Vanessa Stanton.

"I have never waltzed with a princess," the earl said.

"I have never danced with the Earl of Street," Amber replied, making him smile.

When Miles stepped onto the dance floor with Georgiana Devon, Amber felt the first stirrings of jealousy. She wondered if this had been planned.

Amber danced next with Prince Rudolf. Thankfully, Miles partnered Princess Samantha.

And then another statuesque brunette approached their group. This English beauty wore black, its simplicity enhancing her creamy complexion. Diamonds sparkled from her throat, wrist, and earlobes.

"My lord, how pleased I am to see you again," the sultry brunette said, her smile warm and genuine.

Miles bowed over her hand. "Sarah, the pleasure is mine as always," he said smoothly. "Too many years have passed."

Sarah inclined her head. "I was saddened to hear of your loss."

"Thank you." Miles drew Amber forward. "I present Sarah Pole, the Marchioness of Arlington. Sarah's late husband was a hero at Waterloo."

Amber inclined her head, which was beginning to throb from feigned graciousness. "How nice to meet you," she managed.

If her husband had been a commodity, she could have made a fortune. The demand for him exceeded his supply.

Sarah Pole and her group moved on. Amber knew that neither Miles nor she had seen the last of the marchioness. How many old flames did her husband have? How many of them had designs on her husband?

And then Amber noted Vanessa Stanton and her cousin advancing on them. She had no desire to dance with the cousin.

"You will excuse me," Amber whispered, leaning close to her husband. "I need to visit the withdrawing room."

"Are you ill?" Miles asked, concern etched across his face.

Amber forced herself to smile. "I am quite well."

Since Samantha and Isabelle were dancing, Amber made her way alone through the crowded ballroom. Thankfully, no one paid her any particular attention.

Reaching the deserted withdrawing room, Amber sat in a dark alcove. She did not want to be disturbed, and any lady who entered would not see her sitting there.

Apparently, her husband preferred brunettes. Tall, beautiful, large-breasted brunettes. Which made her feel like a blond, flat-chested child. Given a choice, Miles Montgomery would never have chosen her for a mate. Unfortunately for him, he had married her before venturing into society again.

And then the sound of female voices reached her

ears. Hidden in her dark corner, Amber watched three females walk into the withdrawing room. Two of the ladies had already been introduced to her, the Countess of Dorset and the Marchioness of Arlington.

"Miles looks wonderful considering what he has endured," said Georgiana Devon, the Countess of Dorset.

"Princess Amber is very beautiful," remarked Sarah Pole, the Marchioness of Arlington.

The third lady gave a delicate snort. "Gossip is already spreading about her, you know."

"What gossip?" Georgiana asked.

"Before you tell us, Cynthia, where did you hear this gossip?" Sarah Pole asked.

"Vanessa Stanton danced with Count Pushkin," Cynthia said. "Count Pushkin has known Princess Amber for her entire life. He told Vanessa that the princess is Czar Alexander's bastard. Unacknowledged, too. Her legal father murdered her mother and then committed suicide."

"Unendurable shame must have driven the poor man to resort to violence," Georgiana said. "I heard that immoral behavior can be inherited."

"I wonder if Miles knows about his wife's disreputable history," Sarah Pole said, a smile touching her lips.

"Well, someone should tell him to beware," Cynthia said.

Georgiana nodded as the women left the room. "The princess could bring dishonor to the Montgomery family."

Amber felt like weeping. Her past had followed her to England. No one would accept her now. Her presence in her husband's life could only bring him shame. Once her origins became common knowledge, would he divorce her or grow to hate her?

And then her thoughts turned to Sergei. She was a bastard by birth. He was a bastard by nature.

Amber seethed, her anger growing into fury. Her oldest and dearest friend had betrayed her, and she would never forgive him.

Amber would not shame her husband by creating a scene on the night of his return to London society. She could not spoil the moment for him. Schooling her features into an expressionless mask, she left the withdrawing room and wended her way through the crowd to her group. Her husband was dancing with Vanessa Stanton, and Sergei stood with Baron Slominsky nearby.

Amber saw Sergei start walking toward her, and then another gentleman blocked her vision. She looked in surprise at her brother-in-law and smiled with relief. Here, at least, was a friendly face.

"Princess Amber, I believe this is our dance," John Saint-Germain said.

"Thank you for rescuing me from a mean-spirited old friend," Amber said, and stepped onto the dance floor.

"I didn't realize you knew anyone here except your cousins," the duke remarked.

"I have known Count Sergei Pushkin my entire life."

"Ah, yes, I think Miles mentioned him to me."

Amber flicked a glance in her husband's direction. "Tonight has been good for Miles, but I wish we had remained in Stratford."

"Do not worry about his affections waning," John told her. "Those women are in your husband's past."

"Has anyone bothered to tell them?" she asked.

The Duke of Avon laughed out loud, earning curious looks from other dancers. "Take my advice, dear sister-in-law. Tell Miles you want to leave. I guarantee he will whisk you home to Berkeley Square. Your husband will not endanger the mother of his heir."

"I hate to bring his triumphant evening to an early end," she said.

"Do you actually believe he is enjoying himself?" the duke asked. "Trust me, Princess. He would much rather be home with you."

At waltz's end, Amber followed her brother-in-law's advice. She sidled up to her husband, touched his arm, and beckoned him closer.

"The babe wearies me tonight," she whispered.

"We will leave now." Miles placed his arm around her waist and guided her toward the stairs. He leaned close to whisper against her ear, "Will you join me in my bed tonight?"

Her smile could have lit the whole mansion. "I would love to join you, my lord. I thought you would never ask."

Chapter 14

"Why are you blushing?"

Amber looked at her husband across the breakfast table and recalled their bedsport of the previous night. Her blush deepened into a vivid scarlet.

"I enjoyed myself, too," Miles teased her. He pushed the newspaper toward her, saying, "The *Times* mentioned us."

Amber opened the *Times* to the society gossip on page three.

> *The Earl of Stratford returned triumphantly to London society, receiving admiring applause at both the opera and the Earl of Pembroke's ball. Lord Montgomery introduced his royal bride to London's elite, breaking many hopeful hearts.*

Amber could think of three hopeful hearts she had seen the previous evening.

"Are you prepared for today's onslaught?" Miles asked.

Amber gave him a puzzled smile. "I do not understand."

"A hundred invitations will arrive for us today," he

told her. "Many of the people you met last night will visit this afternoon."

"I doubt that will happen."

Miles cocked a dark brow at her.

Amber looked around. Except for the majordomo, she and her husband were alone.

"I am sorry for ruining your life," she said.

"You *gave* me a life," he corrected her. "What has upset you?"

"When I sat in the withdrawing room last night," Amber answered, "I heard some women talking about me. Sergei has spread the gossip about my family history."

"I could kill him," Miles said.

"He only spoke the truth," Amber said. "His betrayal of our friendship hurts and, especially, your loss of social standing."

"Trust me, sweetheart. Your family history has nothing to do with our social status," Miles said. "If you knew the personal history of some of those aristocrats, you would swoon dead away." He dropped the subject, saying, "I don't want to tire you with too much activity or needless anxiety, though. We will refuse all invitations until Inverary's ball."

"I enjoy staying home with you," Amber said. Did he want to forgo social engagements because of her condition, or was he embarrassed by her family history?

Miles beckoned to the majordomo. "I have business meetings all day. Neither my wife nor I will be available to visitors."

"I understand, my lord."

Her stepdaughter, gardening, and knitting a blue blanket for her baby occupied Amber for the remainder of the day. After lunching with Caroline, Amber sent the girl upstairs to nap. She paused in the foyer to speak with the majordomo about the silver trays on a table.

"One tray is filled with calling cards," Pebbles explained. "The other holds invitations."

Amber grabbed a handful of calling cards. Sergei had left one, as had Baron Slominsky.

When someone knocked on the front door, Amber looked at the majordomo. "I am unavailable."

Pebbles inclined his head and then opened the door. Standing to the side, Amber listened to the brief conversation.

"I have a letter for the Earl of Stratford," a masculine voice announced.

"His Lordship is unavailable at the moment," Pebbles said. "I will take it."

"Thank you."

The majordomo closed the door.

Amber eyed the sealed missive. "I will deliver it." When she lifted the letter from his hands, the voluptuous scent of jasmine reached her. Which of the heartbroken three was sending her husband a perfumed letter?

Amber sniffed the letter again. Definitely jasmine.

"Do not mention this letter to the earl."

The majordomo inclined his head. "I understand, Your Highness."

Amber crossed the foyer to the stairs. Another knock sounded on the front door, and she paused while the majordomo opened the door.

A second courier stood there, a letter in his hand.

"I will deliver this to the earl," Pebbles said, lifting the parchment out of the man's hand.

After closing the door, Pebbles handed Amber the letter. "Roses, Your Highness."

"Thank you, Just-Pebbles."

"You are welcome, Your Highness."

Amber climbed the stairs to the drawing room and sat on the settee. She stared at the two letters and wondered what message each contained. Reading letters meant for another was wrong, and yet—

Amber bolted off the settee, tore the two letters into pieces, and tossed them into the hearth fire. Relieved to be rid of the temptation, she sat on the settee again, closed her eyes, and wondered which of the ladies she'd met would dare to send a married man perfumed letters.

Sensing another presence, Amber opened her eyes. The majordomo stood there.

"Yes, Just-Pebbles?"

He offered her a third letter. "Gardenia."

"I did not read the other letters," Amber told him, lifting the letter from his hand. She stood then and tossed the gardenia-scented letter into the fire.

"What a pity," the majordomo murmured. "I would have read them."

"Reading another's mail is wrong."

"That would be almost as wrong as destroying a letter meant for another," the majordomo drawled.

"I did not destroy my husband's mail." Amber gave him her sunshine smile. "I maintained our domestic tranquility."

The majordomo's lips twitched into a smile. "What His Lordship doesn't know cannot anger him."

"Just-Pebbles, you are a treasure."

"Thank you for noticing my finer points of character."

The remainder of the day and evening passed pleasantly. Amber felt snugly secure within the bosom of her family, a security that had eluded her until she married the earl.

Isabelle Saint-Germain and Samantha Kazanov visited the next afternoon while their husbands met with Miles. The three women sat in the drawing room and chatted in easy camaraderie.

"I assume both of you will be attending my aunt's ball tonight," Samantha said.

"John and I would never miss one of your aunt's galas," Isabelle said.

"Miles and I will be attending," Amber said. "We stayed home last night because he worries that too much activity will tire me."

"Let's ride together in Hyde Park tomorrow," Isabelle suggested.

"Then we can shop for baby clothes," Samantha added, reaching out to pat Amber's hand.

"I am carrying a boy," Amber said. "I will only purchase blue items."

"Then you will need to buy blue ribbons to wear in your hair when you deliver your baby," Samantha said.

"Is that an English custom?"

"That is *my* custom." Samantha smiled. "I wore pink and blue for my first baby and delivered twins."

Carrying a silver tray with refreshments, Pebbles walked into the drawing room. He set the tray on a table, served tea and pastries, then paused before leaving. Reaching into his pocket, he produced three sealed missives. He passed her the three perfumed letters. "These arrived within the hour."

Clearly unhappy, Amber stared at the letters. "Thank you, Just-Pebbles."

The majordomo left the drawing room.

"His name is just Pebbles," Isabelle said.

"Yes, I know."

"You look upset," Samantha remarked.

Amber looked at her new friends and held up the missives. "Women are sending my husband perfumed letters."

"Who are they?" Samantha asked.

"Ladies Jasmine, Rose, and Gardenia." Amber stood, then tossed the letters into the hearth fire.

"You do not need to worry that Miles will stray," Isabelle said.

"Do you think destroying his mail is wise?" Samantha asked.

Amber gave them her sunshine smile. "Just-Pebbles says that what His Lordship doesn't know cannot upset him."

Samantha and Isabelle looked at each other and laughed.

"What if Miles somehow discovers what you've done?" Isabelle asked.

"I will explain that I intended to deliver the letters but dropped them."

Samantha giggled. "You dropped them into the fire?"

"Precisely."

"You're wearing *that* to Inverary's ball?"

Standing in front of her cheval mirror for a final inspection, Amber heard the censure in her husband's voice. She watched him crossing the chamber and admired the imposing figure he cut in his black and white formal attire.

Amber studied her appearance in the mirror but could detect no obvious flaw. Her highwaisted black gown had a rounded neckline, its hem ending at her ankles to expose her silk stockings and sandals. She carried a mother-of-pearl fan and a reticule of red morocco and colored beads.

"I do not see—"

"The gown reveals too much skin," Miles told her.

Amber smiled at that. "This is one of my *wrap-yourself-in-pretty-packaging* gowns."

"Wrap yourself in what?"

"When I arrived in London," Amber explained, "Cousin Rudolf bought me a wardrobe. He said if I wanted to attract a husband, I needed to wrap myself in pretty packaging."

Miles laughed and leaned close to plant a kiss on her lips. "I bought the package, my love. You have nothing to sell."

"Vanessa Stanton wore a more revealing gown the other night."

"Vanessa Stanton cannot compare to you."

Amber smiled, pleased with the compliment.

Miles produced a blue velvet box. "I have a belated wedding gift for you."

"I love surprises."

"I thought you did."

Amber opened the package. On a bed of blue satin lay a pair of dangle earrings created from round, marquis, and pear-shaped diamonds set in platinum.

"Thank you, my lord." Amber stood on tiptoes and kissed his cheek. "I have nothing for you, though."

"You have given me my life." Miles slid his hand down to her belly, adding, "And the promise of a future."

Amber placed the palm of her hand against his masked cheek. "You have given me my heart's desire, and I love you."

No one ever refused an invitation from the Duke and Duchess of Inverary. Tonight was no exception. Park Lane was a beehive of activity. Coaches arrived, delivered their passengers, and departed to make space for newcomers.

Amber marveled at the number of carriages in the same place at the same time. "Our baby will have reached his majority by the time we get inside," she said, casting her husband a sidelong glance.

"I doubt we'll be in line *that* long."

Her lips twitched. "How are you at delivering babies?"

Miles laughed. "Don't you dare do that to me."

Thirty minutes later, the Earl and Countess of Stratford walked down the corridor to Inverary's ballroom. Miles and Amber drew interested glances from those members of society unfortunate enough to have missed their appearances at the opera and the Pembroke ball the other evening.

"The Earl of Stratford and Princess Amber, the Countess of Stratford," announced the Inverary majordomo.

Several people descended upon them at the same time. The Duchess of Inverary, their hostess, reached them first.

"Dearest Miles, how wonderful to see you again," the duchess gushed, taking his hands in hers. "I have passed the last four years worrying and praying on your behalf."

This elicited smothered laughter from Rudolf and Samantha, the duchess's niece and nephew-in-law.

"I thank you for your concern, Your Grace," Miles said, struggling against a smile.

The Duchess of Inverary gave Amber her attention. "Our darling princess has managed to bring you back to us."

Amber inclined her head.

"Samantha has shared your happy news," the duchess said. "How divinely exciting. If you ever need advice"—she frowned—"ask Samantha and Rudolf, who, as you know, have several children and are experts on child-rearing."

"Thank you for the suggestion," Amber said.

"Enjoy yourselves, my darlings." With that, the Duchess of Inverary breezed away to greet more guests.

"Miles and you created a stir the other night," Rudolf said, and winked at Amber.

"The *Times* devoted most of its gossip column to your return to society and your marriage again today," Samantha added.

"That was precisely what I did not want." Miles shook his head. "If only those fools had not applauded my appearance."

"Mentioning Amber will bring you-know-who to the surface," Rudolf said. "That is, if he is in London."

Amber knew they were referring to Fedor. She reminded herself once again to read the *Times* each morning on the off chance that the reporter would mention her uncle. Being dangled as bait made her nervous.

"Cousin Amber?"

Prince Viktor and a lovely blond woman stood there. "Amber, I would make known to you my wife, Adele."

"How pleased I am to make your acquaintance," Amber greeted the other woman.

"Thank you, Your Highness. Viktor speaks highly of you." Her gaze skittered away, scanning the ballroom. Apparently, she found what she was looking for.

"I'll speak with you later," Adele said, verging on rudeness. "I see a dear friend I must greet."

Amber watched the blonde making her way through the crowd. The woman attached herself to the Earl of Langley.

"I should never have married her."

Amber caught her cousin's hand. "You must love her."

Viktor shrugged. "I thought I did."

"You should have listened to me," Rudolf said, giving his brother a sympathetic look. "Now you are stuck with that tart."

"I wish Adele was married to her grave," Viktor said, his voice loud enough to draw curious glances from guests near them.

Miles spoke up, breaking the uncomfortable silence, "My lady, will you give me the gift of your first waltz?"

"I would love to dance with you."

Swirling around the ballroom in her husband's arms, Amber spied her three rivals as well as the Russian baron. She did not see Sergei Pushkin, however.

"Vanessa Stanton is dancing with Baron Slominsky," Amber said, watching her husband's expression.

"I suppose Pushkin is here, too?"

I hope not, she thought. "I do not see him." Then, "Vanessa looks especially well this evening."

"You need not feel jealous of Vanessa or any other lady," Miles said, pulling her closer.

"Then do *not* be jealous of Sergei," Amber said.

"I have what he wants," Miles told her, "and I will never let you go."

"Promise?"

"I promise."

Her husband *did* love her. How could he promise to keep her forever and not love her? Or was his loyalty based on the child she carried?

Rudolf claimed her for the next waltz. Stepping onto the dance floor, Amber kept a guarded eye on her husband, who was immediately surrounded by a number of old friends, mostly females. She would not feel secure while his three old flames prowled the ballroom.

"Your gown reveals more than it should," Rudolf remarked, drawing her attention.

Amber smiled. "You purchased it for me."

"Did I?" Rudolf laughed. "I must have suffered a lapse in judgment."

"You said I needed to wrap myself like a pretty package in order to catch a husband," she reminded him.

"You caught the husband," Rudolf teased her. "There is no need to wrap yourself so immodestly."

"I would not wish to waste your gift," Amber said. She cast a worried glance in her husband's direction.

"His mask makes him mysterious," Rudolf explained, his gaze following hers. "The legend of his being injured trying to save his wife enhances his mystique. Trust me, cousin. Your husband has eyes only for you."

"Do you really think so?"

"I have never seen a man more smitten than Montgomery."

"I need a favor," Amber said. "I want you to smell Vanessa Stanton, Georgiana Devon, and Sarah Pole."

Rudolf gave her a blank look. "I beg your pardon?"

"I want you to dance with Vanessa, Georgiana, and Sarah," Amber said, "and then tell me what perfume each wears."

Rudolf grinned. "I will do that if you tell me the reason."

"I want to discover the identities of the three women who sent him perfumed letters."

"Ask your husband," Rudolf told her. "He has nothing to hide."

"I *do* have something to hide," Amber admitted, blushing with embarrassed guilt. "I destroyed the letters before he saw them."

Rudolf chuckled. "I will dance with them, but do not steal your husband's mail again."

"Thank you, cousin. I promise to behave myself."

When the music ended, Rudolf returned Amber to her husband, and the ladies drifted away. She knew that, like sharks, they would return at first opportunity.

"Cousin Amber?"

Miles and Amber turned toward the voice. Prince Stepan stood with a petite dark-haired woman dressed conservatively in a midnight blue gown with a modestly high neckline. *The opera singer.*

"Miles and Amber, I present Miss Fancy Flambeau," Stepan made the introduction. "Fancy, these are Princess Amber, the Countess of Stratford, and her husband, the Earl of Stratford."

"We enjoyed your performance," Miles said.

"God blessed you with an amazingly beautiful voice," Amber added. "Thank you for sharing your gift with us."

"I appreciate your praise," Fancy said, her smile wobbly, her nervousness apparent.

"You will excuse us," Amber said to the men, and led the singer a few feet away.

"I have no designs on your cousin," Fancy spoke first. "I know a relationship between a prince and an opera singer would be impossible."

"Is there something wrong with my cousin?"

The opera singer looked confused. "No, I merely thought—" She shrugged.

"I would appreciate your singing at my home," Amber told her. "That is, if your schedule allows."

"I am sorry," Fancy declined. "I do not usually perform at private parties."

Amber gave her a sunshine smile. "I am not hostessing a party. I want you to sing for my ailing rosebush. My husband's London staff have neglected the poor plant for four years. I am certain the rosebush will thrive and bloom next summer if only you would share the gift of your voice."

Miss Fancy Flambeau laughed. "I would love to save your rosebush," she said. "Your Highness, you are not what I expected in a princess."

"What did you expect?"

"An aristocratic snob."

Amber smiled. "You are not what I expected in an opera singer."

"What did *you* expect?"

"A fat lady."

Stepan appeared pleased by their easy camaraderie. At a signal from the Duchess of Inverary, the prince escorted the opera singer to the top of the ballroom.

Miss Fancy Flambeau sang a haunting song about a

young woman who had given her heart to a handsome nobleman but lost his love to another woman. The poor woman wilted away from unrequited love until, finally, she passed from this life.

Listening to her story, Amber realized the opera singer had known great pain, as she had known in her own life. Had she found a kindred spirit in the young woman? Amber decided to encourage the romance between her cousin and the opera singer.

When she finished her concert, Stepan started to escort Fancy back to Amber and Miles, but Rudolf intercepted them. All three left the ballroom together.

"Miles." The voice belonged to a woman.

Amber saw Vanessa Stanton and Baron Slominsky advancing on them. She cast an anxious look at her husband, who raised his brows at her and then pasted an insincere smile on his face.

"Good to see you again," Miles greeted them.

"Miss Flambeau sang sweeter than any nightingale," Baron Slominsky said.

Amber nodded. "God blessed her with a voice that could melt the devil's cold heart."

"I thought the song too sentimental," Vanessa said. "What do you think, Miles?"

"When it comes to love," he answered, "I suppose one can never be too sentimental."

"You are as diplomatic as ever," Vanessa said. "Romantic, too."

Baron Slominsky spoke up, "Your Highness, would you honor me with this dance?"

Amber hesitated. The last thing she wanted was to leave her husband with the other woman. To refuse the baron bordered on rudeness, though.

"I would like very much to dance with you," Amber lied, and accepted his hand.

No sooner had she and the baron begun their waltz

when Miles and Vanessa stepped onto the dance floor. Amber hoped she could keep her eye on Miles without offending the baron.

"What a relief to be able to speak to someone in my own language," Baron Slominsky said, switching to Russian. "I miss the motherland, my countrymen, and vodka."

"I do not miss Moscow at all," Amber told him, also speaking Russian. "Of course, my four cousins reside in England. I imagine I have more relatives here than there."

"Surely, you miss your father."

"I have no father."

Baron Slominsky looked confused. "Czar Alexander is your father, is he not?"

"Czar Alexander sired me," Amber corrected him, echoing the words her husband had once spoken. "He has never publicly acknowledged our relationship."

"Sergei said—"

"Sergei speaks too freely about matters that do not concern him," Amber interrupted. "I have never met the czar, nor do I intend to meet him." Their conversation was becoming much too personal. "If you do not mind, I would prefer to sit this waltz out."

The baron gave her a conciliatory smile and escorted her off the dance floor. "I will soon be returning home to my wife."

"The baroness must miss you," Amber said, her head beginning to ache from being polite.

"I journeyed to England to procure a certain jewel that interested us," Baron Slominsky said, walking with her down the length of the ballroom. "My wife could not tolerate journeying so far from home."

"Did you procure your jewel?"

"Yes, thank you, I have. My business in England will soon be completed."

Amber realized the baron might know her uncle. "Do you know Fedor Kazanov?"

"I know him by sight," the baron answered, "but I have never made his acquaintance."

"Have you, by chance, seen Fedor in London?"

Baron Slominsky paused to think and then shook his head. "I do not recall seeing him." Nearing the ballroom's entrance, he suggested, "Shall we stroll the garden?"

Amber refused to leave her husband in the company of Vanessa Stanton. "I do not think—"

"You look pale," Baron Slominsky said, refusing to take no for an answer. "A breath of fresh air will bring the roses back to your cheeks."

"Fresh air in London?" Prince Stepan said, his tone sardonic. With him stood Prince Rudolf, his arms folded across his chest. "I need your assistance in a private matter, cousin."

Baron Slominsky inclined his head. "Another time, perhaps."

"Thank you for rescuing me," Amber said, once the baron had left. "How may I help you?"

"Fancy retired to the ladies' withdrawing room," Stepan told her. "Something upset her, and I am worried."

"I will speak with her."

"Wait one moment," Rudolf said, and leaned close. "Georgiana wears jasmine, Sarah wears roses, and Vanessa wears gardenia."

Amber smiled. "Thank you, cousin."

"Keep your distance from Slominsky," Rudolf cautioned her.

"Do you think he is dangerous?"

"I do not like the man. He could be trouble."

"Thank you for the warning." She looked at Stepan, adding, "I will see to your lady now."

Miss Fancy Flambeau stood alone in the withdrawing room. Obviously weeping, she dabbed at her eyes with a handkerchief.

Amber placed a hand on the woman's arm, drawing her attention. "May I help you, Miss Flambeau?"

Fancy shook her head. She seemed to compose herself, but her bottom lip trembled with the effort.

"I have had disturbing news this evening," the opera singer told her. "I have learned who sired me and my sisters."

Amber gave her a blank look. "I do not understand."

"My French aristocratic mother escaped the Terror," Fancy explained. "Penniless and unskilled, she found employment at the opera and caught the attention of a handsome nobleman by whom she had seven daughters."

"You have six sisters?" Amber echoed in surprise.

The opera singer nodded. "At twenty, I am the oldest."

"Your song tonight described your mother?"

"At her death two years ago, my mother still loved her nobleman," Fancy told her, a bitter edge to her voice. "Though she had not seen him in ten years. He sent money by way of his solicitor, but never attended her funeral. Now the villain wants his daughters and intends to secure honorable marriages for them."

"Does this nobleman have a wife?" Amber asked.

"His second wife is childless and wants to mother his girls."

"You do not wish to acknowledge his paternity?"

"The man does not deserve my acknowledgement," Fancy said, "but he threatened to cause problems for me at the opera."

"What will you do?"

"I agreed to send him my six sisters," she answered, "but I will be alone without them."

"You have had more than I ever did," Amber told her. "I have been alone my whole life."

"What do you mean?"

"The life of a princess is not necessarily as wonderful as it appears. I will tell you my story when you visit to serenade the rosebush. Come, Stepan is worried about you."

"The prince wants to make me his mistress," Fancy said, her honesty surprising. "I refuse to become my mother."

"Then do not become your mother." Amber led her out of the withdrawing room. "Fate may be kinder to you."

Rudolf had disappeared, but Miles stood in the corridor and spoke with her cousin. Stepan rushed to the opera singer's side as soon as they appeared.

"I will expect you to visit soon," Amber told her.

When they were alone, Miles asked, "Your Highness, would you care to dance with me?"

"Where are Georgiana, Sarah, and Vanessa?"

"How did I know you were going to say that?" Miles teased her. "Where is Sergei?"

Amber gave him a jaunty smile. "Sergei is nursing a broken heart."

Miles laughed at that.

"I am feeling tired," Amber said. "Do you mind if we leave?"

"Your wish is my command, Your Highness." With his hand on the small of her back, Miles guided her toward the stairs.

"I want to go home to Stratford."

"We will go home, my love, before the end of the month."

Chapter 15

"Where has Caroline disappeared?"

"She and Nanny Smart are practicing the alphabet," Amber answered, without taking her gaze off the paper.

Admiring her profile, Miles stared at her a long moment. "Why are you diligently searching the *Times*?"

Amber lifted her gaze to his. "I want to see if there is any mention of Fedor."

"Rudolf has agents watching all incoming ships," Miles told her. "I think Fedor gave up and remained in Moscow."

"You do not know Fedor Kazanov."

"Will you pass every day of your life wondering if your uncle is about to whisk you back to Russia?"

"Until I get news of his death, yes."

Miles opened his mouth to reply, but Isabelle and Samantha walked into the dining room.

"Good morning," Isabelle called.

"Are you ready?" Samantha asked.

Amber nodded and looked at her husband. "I will return in a few hours," she said.

"Tell the shopkeepers to send me the bills, but try

not to pauper me." Miles looked at the other women. "Do not let her out of your sight."

"I have brought my *large* reticule and you-know-what," Isabelle told her brother.

"And I have a certain sharp object strapped to my leg," Samantha added.

Miles laughed. "Do your husbands know how naughty you are?"

"Yes," they chimed together.

The three women left the dining room. Amber paused in the foyer to don her cloak.

"Your Highness," Pebbles called, hurrying after them. He drew three letters from his jacket pocket and passed them to her. "These arrived earlier."

"Jasmine, Rose, and Gardenia are certainly persistent," Amber said, and stuffed the perfumed letters into her reticule.

"Enjoy your excursion," Pebbles said, opening the door for them.

After the women had gone, Miles walked upstairs to his office. He tried to concentrate on ledgers, but thoughts of his wife kept intruding.

Amber needed and deserved to hear the words *I love you*. What prevented him from saying them? If he said the words out loud, would fate find a way to hurt him?

There was also the matter of Fedor Kazanov. In spite of what he had said to his wife, Rudolf felt positive that Fedor would not give up his plan for Amber, especially with money involved. Fedor was in London already. *Where?*

Someone was hiding the villain. *Who?* His first thought had been Sergei, but Rudolf said Pushkin enjoyed an outstanding reputation, never a hint of scandal or underhandedness.

And then there was Sergei Pushkin's gossip. Knowing his wife had plans with his sister, Miles had sent the Russian a note, summoning him to Berkeley Square, but had no idea if the man would show.

"My lord?"

Miles looked at his majordomo.

"Count Pushkin has arrived."

"Escort the count to me."

Miles wandered to the window while he waited. A moment later the Russian count walked into his office.

Miles turned around, his gaze cold on the other man. He gestured to a chair, saying, "Please sit down."

"I prefer to stand," Sergei refused.

Miles inclined his head. The two rivals for the princess's affection faced each other across the chasm of the desk.

"I will come directly to the point," Miles said. "Keep your mouth shut about my wife's family history, or I will kill you."

"You can *try* to kill me," Sergei replied. "Does her family history embarrass you?"

"Amber considers you her oldest, dearest friend," Miles said. "Your betrayal hurt her deeply."

"I spoke without thinking," Sergei said, less belligerently. "I never meant to hurt her."

Miles nodded in understanding. "Would you consider writing her a note of apology?"

"If you give me parchment and quill," Sergei said, sitting in the chair, "I will do that now."

"Thank you."

While Miles and Sergei were speaking, the ladies rode in the duchess's open carriage in Hyde Park. Isabelle looked over her shoulder and instructed her driver, "Stop over there, Johnny."

"Why are we stopping?" Amber asked. "Do you not think we should shop first?"

"We have hours to shop," Samantha said.

"I cannot believe women are sending *my* brother perfumed letters," Isabelle said. "Let's read them."

"That would be wrong," Amber said.

"You stole your husband's mail," Samantha said. "We may as well read them."

"Well, if you really think—"

"We do," Isabelle and Samantha interrupted.

Amber opened the jasmine-scented letter. It said,

I must speak privately with you and will call at one o'clock today. Georgiana.

"Do you think Georgiana will mention the letters?" Amber asked, alarmed.

"I am certain she thinks Miles ignored her letters," Isabelle answered.

"She won't mention them," Samantha agreed. "Open the next one."

Amber opened the rose-scented letter. It said,

I have urgent news for you and will call at Berkeley Square at two o'clock. Sarah.

"I do hope Georgiana stays late and Sarah arrives early," Isabelle said.

"That would be a delicious situation," Samantha said.

Amber said nothing, concerned that her crimes were about to be exposed. She opened the gardenia-scented letter. It said,

I desperately need your advice about a financial investment and will visit you at three o'clock today. Vanessa.

"That woman is dangerous," Isabelle said.

"I need to go home before they arrive," Amber said, *knowing* she was caught.

"You must delay as long as possible," Isabelle advised her.

"If we don't shop for baby clothes, Miles will become suspicious," Samantha said.

"Good afternoon, ladies." Baron Slominsky had halted his mount beside their carriage. "Something is making for interesting reading."

"We are indulging in silly women's gossip," Isabelle said.

Amber stuffed the letters into her reticule. Then she smiled at the watching baron.

"Will I be seeing you ladies at Vanessa Stanton's costume ball?" the baron asked.

"Yes," all three answered at the same time.

"I am requesting that each of you save me a waltz," he said.

"We will," they chirped, sounding like schoolgirls.

Baron Slominsky laughed. "Good day to you." With that, he rode away.

"My lord?"

Miles looked at his majordomo.

"The Countess of Dorset requests an interview."

Georgiana Devon? That surprised him.

"Escort the countess to me."

"Shall I serve refreshment?"

"That will be unnecessary."

"Very good, my lord."

Miles stood when Georgiana walked into his office. He smiled in greeting and gestured to the chair in front of his desk. "My lady, please be seated."

Georgiana sat down and smiled at him.

"To what do I owe this unexpected pleasure?" Miles asked.

"You did not receive my note?" Georgiana asked, looking puzzled.

"You sent me a note?"

Georgiana nodded. "I sent you several notes. The latest was this morning."

That surprised Miles, though his expression remained blandly placid. "Pebbles is getting old. I must have been occupied when your note arrived, and he simply forgot to deliver it."

"No harm done," Georgiana said.

"What can I do for you?" Miles asked.

"That, my lord, is a loaded question," she said, her smile flirtatious.

Georgiana Devon could not be making a play for him. Could she?

"Tell me the purpose for your visit," Miles said smoothly, "except, of course, for brightening my day."

Georgiana blushed right on cue. Miles had always admired her ability to do that.

"I have heard disturbing news about your wife and thought you should know."

"Enlighten me," Miles said, knowing what she would say.

"Princess Amber is illegitimate issue," Georgiana said, lowering her voice. "Her legal father murdered her mother and then committed suicide."

"Yes, I know." Miles stood in a gesture of dismissal. "Our parents' actions, right or wrong, have nothing to do with our worth. Come, Georgiana. I'll walk you to the foyer."

Clearly unhappy, Georgiana stood and left the study with him. "Perhaps we could ride together one morning."

"I would love to ride with you," Miles said. "Unfortunately, my wife needs me in the morning. Amber is carrying my heir, and mornings are difficult for her."

"I commend your sensitivity," Georgiana said. "Too bad all husbands are not as sympathetic as you."

Miles kissed her hand and then opened the front door for her. He turned to the majordomo, asking, "Did Lady Devon send me a note?"

"Oh, my lord, I am so sorry," Pebbles answered. "You were unavailable, and the note slipped my mind. I'm not sure I even remember where I put it."

"Don't concern yourself about that."

Miles walked upstairs to his office and opened one of his business ledgers, but his thoughts strayed from profits and losses. Georgiana had sent him several notes, but he had received none. He could not believe that Pebbles had forgotten to deliver several notes.

Nearly an hour later, Pebbles walked into his office. "My lord?"

"Yes, Pebbles?"

"The Marchioness of Arlington requests an interview."

Sarah Pole? What could she possibly want?

"Escort the marchioness to me."

"Shall I serve refreshment?"

Miles smiled, realizing they were replaying the earlier scene. "That will be unnecessary."

"Very good, my lord."

Miles stood when Sarah walked into his office. "My lady, please be seated," he said, gesturing to the chair in front of his desk.

Sarah Pole sat down and smiled at him.

Miles sat when she did and then asked, "Did you send me a note?"

"I sent you several notes. Did you receive them?"

"Alas, poor Pebbles is forgetful in his advancing years," Miles said. "Let me guess. You have heard disturbing gossip about my wife."

"You know about her disreputable family?" Sarah asked, lowering her voice to a whisper.

Miles inclined his head. "Princess Amber revealed her family history before we married," he said. "I would appreciate your silence regarding this. After all, Amber carries my heir, whom I would not want tarnished by gossip before he is even born."

"You can depend upon me."

Miles stood in a gesture of dismissal. "Come, Sarah. I will escort you to the foyer."

Sarah Pole stood and left the office with him. "Perhaps we could dine some evening?"

"I would love to dine with you," Miles said. "Send Amber the invitation, and we will certainly attend your dinner party."

Miles kissed her hand and then opened the front door for her. He turned to the majordomo again, asking, "Did Lady Pole send me a note?"

"Oh, my lord, I am so sorry," Pebbles repeated his earlier words, his face a brilliant red.

Embarrassment or guilt? Pebbles had never forgotten anything before. If he questioned his wife, would Amber redden with guilt or embarrassment, too?

Miles suppressed the urge to laugh in his majordomo's face. Georgiana Devon and Sarah Pole always scented their notes with perfume. Amber had enlisted his majordomo's aid to intercept those notes. He didn't know if he should be angry or flattered by her jealousy.

"Don't worry about it," Miles said. Then he returned to his office to work on his profits and losses.

"My lord?"

Another visitor? Miles shifted his gaze to Pebbles.

"The Countess of Tewksbury requests an interview."

Vanessa Stanton? Somehow that did not surprise him. Were there more undelivered notes?

"Escort the countess to me."

"Shall I serve refreshment?"

"The lady won't be staying that long," Miles answered. "In fact, interrupt us in ten minutes."

The majordomo grinned. "Very good, my lord."

"Pebbles?"

"Yes, my lord?"

"You always disapproved of Vanessa Stanton, didn't you?"

"I would never say that, my lord."

"What *would* you say?"

"I would say that I dislike her in the extreme."

Miles knew that Vanessa was hunting as soon as she stepped into the room. Her smile was seductive and her bodice cut too low for a morning call.

"To what do I owe this unexpected pleasure?" Miles asked, standing at her entrance. "Do you have urgent news for me?"

"I desperately need your financial advice," Vanessa answered, advancing on him, her hips swaying.

Miles felt like a Russian waiting for Napoleon's attack. He saw the determined gleam in her eyes, but she would leave as disappointed as Napoleon retreating before the Russian winter.

Vanessa gestured for him to sit. He realized his mistake when she circled the desk to perch close to him.

Miles caught her gardenia scent and recalled the pleasureable moments passed in her company. Looking at her now, he could not remember what had attracted him.

"Ask away," Miles said, leaning back in his chair to put distance between them.

"I have been considering investing in thoroughbreds," Vanessa told him.

Miles raised his brows. "Have you developed an interest in racing?"

"Whatever happened to us?" She changed the subject so abruptly, he needed a moment to leap from one thought to another.

"You married Stanton, and I married Brenna."

Vanessa sighed dramatically.

Miles thought, *Here it comes.*

"We were so good together and could be again."

He wasn't even tempted.

Miles stared at her, wondering how to let her down gently. Society affairs were common enough, he supposed, but not for him. Never for him. Still, there was no good reason for unnecessary cruelty.

"I have given the Stantons their heir and secured the estates," Vanessa said. "I have no need to marry at the moment. Your Russian princess is a child, a dishcloth when compared to me."

Miles smiled in spite of the situation. "Modesty was never your strong suit."

Vanessa gave him a feline smile. "I believe in honesty."

"And so do I." Miles stood. "Your interest flatters me, but I love my wife and intend to remain faithful to her." *Why could he say those words to Vanessa but not his own wife?*

"Your lips say no, but your eyes say yes." Vanessa gave him a smoldering look. "I want your stallion to cover my mare . . ."

"Good afternoon, Your Highness," the majordomo greeted her, opening the front door. "Let me take your packages."

"Thank you, Just-Pebbles." Amber let him lift the packages from her arms. "Where is my husband?"

"His Lordship is in his office," Pebbles answered. "The Countess of Tewksbury is conferring with him."

Lady Gardenia? She would put an end to this conference.

Amber marched across the foyer, missing the majordomo's satisfied smile, and climbed the stairs to her husband's office. She reached for the doorknob but paused when she heard the countess's voice.

"I want your stallion to cover my mare . . ."

There was no mistaking the meaning of those words. The tart had come into her own home to seduce her husband.

Amber took a deep breath and prepared for battle. She tapped lightly on the door and then walked inside without invitation, completely missing her husband's relieved expression. At least the two were not locked in an embrace.

"Lady Stanton, what a surprise to find you here," Amber said.

"I had business with Miles."

"Regarding what?"

"An investment I'm considering." Vanessa smiled. "You wouldn't understand."

Amber smiled even more insincerely than the tart. "I understand more than you think."

The other woman's confidence slipped a notch. "Miles and you must attend my costume ball," Vanessa said, walking toward the door. "I will be expecting you."

"I'll escort you downstairs," Miles said.

Amber watched the two of them leave, walked upstairs to her bedchamber, and sat on the edge of her bed. She had no choice but to compete with his first wife; however, she had no intention of competing against Ladies Jasmine, Rose, and Gardenia.

The door opened, admitting her husband.

"You are not taking her home?" Amber asked him.

Miles looked unhappy with that remark. He sat beside her on the bed. "I was as surprised as you to see Vanessa in my office."

Amber believed him. No sane man entertained women in his wife's home. Besides, she had stolen the note.

Miles reached into his pocket, produced a sealed letter, and offered it to her. "This arrived earlier."

Feeling guilty about her own crimes, Amber stared at the letter as if it could bite. Finally, she lifted it from his hand. The letter was addressed to her.

"Open it."

Amber opened the letter. It said,

> *Please forgive my lapse in good judgment. I spoke about your family without considering the consequences and regret hurting my dearest friend. Yours always, Sergei.*

Amber offered the letter to Miles, saying, "Sergei apologizes for spreading gossip."

"I trust you, darling," Miles said, "and do not need to read your mail."

His words made Amber feel worse than she already did.

"Do you think you will ever trust me?" he asked.

"I trust you now."

"I know you intercepted my mail."

Amber looked him straight in the eye. "I trust you, but I do not trust those women."

Miles laughed, much to her relief, and drew her into his arms. "I have no interest in any other woman."

Amber leaned closer, offering her mouth.

Their breaths mingled.

Their lips touched.

"I want your stallion to cover my mare," she whispered.

Miles laughed in her face. "Shall we attend her costume party as a stallion and a mare?"

"I will dress as Little Bo Peep," Amber said, "and you will play the randy old ram."

"How do you know about Little Bo Peep?"

"I read about her in Caroline's storybook."

"How about it, Princess?" Miles gently set her back on the bed and leaned over her. "Will you let my stallion cover your mare?"

"Perhaps."

Chapter 16

"I wish tomorrow was tonight," Amber said, slipping her stockinged feet into gold sandals. "Then we would be riding to Stratford instead of dressing for Vanessa Stanton's costume ball."

"You don't like London," Miles said.

"I prefer Stratford," she answered. "I want to hold our baby in my arms."

Amber felt uncomfortable about attending the party, feeling something bad would happen. In fact, she had practically begged her husband to leave London today, but he had insisted the hour was too late for traveling and the staff needed to finish packing. Tomorrow would be soon enough for returning home.

"We will need to wait more than five months to hold our baby," Miles reminded her. "By the way, are there any blue blankets and buntings left in London?"

"I do not believe I missed any." Amber smiled at him. "London's newborn boys will be wearing pink for a few months."

Miles laughed at that. "What an insult to their manhood."

Amber inspected her husband up and down. As Satan, Miles had dressed completely in black.

"You look diabolical."

"You look angelic."

Dressed as an angel, Amber wore a white silk gown with flowing sleeves shaped like a bell. Attached to the back of her gown were two small wings fashioned from swan feathers. A rhinestone tiara served as a halo, and a white demi-mask covered the top half of her face. Her reticule was gold, and her fan, when opened, had been painted like a harp.

"How many swans died for your wings?"

"Madam Janette told me the feathers came from deceased swans."

"When did those swans become deceased?"

Amber looked appalled. "I told her not to hurt any birds."

"I am teasing you," Miles said. "Madam Janette would never even hurt a flea . . . . A defenseless swan maybe."

"Miles!"

The ride to Vanessa Stanton's estate on the outskirts of London took less than an hour. Once inside the foyer, they met Rudolf and Samantha, dressed as Romeo and Juliet.

"You make a lovely angel," Rudolf greeted her.

Amber inspected her cousin from his velvet doublet to his pantaloons and tight leg hose. "What attractive legs you have," she said, then giggled.

"I love the codpiece," Miles said, falling in with his wife's merriment. "Did you pad it?"

"I assure you," Samantha answered, "my husband did not pad the codpiece."

"If we are finished discussing my private body parts," Rudolf said, "perhaps we could attend the party."

Dressed as Marie Antoinette, Vanessa Stanton greeted them almost as soon as they walked into the crowded ballroom. She wore a white wig and a scandalous gown that exposed the top of her breasts almost to her nipples.

The Countess of Tewksbury was definitely prowling for a lover.

"How sweet you look," Vanessa complimented Amber, her gaze fixed on Miles. "You, my lord, look divinely diabolical, tempting enough to follow through the gates of you-know-where. Oh, you've brought Romeo and Juliet with you."

"Are you an apparition?" Amber asked, making her husband smile.

The other woman's gracious expression slipped. "I am Queen Marie Antoinette."

"The late French queen was before my time," Amber said, her smile angelic, "but I am certain you remember her." Leaning close to her husband, she asked, "Will you dance with me?"

"I would love to dance with my wife."

Miles escorted Amber onto the dance floor. She stepped into his arms, but could not stop herself from peeking at her own bosom. Compared with the countess, she was certainly lacking.

When her husband laughed, Amber lifted her gaze to his. "What do you find so amusing?"

"You."

"I will take that as a compliment."

"Please do."

Amber danced next with Prince Rudolf. She nearly sighed with relief when Miles and Samantha stepped onto the dance floor.

"I do not see Viktor, Mikhail, or Stepan in attendance," Amber remarked, swirling around the ballroom in her cousin's arms.

"Stepan is missing," Rudolf said. "Miss Flambeau is also missing."

That surprised Amber. "Have they gone away together? Miss Flambeau refused to become Stepan's *you-know*."

"I believe my impetuous baby brother has snatched the lady in an effort to change her mind," Rudolf said. "Though Stepan did mention the word *marriage* in connection with the opera singer. As for the other two, Mikhail is out of town, and Viktor preferred passing the evening at White's."

Amber was surprised and relieved that Vanessa was keeping her distance from Miles. Dressed like a pirate, Sergei Pushkin arrived. And there was Princess Adele, clinging to the Earl of Langley.

"Princess Adele did not wear a costume," Amber said. "Neither did the Earl of Langley."

"Adele insisted on dressing as a whore and Langley as a jackass," Rudolf said. "That is the reason they look as usual."

Amber giggled. "That is really too bad of you, cousin."

Rudolf grinned. "You are leaving for Stratford in the morning?"

"I would have preferred to remain in Stratford." Amber blushed, adding, "Thank you for bringing me to Miles. I love him."

"You are very welcome," Rudolf said, escorting her off the dance floor. "No one deserves happiness more than you and Montgomery. I only regret not flushing Fedor out of his hole."

Amber patted his hand. "I believe Fedor remained in Moscow. He must have realized how protected I would be."

Amber danced with her husband, her cousin, several of her husband's acquaintances, and the Duke of Inverary. After supper, Vanessa Stanton cornered Miles and insisted upon a dance. Only then did Sergei approach.

"I have wanted to speak privately all evening," Sergei said in Russian. "Can you ever forgive my insensitivity?"

Recognizing the misery couched in his eyes, Amber softened her gaze on him. Regret for losing her childhood friend swelled in her heart. From her earliest memory, Sergei had supported and defended and protected her. She had repaid him by marrying another man.

"I am leaving soon for Moscow," Sergei told her. "Will you walk with me in the garden so I may bid you a private farewell? We may never see each other again."

Amber glanced in her husband's direction. He was otherwise occupied with Vanessa Stanton. She inclined her head. "Yes, I will walk with you in the garden."

Sergei and Amber stepped outside the French doors onto the balcony. Then they descended the stone stairs into the garden. The pathways were deserted, the guests preferring to remain within during this season of the year.

"Are you cold?" Sergei asked.

Amber shook her head. "I am sorry you traveled across Europe only to be disappointed."

Sergei paused and turned her to face him. "I love you, Princess. If you are happy, then I am happy."

Amber felt tears welling up in her eyes and then heard a sound behind her. Seeing Sergei's gaze shift, she started to turn around, but a hand holding a cloth covered her mouth and nose. An arm encircled her body and lifted her off the ground.

Caught off guard, Amber could not cry for help. She struggled to escape the foul-smelling cloth, her legs flailing in the air.

And then she lost consciousness.

* * *

Dancing with Vanessa, Miles scanned the ballroom for his wife. He knew the moment Amber and Sergei stepped outside.

Through force of will, Miles stopped himself from acting impulsively. His first instinct was to go after them, but common sense prevailed.

The Russian had been his wife's childhood friend. If she wanted to steal a private moment to bid the man farewell, he could accept that. She would be returning to Stratford with him and, in a few months, deliver their child. Sergei was the loser, not he.

Ten minutes passed. And then another ten. His wife had been gone too long for a final farewell.

"Excuse me," Miles said, leaving Vanessa in mid-sentence.

Miles left the ballroom by way of the French doors and then descended the balcony's stone staircase. He walked down a deserted path.

"Amber!"

No answer.

Miles felt the first twinges of apprehension. Searching the other paths would be a waste of time. If his wife was in the garden, she would have answered him.

Unless she wants to stay hidden.

Miles returned inside to search the ballroom. Next came the cardroom where Rudolf and Samantha sat with the Duke and Duchess of Inverary.

"I can't find Amber," Miles told them.

"I will look in the ladies' withdrawing room," Samantha said, rising from her chair.

She returned a few minutes later and shook her head. "She isn't there."

"When did you last see her?" Rudolf asked, rising from his chair, preparing to search the house and grounds.

"I saw her and Sergei Pushkin leave the ballroom for the garden," Miles answered.

"Lord Montgomery?"

Both men turned to see the Stanton majordomo. "Lady Montgomery asked me to tell you that she will see you at home later."

Miles looked at Rudolf. "Amber left with Sergei."

"My cousin would never do that."

"She *did* do that, though."

Without another word, Miles left the cardroom and walked outside to call for his coach. Cold anger grew into scorching fury.

Amber left with Sergei pounded in his head. Reaching the Berkeley Square mansion, he walked upstairs without greeting Pebbles. He went directly to his wife's empty chamber and sat on the chaise to wait for her return.

Was Amber giving Pushkin a farewell gift of her body? She was already pregnant. How could he ever be certain she hadn't lain with her old friend? Pain sliced through him as he conjured the erotic image of their naked bodies entwined.

He loved her. And had believed her words of love.

He should have known she could never love a disfigured beast.

Heavyhearted, Miles leaned his head back against the chaise. The lateness of the hour and several glasses of wine conspired to send him into a troubled sleep.

When he awakened hours later, sunlight streamed into the room. Miles focused on the empty chamber and realized the bed was unused. His wife had left him for another man.

So be it.

Amber awakened disoriented. She opened her eyes and stared at the unfamiliar bedchamber.

Where am I? She remembered speaking with Sergei

and hearing a noise behind her. A hand covering her mouth. An arm grabbing her around the waist.

Amber sat up slowly and realized she wore only her chemise. Who had undressed her? She slipped off the bed and tried the door.

Locked.

Turning around, Amber walked to the windows. She was locked in a third-floor chamber. Her only hope—if she dared—was the oak tree, one of its thick branches reaching out to the window.

Did Sergei love her so much he would steal her from her husband? Or had Fedor and Gromeko found her? If that was the case, what had they done to poor Sergei?

Amber whirled away from the window when she heard the door being unlocked. Her heartbeat quickened, and her hands began to tremble.

Baron Slominsky? Carrying a breakfast tray, the Russian baron walked into the room and kicked the door shut. He smiled at her, set the tray on the table, and pulled a chair out.

"Come, Princess," the baron said. "You will eat breakfast now."

"What have you done?" Amber cried, trying to cover herself with her hands.

"Allow me to reintroduce myself," the baron said. "I am Count Gromeko and forgive you for the merry chase you have led me." Gromeko took a step toward her but halted when she shrank back against the window. "You need not fear me, Princess. I will never hurt you."

"You murdered Sergei," she accused him.

"I assure you that Count Pushkin is enjoying his breakfast downstairs."

"I do not believe your lies. Sergei would never betray me."

"Unfortunately, Sergei and his family are heavily in

debt," Gromeko told her. "Perhaps under normal circumstances he would not have considered betrayal,
but—" The count shrugged.

"I only want to have my baby," Amber pleaded, beginning to weep. "Please do not do this."

"Princess, do not cry," Gromeko said, his tone soothing. Gently, he forced her toward the table. "You must
eat now. I promise you will have your baby. You will have
many babies and make me a wealthy man."

Anger surged through Amber. She would die before
accepting this fate. In a flash of movement, she swiped
the breakfast tray off the table.

The door opened at the same moment the tray and
its contents hit the floor. Fedor Kazanov stood in the
doorway, fury etched across his face.

"You stupid, worthless slut," her uncle shouted,
crossing the chamber toward her.

Fedor raised his hand, but Gromeko grabbed his
arm, preventing the strike.

"Do not forget your niece belongs to me," Gromeko
warned. "If you touch her, I will kill you." The count
turned to her, ordering, "You will sit here, Princess. *Now.*"

Amber sat.

Fedor placed parchment and quill on the table in
front of her. "You will tell Montgomery that you are returning to Moscow with Sergei and want the czar's acknowledgement."

"I will not do that," Amber refused, folding her
hands on her lap. "My husband will search for me, and
when he finds me, he will kill you."

"If Montgomery finds you, I will kill him," Gromeko
threatened. "Do you wish to cause his death?"

Amber stared at the parchment and quill. Her husband had known more than his share of suffering. She
could not risk his life. Writing the note did not pre-
clude escaping what Gromeko had planned for her.

With an idea forming in her mind, Amber drew the parchment toward her and lifted the quill. Cousin Rudolf had taught her Germanic runes so they could secretly communicate. She would use that knowledge now and pray that her husband showed her cousin the note.

Amber wrote the message Gromeko dictated. Then she affixed her name, adding four scribbles beneath her signature.

"What is this?" Fedor asked, lifting the note from the table.

Amber looked where he pointed. "I have a habit of scribbling when finished writing."

Gromeko looked at the note. "Send a courier to deliver this to Montgomery," he instructed her uncle.

Alone with the count, Amber sat perfectly still and stared into space. She sensed him moving closer and prayed he would not touch her.

"How beautiful you are," Gromeko whispered against her ear.

Amber froze at his closeness. She shut her eyes against the feeling of him stroking the back of her head.

"You need not fear mistreatment," he told her. "I wish to tell you about your mate."

"Miles Montgomery is my mate," Amber said, looking straight ahead.

Gromeko ignored her words. "My stud is a big, handsome man. I have watched him mating with my female slaves, and even the most reluctant soon cry out in pleasure. His seed is potent and, from this moment, reserved exclusively for you.

"You will enjoy a pampered life and want for nothing. Indeed, you could grow fat from indolence and pregnancy.

"Who knows? When you are with child, I may take you into my bed. I can be a skillfull and generous lover."

Amber turned her head to look at him, a murderous gleam in her eyes. "I prefer coughing up blood."

Miles sat in the dining room at his Berkeley Square mansion. Ignoring the cup of coffee on the table in front of him, he stared straight ahead at nothing in particular. His rioting emotions made him feel ill, as if he had been severely beaten.

The morning routine progressed as if nothing had happened. Everything seemed different, though. How could the servants perform their usual tasks when the woman he loved had deserted him? Why hadn't the earth stopped spinning?

Miles knew he felt even worse about the loss of Amber than the loss of his late wife. The happiness the princess had brought into his life had been more intense because of the abject misery he'd known after Brenna's death.

"My lord?"

Miles turned his head to look at the majordomo.

"I urge you to search for the princess," Pebbles said. "Do not let her return to Russia."

"Go away," Miles growled.

"Would the princess have stolen those perfumed letters if she didn't care for you?"

"Her Highness was playing a game," Miles said. "When given a choice, she preferred an unscarred husband, a man who does not need to wear a mask lest his face frighten the unaware."

"Her Highness does not see your scars."

A knock on the dining room door drew their attention. The majordomo crossed the room, lifted a parchment from a footman's hand, and closed the door again.

Pebbles passed Miles the letter. Then he stood nearby,

silently refusing to leave his employer alone in his hour of need.

Miles stared at the sealed parchment and then opened it. He read,

I regret that I have changed my mind about returning to Moscow. The czar's acknowledgment means everything to me. I plan to marry Sergei and hope you will forgive me. Amber.

Beneath her name, the princess had written four scribbles. He assumed that was her name in the Russian alphabet.

Miles folded the note and pocketed it. He planned to keep it forever as a reminder of her betrayal. He would never trust another woman. "Pour me a whisky," he ordered.

"My lord, the morning is hardly—"

"Damn it, man. Get me a whisky, and bring the bottle."

Pebbles placed a shot glass and a bottle of whisky on the table. Then he retreated to the sideboard to watch his employer get drunk.

Miles gulped the whisky down in one swig and poured another. He would remain in London and make the rounds with Georgiana, Sarah, and Vanessa. Amber read the *Times* every morning and would read about his social activities. She would believe he had never cared about her, the same way she had never cared for him.

"Instruct the servants to start unpacking," Miles said. "Send a message to my barrister that I want him in my office this afternoon." He stood to leave the dining room. "Tell him it is urgent that I file for divorce and serve her the documents before she leaves for Moscow."

"But my lord—"

"Bring Caroline to my office in thirty minutes," Miles interrupted before quitting the dining room.

Miles went directly to his office and sat at his desk. What the bloody hell was he going to tell Caroline? The princess was hurting his innocent daughter, and that was beyond forgiveness.

Thirty minutes later, Pebbles opened the office door for Caroline. The little girl ran across the room to her father.

"Good morning, Daddy."

Miles managed a smile and pulled her onto his lap. "Good morning, Caro." He put his arms around her as if to protect her from his words. "I want to speak with you about something serious," he began. "Can I do that?"

Caroline nodded, her expression expectant.

"Little girls and little boys have little problems," Miles told her. "Big girls and big boys have big problems." He paused a moment and then continued, "Sometimes adults have divided loyalties that cannot be reconciled. Do you understand?"

Caroline shook her head.

"Let me begin again," Miles said. "Mummy needed to return to Russia, where she lived before. Her daddy is sick and wants to see her before he goes to heaven."

"Mummy is gone?" Caroline cried, alarmed.

Miles could not speak through the lump of emotion in his throat. Pain constricted in his chest, making breathing difficult. He reminded himself to remain calm for his daughter's sake.

"Mummy felt bad about leaving you without saying good-bye," he said. "Mummy loves you very, very much."

"Will Mummy come home after her daddy goes to heaven?"

"I am sorry, but Mummy will never return to us."

Caroline buried her head against her father's chest and wept. "I want Mummy," she sobbed. "I love her."

Miles held her close. "I love Mummy, too."

And then the Earl of Stratford wept with his daughter.

Chapter 17

Amber looked out the window. The chamber faced the garden. If she called for help, would anyone hear her? Gromeko would silence her before anyone could guess the whereabouts of the cry. That left only the choice of climbing down the oak tree from three stories up. She needed a gown to wear before she could do that.

With a sigh, Amber lay on the bed. Even now, Miles would be searching for her. She hoped he would think of Sergei Pushkin and Baron Slominsky.

At the lunch hour, Amber heard the door being unlocked. Gromeko entered and set the tray on the table.

"I wish you would eat," he said before leaving. "Consider the health of the babe you carry."

Amber knew the count was right. She needed to eat or her baby would suffer. She ate the soup and a slice of bread. After eating, she wandered to the window and looked down. The ground semed very far away. She could not escape wearing her chemise. Or could she? If she slipped and fell, her baby would die, and she was not ready to chance that. *Yet*.

Amber lay on the bed again. She would wait a while longer for her husband to rescue her.

At the dinner hour Amber heard the door being unlocked. She assumed the count was serving her dinner but refused to look at him.

"Good evening, Princess." The voice belonged to Sergei.

Amber rolled over and rose from the bed. Advancing on him, she recognized the desire couched in his gaze.

"You betrayed me."

"My family needs money," Sergei said. "I had intended to make you my mistress, but—" He shrugged.

"You said you loved me," she reminded him. "You loved me so much you wanted to make babies with me."

"I spoke truthfully and would have made babies with you," Sergei told her. "Unfortunately, I could not offer marriage to an unacknowledged bastard."

"You are the bastard, not I."

Sergei stepped closer. "Your husband consoled himself by passing the night in Vanessa Stanton's bed."

"Liar." Amber slapped him so hard his head jerked to the right.

Sergei snaked his hands out to grab her and yank her against his body. "You are already with child. Gromeko will not complain if I sample what should have been mine."

Sergei captured her mouth in a bruising kiss.

Amber bit his lip.

"Bitch." Sergei slapped her hard and shoved her away. Amber landed on her rump.

"Help!"

Gromeko was there in an instant. He looked from Sergei to Amber and the red imprint of a hand on her cheek.

"If he comes near me again," Amber warned the count, "I will kill him, and then I will take my own life."

Gromeko flicked a wrist at Sergei, ordering him to leave. Then he lifted her into his arms and carried her to the bed. "Pushkin will not bother you again." He left the room.

Amber turned her face into the pillow and wept.

How would he explain his wife's absence? Miles wondered, dressing for the evening.

Donning his mask and grabbing his cravat, he crossed the bedchamber to the cheval mirror. He tied the cravat with the nimbleness of a man who had performed that minor task thousands of times. At the moment, he would have preferred hanging himself with the cravat rather than tying it for a night out.

If anyone asked, he would say his wife was resting at home. Her delicate condition, you know.

Leaving his bedchamber, Miles went to check on Caroline, who had been inconsolable all day. His daughter was sobbing in her sleep. He kissed her forehead, and she quieted for a moment. He would never forgive the princess for hurting his daughter so badly. Would she ever recover from losing two mothers?

Stopping in the foyer, Miles sorted through the pile of invitations that had arrived during the day. He selected three and turned to leave.

Pebbles blocked his path to the door. "My lord, I urge you to—"

"Get out of my way." His expression and tone told the older man not to argue.

"As you wish, my lord." Pebbles stepped aside but muttered as he passed, "And may God have mercy on your conscience."

A short time later Miles stood at the top of the stairs at the home of the Earl and Countess of Malton. He nodded at the majordomo and pasted a smile onto his face.

"The Earl of Stratford," the Malton majordomo announced.

Miles started down the stairs and was immediately surrounded by friends and other well-wishers. No one asked about Amber, a nobody princess from a nowhere country. After ten minutes, he broke free from the group and began circulating.

And then Miles spied Georgiana Devon. She wore an emerald green gown, cut so low it barely covered her nipples.

"I see you've lost the princess," Georgiana said.

"I was hoping to see you tonight," Miles said. "Shall we dance?"

Georgiana inclined her head, stepped onto the dance floor, and into his arms. "Where is she tonight?"

"My wife is feeling under the eaves," he answered. "Her delicate condition, you know. Where is Grover Dalrymple?"

Georgiana laughed throatily. "I do believe Grover had other plans for the evening."

When the music ended, Miles escorted her off the dance floor. He lifted her hand to his lips. "I regret I have another engagement but will call upon you soon."

Georgiana smiled. "I will look forward to that, my lord."

His next stop was the home of the Earl and Countess of Lynton. As he had done earlier, Miles pasted a smile on his face and walked down the stairs into the crush of aristocrats.

He saw Sarah Pole almost immediately. She smiled when he walked in her direction.

"Sarah, I hoped to see you tonight," Miles said, lifting her hand to his lips. His dark gaze fixed on the generous cleavage bared by the cut of her ruby gown.

"Where is the princess?" Sarah asked.

"I would much prefer to dance with you than discuss my wife," Miles said.

Sarah inclined her head and stepped onto the dance floor. Miles pulled her close as they began to swirl around the ballroom.

"If I hadn't met Brenna," he told her, "I would have offered for you."

"We were good together, weren't we?"

Miles managed a smile and inclined his head. At waltz's end, he escorted her off the dance floor. "I regret I have another engagement," he said. "I would like to call upon you soon."

"I would love to entertain you," Sarah said.

The home of the Earl and Countess of Worcester was his final destination. As he had done at the previous two balls, Miles smiled at the world and mingled with society. His face was beginning to hurt from forcing smiles he didn't feel.

"I see you have come to your senses," Vanessa Stanton said, sidling up to him.

Miles looked at her. She was a vision in white silk, her gown nearly transparent and her nipples almost visible. Her rouged nipples, if he wasn't mistaken.

"You are drooling, my lord," she purred.

"I am imagining," he parried smoothly.

"Why limit yourself to imagining when you can experience," Vanessa said.

"Unfortunately, I have another engagement," Miles said. "I will call upon you to discuss an important matter."

"You do not need a reason to call upon me," Vanessa said. "What did you wish to discuss?"

"I believe it was something about a stallion and a mare," Miles answered, dropping his gaze to her breasts.

"I will enjoy that particular discussion."

"Until then."

Within minutes, Miles sat alone in his coach for the return ride to Berkeley Square. He leaned back, closed his eyes, and decided that he should be feeling a certain measure of satisfaction. Why the bloody hell did he feel worse?

I need to save myself. Amber awakened in the morning, determined to escape. She would not wait for Miles to rescue her. If she could get away on her own, her husband would be in no danger.

The villains would never suspect what she planned if she pretended obedience. On the other hand, she should not arouse their suspicions by overplaying her role.

Amber heard the door being unlocked. Gromeko entered, carrying a tray with her breakfast.

"Good morning, Princess. I hope you slept well."

Amber ignored him. She crossed the chamber and sat at the table to eat her breakfast.

"I am pleased that you are not starving yourself," Gromeko said, watching her eat. When she made no reply, he turned to leave.

"Gromeko." Amber looked over her shoulder at him. "I need something warmer to wear. Will you bring me a dress? Pink, I think. And matching ribbons for my hair."

Amber tried to sound as stupid as possible. If the count believed she was concerned with gowns and ribbons, he would never imagine she planned to escape.

Count Gromeko stared at her for a long moment, as if considering her request. Finally, he nodded. "I will see what I can do."

Hours later, Gromeko returned with her lunch tray. Slung over his arm, he carried a gown and a shawl.

"I apologize for the lack of pink," the count said. "You will forgive me for choosing a gown and a shawl to match your violet eyes."

Amber willed herself to blush. "I forgive you," she said, lifting the gown and the shawl from his hand. "Oh, you have forgotten the ribbons."

"I will bring you the ribbons at dinner," he said. "If you cooperate and eat your lunch."

Much to her mortification, Count Gromeko insisted on playing the lady's maid. He helped her into the gown, brushing his fingertips across the upper swell of her breasts, and then fastened the buttons. Finally, he wrapped the cashmere shawl around her shoulders.

"You are exquisite," the count said, his voice husky. "I believe I am jealous of my own stud. He will be pleased with the gift I bring him and, I am certain, will perform most admirably. I will watch you mate and pretend that I am the one riding you."

Revulsion and embarrassment mingled in Amber. She had never heard anyone speak so shockingly. She made no reply but moved to the table, sat down, and began to eat.

When the count turned to leave, she forced herself to say, "Will you sit with me while I eat?"

Gromeko inclined his head and returned to the table.

"What will happen to my husband's child?"

"Once the babe is weaned, I will send the earl his heir," Gromeko assured her. "If you cooperate."

"What will happen to my other babies?"

"I will not tear them from your breast. You will keep them until they reach an age to sell."

How generous. Amber suffered the almost overwhelming urge to strike him.

"They will be weaned off your milk within a few weeks," Gromeko continued. "You will recover from childbirth more quickly that way and resume your relationship with my stud." He stroked the back of her hand. "You need not worry, though. I own wet nurses and will let you choose which woman will feed your babies."

Amber ignored that. "I presume the letter from the czar was a forgery."

"We were hoping you would come willingly." Gromeko chuckled. "Pushkin misjudged your feelings for him and your desire for the czar's acknowledgment." He stroked her silver-blond hair. "You are your mother's image."

His remark surprised Amber. No one had ever spoken about her mother. Fedor had always brushed her questions aside, saying, "Your mother was the czar's whore."

"Tell me about my mother."

"I did not know her personally, but every man—including myself—would have sold his soul for one night in her bed." Gromeko left her after that, taking the empty tray with him.

Amber listened to his retreating footsteps and then hurried to the window. She stared at the oak tree, its outstretched branches calling to her. She needed to climb onto the closest branch.

Fear gripped her. She had never climbed a tree in her life. One false move would send her to her death. *Death before defilement,* she told herself. *Take one branch at a time.*

Amber opened the window and sent up a silent prayer of thanks that it did not squeak. Determined not to look down, she climbed rear-end first out the window and sat on the thick branch as if astride a horse.

Holding on with both hands, Amber concentrated on keeping her balance and inched backward toward the tree trunk. Then she lowered her left leg to the branch below as if dismounting a horse. Branch by branch, she descended the oak tree until she sat on the lowest branch. Only then did she look to judge the distance to the ground.

Count Gromeko and Uncle Fedor stood there, watching her.

"I warned you to beware of her," her uncle told the count. "She is her mother's daughter."

"Princess, come down," Gromeko ordered. *"Now."*

Amber closed her eyes against the reality of being caught. Then she dropped to the ground, landing on her feet.

"You conniving witch," Fedor shouted, his right fist connecting with her left cheek.

Amber dropped, unconscious, to the ground. . . .

Something cool covered her throbbing cheek.

Amber opened her eyes. She was lying on the bed in her chamber. Wearing a concerned expression, Count Gromeko perched on the edge of the bed. "I apologize for your uncle's barbaric behavior. I would never hurt you." He stood to leave. "Keep the cloth on your cheek. Though I appreciate your ingenuity, do not climb out the window again."

Once alone, Amber dropped a hand to her belly and whispered, "Do not fear, my little one. I will protect you."

Dressed in formal attire, Miles walked downstairs to the foyer that evening. He looked through the pile of invitations and decided on the Stroud, Enfield, and Brentwood balls after the opera. Hopefully, Georgiana, Sarah, and Vanessa would not attend the same ball. If that happened, he would take himself to White's for a drink and cards.

Miles noted his majordomo's disapproving expression and paused. "If you do not approve of my actions, feel free to find yourself another job." He turned away but stopped short when the other man spoke.

"First you discard your wife and then you discard me," Pebbles muttered. "I liked you better sitting in the dark."

"I did not discard my wife," Miles said. "She discarded me."

"You have not searched—"

"*Enough!* I want you packed and gone by the time I return," Miles said, giving his anger free reign.

"You cannot fire me," Pebbles said, looking down his nose at the younger man. "*I quit!*"

Miles slammed the door on the way out. He climbed into his coach and called out, "The Royal Opera House." Twenty minutes later, the coach stopped in front of the opera house. His driver opened the door, but Miles did not move. His mood precluded enjoying an opera performance.

"I've changed my mind," Miles told his driver. "Take me to the Earl of Stroud's in Grosvenor Square." Fifteen minutes later, the coach halted in front of the Stroud residence. Again, Miles did not move.

"I've changed my mind," he told his driver. "Take me home." Loosening his cravat, Miles leaned back and rested his head against the back of the coach. He could not engage in an affair with Georgiana, Sarah, or Vanessa. He wanted his wife. Unfortunately, his wife didn't want him, but he would have his son.

Miles came to a decision. In the morning he would send a note to his barrister to procure a court order preventing his wife from leaving England while she carried his child. Once she delivered and relinquished the babe to him, Amber Kazanov could go wherever she wanted with whomever she wanted.

The coach halted in front of Montgomery House in Berkeley Square. His driver opened the door, but Miles did not move. His gaze had fixed on his majordomo. With suitcase in hand, Pebbles descended the front stairs and walked down the street in the direction of Park Lane.

"Don't tell me you've changed your mind again," his driver said, irritation tinging his voice.

Without bothering to reply, Miles climbed out of the coach and jogged down the street after his majordomo. He touched the older man's arm, asking, "Where are you going?"

"I am leaving," Pebbles said.

"I've changed my mind," Miles told him.

"You cannot change your mind."

Miles snapped his brows together. "Why not?"

"I have found employment elsewhere," Pebbles answered.

"With whom?"

"My lord, I do not see how that—"

"Humor me!"

"Lady Isabelle has responded favorably to my request for employment," Pebbles answered.

"My own sister?"

Pebbles inclined his head. "Send me a note when you bring Her Highness home. I may reconsider."

"Her Highness is not coming home."

"Then I suggest that Joseph will make an excellent majordomo."

"I don't want Joseph. I want you."

"Tough." At that, Pebbles turned his back and walked away.

Miles watched until the older man disappeared around the corner. He had lost everything . . . Brenna, Amber, his face, and now even Pebbles, a man more like a father than a retainer.

Awakening in the morning, Amber inspected her reflection in the cheval mirror. A bruise discolored her left cheek. She heard the door being unlocked but refused to turn around. Footsteps crossed the chamber, and someone set a tray on the table.

"Eat this, or I will cram it down your throat," Fedor said. "We cannot get babies out of a dead woman."

"The sight of you sickens me," Amber said, rounding on her uncle. "I will not eat until you leave this chamber. Do not forget to lock the door on your way out."

Amber knew she needed to eat for the sake of her

baby. Taking her seat, she unrolled the napkin holding her utensils and stared in surprise at them.

The cook had sent her a fork and a knife. The blade looked sharp enough to slice the steak on her plate. Apparently, Count Gromeko had neglected to tell the cook to slice the steak before serving. For the rest of her life, Amber knew her favorite meal would be steak and eggs.

Amber lifted the blade and tested its sharpness with the tip of her finger. Then she smiled. *And waited.*

Uncle Fedor returned an hour later and noted the uneaten food. "I warned you—"

Amber touched the back of his neck with the blade. "Move or call for help, and I will kill you. Remember, dearest uncle, I relish the thought of your blood spurting all over this chamber until you are drained. Do you understand?"

"Yes."

"Yes, *Your Highness,*" she corrected him. "Say it."

"Yes, Your Highness."

"Your continued good health depends upon listening to my instructions," she warned him. "We will proceed slowly and silently to the servants' staircase. One false move, and my blade will skewer you."

With her hostage in the lead, Amber walked down the corridor to the narrow staircase. The tip of her blade never left the back of his neck.

Without warning, strong arms wrapped around her from behind and lifted her off the floor. The blade slipped from her hand and dropped to the floor.

"My family's fortune depends upon your fruitfulness," Sergei whispered against her ear. He carried her back to the bedchamber.

"Gromeko!" Amber screamed, fearing her uncle would beat her again and harm her baby. Gromeko appeared as Sergei dragged her, struggling, into the bed-chamber. Fedor grabbed the front of her gown and ripped it off her body.

"I told you she would escape if you gave her a gown," Fedor said. "Lock her in the closet."

"No!" Amber paled to a deathly white. "Please do not put me in there."

"Regretfully, Princess, you have proven untrustwor-thy." Gromeko nodded at Sergei, who tossed her into the closet and slammed the door.

Amber banged on it, calling, "I am cold in here."

"Toss her the shawl," she heard Gromeko say.

"Let her suffer," Fedor said.

"The princess belongs to me," the count told her uncle. "If she dies from a chill, I will lose my investment. *Give her the shawl.*"

The door opened a crack, and a hand tossed the shawl inside. Then she heard the sound of the lock turning.

"Gromeko," Amber cried. "Please, I promise—"

The bedchamber door slammed shut.

Amber wrapped the shawl around her shoulders and sat, trembling, in the dark.

Where are you, Miles? I need you.

Chapter 18

Where is she?

Warming the Russian's bed? Spreading her—?

That road led to madness.

Unshaven and unkempt in his evening attire from the previous night, Miles sat at his desk the third morning after his wife had left him. He poured himself another whisky and gulped it down in a single swig. Then he unfolded his wife's note, dismissing him from her life.

> *. . . The czar's acknowledgment means everything to me. I plan to marry Sergei . . .*

Miles focused on her intended marriage to the Russian and then stared at the ring she had given him. Why had she gifted him with the czar's ring if she loved another man? Why hadn't she gone to Sergei for help with her problem? Why had she brought love into his life only to take it away?

If the devil had the power to assume a pleasing shape, then the devil was Princess Amber Kazanov. An enticing liar and betrayer of men, a mirror image of her adulterous mother.

Miles tossed the ring on the desk and pocketed the note. He intended always to keep it close as a reminder to beware of women, especially those who professed their love.

Standing, Miles wandered to the window to stare at the garden below. His heart wrenched at what he saw. Caroline sat with Nanny Smart on a stone bench. His daughter looked sad, as if she had lost her best friend in the world. He regretted telling her that her new mummy had gone away. Forever.

Having survived the loss of his first wife, Miles knew he had the strength to shoulder the pain of this betrayal, but his daughter was a different matter. He would never forgive Amber Kazanov for hurting Caroline.

Miles watched his daughter rise from the bench. With head bowed, Caroline crossed the garden to the rosebush his wife had intended to nurse back to health.

The sight of the rosebush sent his simmering anger exploding into fury. How sickeningly sweet the princess was to worry about a plant. She thought nothing of turning her back on her husband and the little girl who loved her.

Damn her. She was carrying his baby and stealing his heir. Miles whirled away from the window and marched downstairs. Like an unexpected storm, he surprised the retainers he passed.

Passing through the kitchen, Miles grabbed an enormous butcher knife. He advanced on the rosebush, shouting at his daughter, "Get out of the way!"

Caroline watched in horror as he lifted the butcher knife to the rosebush. "No, Daddy!" She burst into tears.

Miles ignored her cries. He hacked branch after branch off the rosebush, mutilating it beyond recognition.

"Montgomery!"

The sound of a voice calling his name seeped into his brain.

"What the bloody hell are you doing?"

Miles whirled around, the butcher knife raised in his hand, a murderous gleam in his eyes.

Prince Rudolf stood there. With his gaze fixed on the blade, the prince held his hands up.

Miles shook his head to clear his brain and focused on the prince. He lowered the butcher knife, but the prince remained motionless. Only when he tossed the blade down did the prince step closer.

Miles gestured at Nanny Smart to take Caroline inside.

"I do not understand what is happening," Rudolf said, glancing at the mutilated rosebush, "but I carry news that will put you in a better frame of mind."

"And what news is that?"

"I passed Pushkin's residence and saw his servants packing the coaches," Rudolf said. "He will be leaving England on the evening tide. I heard you were still in residence and knew you and Amber would rejoice at the news."

Miles cocked a brow at him. "I have not seen Amber since the Stanton party."

"Amber is missing and you never sent me word?"

"My wife is not missing. She left me for the Russian."

"Amber would never do that," Rudolf insisted. "When I danced with her the other night, she proclaimed her love for you. She thanked me for bringing her to you."

Miles looked as surprised as he felt. Why would the princess leave the man she professed to love?

"Amber sent me a note," Miles said, reaching into his pocket.

"Are you certain she wrote it?"

Miles handed the crumpled parchment to the prince.

"The handwriting is hers," Rudolf said, perusing the note, "but look at this." He pointed to four scribbles beneath her name. "I taught Amber Germanic runes so that we could communicate secretly. She has written the word *help*."

"Oh, Christ." Miles ran toward the mansion.

"Joseph, send a footman to my brother-in-law—"

"Send another to Prince Viktor's," Rudolf interjected.

"Tell John and Viktor to meet us in front of Sergei Pushkin's mansion," Miles ordered, yanking the front door open. "The Russian has abducted my wife."

Twenty minutes later, the four men stood in front of the mansion. All four carried pistols.

Miles raced up the stairs and barged into the foyer, the others following behind. Surprised, Sergei Pushkin and Baron Slominsky whirled toward the door.

"What is the meaning of this?" Sergei demanded. "You cannot force your way into my home."

Four pistols leveled on him.

"Gentlemen, violence is unnecessary," Baron Slominsky intervened, his smile ingratiating. "If you state your business, then we can settle the matter and leave for our ship. Pushkin and I are leaving on the evening tide."

"Amber!" Miles shouted. "Where are you?"

"You are insane," Sergei said.

Miles struck him with the butt of the pistol, sending him crashing to the floor. "If you've touched her, I'll use the other end."

No one spoke.

"Amber!"

Hearing the sound of muffled cries, Miles raced up the stairs two at a time. Rudolf followed one step behind.

Miles burst into the chamber at the end of the corridor and faced a stranger. Then he heard the prince say, "Fedor."

"This invasion is illegal," Fedor Kazanov said, trying to block their way. "I will send for the authorities."

"Abduction is also illegal, *Father.*"

"I am not your father."

"Thank God for His blessings," Rudolf shot back.

Miles heard his wife weeping and pleading. *Her uncle had locked her in the closet.*

"Give me the key," Miles demanded.

"I am punishing a recalcitrant maid," Fedor said. "My discipline is none of your business."

"This is for my mother." Rudolf closed his fist and struck his father, sending him staggering toward Miles.

"This is for my wife." Miles closed his fist and struck Fedor again, sending him crashing to the floor. He searched the dazed man's pockets and found the key.

Miles opened the closet door and felt his heart breaking. His weeping wife was curled up on the floor, rocking back and forth. Removing his jacket, Miles knelt beside her and wrapped it around her. Then he scooped her into his arms.

"Why did you make me wait so long?" Amber cried, clinging to him like a drowning woman. "I needed you."

Miles wondered how he would ever live with himself again. His blind stupidity had nearly cost him his wife.

Gingerly, Miles set Amber down on her bed, but she refused to let him go. "Hold me," she sobbed, clinging to him.

He pulled the coverlet up to cover her. Then he sat on the bed, leaned back against the headboard, and held her protectively close. "I am sorry I failed you," he whispered, his voice raw with emotion.

"You did not fail me," Amber sobbed. "You rescued me."

Guilt consumed Miles. He could never tell her that

he had doubted her love and her faithfulness. He could never tell her that she had suffered because of his pig-headedness. He could never tell her that she had only narrowly escaped a lifetime of sexual slavery. If Rudolf had not chanced by, his wife would have been lost to him forever. How did a man live with that?

"Let me see your face," Miles said, tilting her chin up. He winced at her bruises and swollen eyes.

"Fedor beat me when I tried to escape."

"The fault is mine."

She shook her head. "The fault belongs to Fedor, Gromeko, and Sergei."

A knock on the door drew their attention. Amber clung to him in a panic. "I do not want to see anyone. Please do not leave me."

Miles tightened his hold. "Do not enter this chamber," he called.

"My lord, may I serve you in any way?" The voice belonged to Joseph.

"Bring a bowl of soup, a cup of tea, and a shot of vodka."

"Yes, my lord."

Amber looked up. "You will not leave me today?"

"I have no intention of leaving the house."

"Do not leave this room," she cried.

"I promise to stay by your side."

A short time later, another knock sounded on the door. "My lord?" Joseph called.

"I am walking to the door to get the tray," Miles told Amber. He rose from the bed and opened the door only far enough to take the tray.

"Do not disturb us for the remainder of the day," Miles instructed his man. "Bring a tray for two at the dinner hour. If Prince Rudolf returns, tell him I cannot leave the princess and will speak to him in the morning."

"Yes, my lord."

Miles returned to the bed. He placed the tray on the bed and handed Amber the shot of vodka.

"Drink this. The vodka will relax you."

"But the baby—"

"One shot of vodka will not hurt the baby."

Amber drank the vodka down in one gulp. She shivered as it burned a path to her stomach.

Miles dipped the spoon into the soup and then raised the spoon to her mouth.

"You do not need to feed me," she said.

"I want to feed you." When she finished the soup, Miles passed her the teacup. "Now drink this."

Amber sipped the tea. She glanced at the evening jacket wrapped around her shoulders and then at his formal attire. "You were awake all night searching for me."

Miles dropped his gaze. "I was awake all night."

"You look terrible."

"You look beautiful." Miles set the tray on the floor and returned to his perch leaning against the headboard. He gathered her into his arms. "Sleep now."

"You will not leave me?"

"I will never leave you." Miles clutched her against his chest and stroked her back soothingly. When her breathing evened, he knew she slept.

Miles closed his eyes. God forgive him for his lies, but he could not hurt his wife more by admitting he had doubted her. The problem was his, not hers. The damn scars had colored his judgment.

Amber felt more secure the next morning. She was willing to let her husband leave her bedchamber, though not the house.

"How do you feel this morning?" Miles asked, sitting on the edge of the bed.

"Much better." Amber glanced at his clothing. Her

husband still wore his evening attire. "You can leave this chamber if you want."

"I would like to clean myself," Miles said. "I locked your door, and there is warm water on the table. Joseph will deliver breakfast to my chamber. I'll call you when it arrives."

After he disappeared into his own chamber, Amber rose from the bed and checked the lock on her door. Then she washed and changed into a fresh nightgown. She had no intention of leaving her bedchamber, so there was no reason to dress.

"Breakfast is served," Miles called, knocking on the connecting door.

Amber walked into her husband's chamber and sat at the table placed in front of the hearth. The sunshine was missing from the smile she gave her husband.

"Are you certain you feel better?"

"I feel much better." To prove her words, Amber lifted her fork and began to eat the eggs and ham on her plate.

"Rudolf will want to speak with me this morning," Miles said. "I will need to leave your chamber but will remain inside the house. I promise you have nothing to fear."

"Could Just-Pebbles guard the corridor outside my door?" Amber asked.

Miles felt his heart wrench at her question. His wife was *not* better if she needed a guard outside a locked door. He wondered if she would ever recover.

"Pebbles and I argued," Miles told her. "He is no longer in my employ."

Amber felt her panic rising. The old majordomo was her friend. She needed him.

"Where has he gone?"

"My sister is harboring the old codger." Miles gave her a rueful smile. "I will send a footman to bring him home and offer him a pay raise."

"Thank you."

"Caroline will want to visit today," he said. "She missed you terribly."

"I would like to see Caroline."

Later that morning, Amber lay on her bed and tried to forget what had happened. When someone knocked on the door, she leaped off the bed in alarm and wrapped herself in her bedrobe.

"Who is it?"

"Pebbles, Your Highness."

Amber unlocked and opened the door. She threw herself into the stunned majordomo's arms. "Thank God you have returned."

"I am relieved to see you," Pebbles said, patting her back, offering fatherly comfort.

"You must have seen how frantic Miles was to find me," Amber said, looking up at the older man. "You should not have deserted him."

"I apologize, Your Highness, and promise never to leave His Lordship again."

"Thank you, Just-Pebbles. That eases my mind."

Caroline visited her after lunch. The little girl dashed across the chamber, climbed on the bed, and threw herself in Amber's arms.

"I missed you, Mummy," Caroline told her. "I cried every night."

"I missed you more," Amber said. "I cried every night, too."

"Daddy said you were gone forever and never coming home," Caroline told her, "but I knew you loved me too much to leave me."

The girl's remark puzzled Amber. Why had her husband told his daughter that she had gone forever? Had he become frustrated in his search for her and feared he would never find her?

"How is your daddy?" Caroline asked.

Amber gave her a blank look. "I do not understand."

"Daddy said that your daddy wanted to see you before he went to heaven."

Amber was relieved that Miles had made up a story for her stepdaughter's benefit. Caroline would have been frightened to learn she had been abducted.

"My daddy feels much better." Amber managed a smile for the girl. "He has postponed his trip to heaven."

"Will you need to see him some day?"

"No, Caro, I promise to stay in Stratford with you and your baby brother."

Later that afternoon, Miles walked into her chamber and perched on the edge of the bed. "Wouldn't you like to dress and sit with Caroline in the garden?"

"No, thank you." Amber refused to leave the safety of her bedchamber.

"Fedor, Pushkin, and Gromeko are locked in the Russian embassy," Miles told her. "They cannot harm you."

"I will sit in the garden tomorrow."

On the third day, Amber forced herself to get out of bed and dressed. The Duke of Inverary had used his influence to save her from the humilation and scandal of testifying in open court. Her presence in her husband's office was required to give a deposition to the magistrate and the Russian ambassador.

"Everyone has arrived," Miles said, walking into her bedchamber. "Are you strong enough for this? We can postpone it for a few days."

Amber managed a faint smile, but her complexion was pale. "We cannot return to Stratford until I do this, and I want to go home."

"You need fear nothing," Miles promised, holding her hand to escort her downstairs. "I will remain by your side. Let me know if you want to leave."

The English magistrate sat behind the desk. Count

Korsekov, the Russian ambassador, sat nearby while Rudolf stood near the windows. Two chairs had been placed in front of the desk.

Amber trembled when she saw the chairs, feeling as if she was on trial. What if they did not believe her? What if the authorities released Gromeko? Would she always be looking over her shoulder?

Amber cast a nervous glance at her cousin. Rudolf winked at her.

And then she knew. Her abductors would remain healthy in custody. But if they were freed, Rudolf would deal with them as he had Terrence Pines.

"Your Highness, are you well enough to speak to us?" the magistrate asked.

"Yes, my lord."

"I thank you for the elevation in position," the magistrate said with a kindly smile. "I am merely a sir."

Amber blushed at her mistake.

The magistrate looked at Miles. He inclined his head, giving the man permission to continue.

"Abduction and attempted bondage are serious charges to bring against a prince and two counts," the magistrate said. "Because of their ranks, Pushkin, Gromeko, and Kazanov are confined to the Russian embassy."

"I understand."

Amber did not understand at all. A criminal was a criminal, no matter if he was a mister, a lord, or a royal.

"Please tell us what happened," the magistrate said.

Amber hesitated, uncertain of where to begin. Then she felt her husband give her hand a gentle squeeze.

"Start at the very beginning," Miles said.

"Last March I overheard Uncle Fedor selling me to Count Gromeko," she said, staring at her lap. "Gromeko wanted to mate me with one of his slaves and sell my babies in the East."

Amber glanced at the Russian ambassador. "Because my father had never publicly acknowledged me, I could not seek his help. I sought refuge with my cousins in England.

"Rudolf introduced me to Lord Montgomery, and we married. When we came to London for a visit, Sergei Pushkin appeared at our door and carried a letter from the czar, who indicated he wanted me to return to Moscow."

Miles passed the note to the magistrate who, in turn, handed it to Ambassador Korsekov.

"This is a good forgery," the ambassador said.

"I had yearned for my father's acknowledgement my whole life," Amber said, "but the offer came too late." She gave her husband a smiling glance. "I was a married lady and expecting my first child. My love and my allegiance belonged to my husband."

"Tell us what happened on the evening in question," the magistrate said.

"I danced with Count Pushkin at the Stanton ball. He said he was leaving England and wanted a private word with me. Someone hiding in the garden attacked me, and I awakened to find myself a captive."

"Did any of them *touch* you?" Ambassador Korsekov asked.

"Fedor struck me and would have beaten me more, but Gromeko stopped him," Amber answered. "Sergei tried to force himself on me, but I bit him."

All the men smiled at that.

"Count Gromeko abducted you but did not attempt assault?" the ambassador asked.

"Gromeko was waiting until I reached his—wherever he keeps slaves."

"Did he tell you this?"

Amber blushed, humiliated almost beyond endurance. "Gromeko said he would take me into his bed whenever

I was pregnant." She looked in distress at her husband. "I want to leave now, Miles."

"Thank you, Your Highness," the magistrate said, standing when she did. "The earl and the prince can answer anything else."

Ambassador Korsekov bowed over her hand. "Czar Alexander has never publicly acknowledged you, but he does care for you. The czar mentioned you many times to me, and I brought you his yearly gift when you were too young to remember."

Tears welled up in her eyes and streamed down her cheeks. "Thank you for saying that. What will happen to them?"

"I will personally escort them to Moscow and present your deposition to the czar," the ambassador answered. "They will face Czar Alexander's justice."

"You need never fear them," Rudolf spoke up. "Returning to England would be unhealthy for those three."

"I did not hear that," the magistrate said.

"Neither did I," the ambassador agreed.

"Shall I help you upstairs?" Miles asked her.

"I can manage on my own."

Amber went to her chamber to wait for the magistrate and the ambassador to leave. She wanted to be done with this nightmare. She wanted to go home. She wanted to feel safe.

Standing at the window, Amber gazed at the barren garden. Then she noticed the rosebush, mutilated almost beyond recognition.

Amber hurried downstairs. The foyer was deserted, and someone was knocking on the door. She hesitated a moment, summoning the courage to open the door.

"Your Highness," her husband's barrister said in obvious surprise, stepping into the foyer.

"Good afternoon, Mr. Smythe," Amber greeted the man. "Did you wish to speak with His Lordship?"

"Actually, I need to give you these documents," Smythe answered, passing her the sealed papers. "Read and sign those, please. Then return them to my office, if you will. Thank you, Your Highness, and good day to you."

Amber stared at the sealed papers in confusion. Who would be sending her legal documents? She looked up when the majordomo walked into the foyer.

"I thought I heard the door," Pebbles said.

"Mr. Smythe brought me these," Amber said, holding the documents up, "but he did not wish to speak to the earl." She started down the corridor in the direction of the garden door.

"Your Highness, those are not for you," Pebbles called.

Amber heard him but did not stop. She needed to see that rosebush.

"My lord—" came the majordomo's distant shout.

Amber ignored it. She stepped into the garden and did not stop until she stood in front of the dead rosebush.

"Amber?" Miles arrived in the garden a few minutes later. He put his arm around her and drew her against the side of his body. "We can leave for Stratford whenever we want."

"Who did this?" Amber asked, her gaze on the rosebush.

"I believed you had betrayed me," Miles admitted. "In anger, I hacked the rosebush to death."

Amber stepped away from him. "You believed I had betrayed you?"

"Yes."

Daddy said you were gone forever and never coming home. Pain ripped through her, making speaking difficult. "You did *not* search three days for me?"

Her husband remained silent. Which answered her question.

"Why did you search for me that day?"

Misery was etched across her husband's face. He stepped toward her.

Amber was not inclined to forgive. She held her hand up in a gesture telling him to remain where he stood. "Answer my question."

"Rudolf stopped by that morning," Miles said. "He read your secret cry for help in the runes."

"You were willing to lose me."

"I was *not* willing."

Amber could not control the shudder that shook her body. "If Rudolf had not chanced to visit, I would be on my way—" She left the frightening thought unfinished.

"I regret you suffered three days because of my inaction," Miles said. "Believe me, love, I am sorry."

"I am sorry, too. Do not use the word *love* in my presence again."

"We will return to Stratford and begin again," Miles said. "I will never forgive myself, nor will I ever mistrust you again." He dropped his gaze to the papers in her hand. "Pass me those documents, and we will go home."

Amber looked from her husband to the documents and then back at him. "Smythe told me to sign and return these to him."

"Smythe made a mistake," Miles said, and held his hand out. "Give them to me."

Her husband did not want her to see what the documents contained. Amber broke the seal and stared in horror at what was written. The first was her husband's petition for divorce, the second a court order forbidding her to leave England until she gave birth and relinquished the baby to her husband.

Amber trembled with horror and heartbreak. She let

the documents slip from her hand and, without another word, walked away.

Her husband wanted to divorce her.

Her husband intended to take her baby.

Her husband did not love her.

Chapter 19

I've failed her. Miles watched his wife disappear inside the mansion. He was getting what he deserved for doubting her, for planning a divorce, and for intending to take the baby.

The late October afternoon faded into twilight, making the barren garden seem melancholy. Miles wished his troubles would fade away like the daylight. Why did people fail to recognize a treasure until it was gone?

Miles picked the divorce papers and court orders off the ground. How stupid could one man be? Why hadn't he tried to find her to speak with her before taking such a foolish action? He could have saved himself and his wife much heartache.

All roads led back to the damn scars. He hadn't bothered to search for her because he had been so certain of her rejection. A self-fulfilling prophecy.

What should he do now? How could he ever make things right between them? Amber would never forgive him. He could not fault her for that. Men had been the bane of his wife's entire life. A father who had never acknowledged her, making her a social outcast. A stepfather who had murdered her mother, making her an orphan. A ruthless uncle who sold her into sexual slavery. A beloved friend who had betrayed her for money, and a husband who had distrusted her.

The princess's remarkable ability to love was one of God's miracles. She should have been bitter and suspicious. Instead, she had handed him her heart and placed her trust in him.

Yes, he had failed her. He had trampled on her heart. He was no better than the other self-centered, cold-hearted bastards in her life.

Miles returned to the mansion and, walking into the foyer, sat on the bottom stair. He looked at the major-domo.

"She read the documents," he said with a groan.

"I know."

Miles looked at his old retainer. "Don't you want to say I told you so?"

Pebbles sat on the stair beside him. "Will you feel better if I do?"

"How do I fix this?"

"Take Her Highness home to Stratford and give her time to heal," the majordomo advised him. "She will forgive you. Eventually."

"What if she doesn't?"

"How could she not forgive you, my lord? You are so *damn* lovable."

In spite of his misery, Miles smiled at the older man. He stood then and climbed the stairs to the third floor. He tapped lightly on her bedchamber door. No answer. He tried the doorknob. Locked. He walked into his own bedchamber and, instead of entering his wife's chamber without permission, knocked on the connecting door.

"Amber?"

"Yes?"

"I want to speak with you."

"Speak."

"I want to look at you while I speak," Miles said. "May I come inside?"

"You own this house, my lord."

Miles winced at her answer. "I will not force my presence on you."

Silence.

Amber opened the door, saying, "You may come inside."

With the offending legal documents in hand, Miles walked into her bedchamber and saw her gaze drop to the papers. He tossed them into the hearthfire and watched them burn.

He turned around. She was watching him.

"I do not want a divorce, nor do I want to take our baby from you," Miles said. "I regret betraying your trust and hope you can forgive me."

Amber squared her shoulders proudly but refused to meet his gaze. "You have done nothing that requires my forgiveness," she said, her tone coolly polite. "We made a bargain. You would give me your name, and I would give you an heir. What you do with your heart is no concern of mine."

"You don't love me anymore?"

"Love is the child of an idle brain," Amber said, her smile bitter. "Those who seek it do so at their own peril. I will not allow insubstantial love to destroy me as it did my mother."

Miles said nothing. If he professed his love, she would believe he was lying.

"We will go home to Stratford in the morning." Miles paused, hoping she would say something.

"Is there anything else?"

"Will you dine with me?"

"I think not tonight."

"Good night, Princess."

* * *

Silence is golden, Amber thought, *but decidedly uncomfortable when trapped in a coach.* The journey to Stratford was the most silent, tense ride she had ever taken in the company of others. If her stepdaughter had not been present, no words would have been spoken.

Amber could not force herself to converse as if nothing had happened between them. She knew her husband felt guilty, but his remorse could not change their circumstances. Once done, some things could not be undone.

A loveless marriage was better than what Gromeko had planned for her. She intended to be a dutiful wife, enjoying her husband's protection, his home, and his children. She would have everything she ever wanted. *Except love.*

Oppressive silence echoed in the dining room at Arden Hall that evening. A fog of tension, emanating from the lord and his lady, swirled around everyone.

Miles and Amber ate in silence. The footmen tiptoed around the room. Even Caroline was unusually subdued.

Amber focused on her husband's hand when he lifted the wineglass to his lips. He wore the czar's ring again.

"I am wearing your father's ring," Miles said, noting where her gaze had fixed.

Anger shot through her. Did he actually believe wearing a ring held any significance now?

"I wear no rings," Amber said, holding her hands out for him to see. She caught his gaze on the third finger of her left hand. He did not need to know she had removed her wedding band that morning because pregnancy had swollen her fingers.

"You will want to start decorating a nursery," Miles said, refusing to comment on her lack of a wedding band. "Stratford has many fine shops. Spend whatever you want."

"I will not venture into Stratford any time soon."

"If you aren't well enough to shop, give Pebbles a list."

"My lord, please use the man's correct name. Doing otherwise is rude and may cause him to seek employment elsewhere."

Miles, the two footmen, and the majordomo smiled. Which confused her.

Caroline yawned, drawing their attention.

"Come, Caro," Amber said, standing. "I will put you to bed."

"I'm not tired."

"You are yawning in your plate."

"No, Mummy, I was growling like a lion."

"I will tell you a story about a princess and a pea," Amber coaxed her.

That appealed to Caroline. She stood and kissed her father's cheek. "Do you want to hear the story, Daddy?"

"Mummy will tell me later." Miles shifted his gaze to Amber. "Will I see you in the drawing room?"

"I am sorry, but traveling has tired me."

After her stepdaughter slept, Amber went to her own bedchamber. She found her husband waiting there.

"May I help you?"

"I have come to help you," he said. "If you turn around, I will unfasten your gown."

"I have undressed myself for many years and do not need your assistance."

Amber did not want him to touch her. The situation would have been different if her husband had searched for her. If he had not planned to divorce her and take her baby.

"How long are you planning to punish me?"

"I am not punishing you." Amber looked him straight in the eye. "I need time to accept that the father of my baby had no faith in my word."

"Amber—"

"Please, Miles. The babe tires me."

He inclined his head. "As you wish."

The morning dawned depressingly gray and bleak. Which suited Amber's mood. She decided she would be civil to her husband but distance herself from him emotionally. She would not give her love to a man who could not return it. Accordingly, she sent a maid to bring her a late breakfast in her chamber, avoiding her husband. And she ate enough to keep herself from being hungry at lunch.

Unfortunately, Amber could find no good reason to miss dinner. She collected Caroline and walked downstairs to the dining room. Nothing personal would be said with the child present.

Amber suppressed an urge to sit at the far end of the dining table—that would be childish. She and her stepdaughter took their usual places.

"How are my two favorite girls?" Miles asked, sitting at the head of the table.

"Mummy told me a story about a princess and a pauper girl," Caroline said. "The mean princess treated the pauper girl very badly. So the king made his daughter change gowns with the pauper girl. He wanted her to know that other people had feelings."

"Did the princess learn her lesson?"

Caroline nodded. "The princess felt sorry and shared all of her gowns with the pauper girl. Everyone lived happily ever after."

"I am glad that someone lives happily ever after," Miles said, and glanced at his wife. "Come spring, I plan to renovate the east wing and hope you will decorate it."

Amber looked up from her plate. "I have no interest in decorating the east wing."

Miles knew he deserved whatever punishment she gave him. He had nearly lost her, inadvertently almost cast her into slavery.

"I understand."

"You understand nothing." Setting her napkin on the table, Amber rose from her chair and walked toward the door.

Miles knew he couldn't let this continue but did not know what to do. Had he lost her love forever?

"Mummy, where are you going?" Caroline called.

Amber paused. "I need to use the water closet."

"Don't forget to wash your hands."

Amber smiled and walked back to the table. She put her arm around the little girl and planted a kiss on her cheek.

"I love you, Caroline," she said. "I promise to wash my hands."

Caroline smiled. "I love you, too, Mummy."

Miles watched this byplay between his two ladies. He should feel grateful that the princess loved his daughter, but he needed her love, too.

Amber managed to avoid her husband again at breakfast and lunch the next day but knew she needed to appear for dinner. She inspected her appearance in the cheval mirror, wondering why she bothered. Why should she care about her appearance when she was dining with a man who had no feelings for her?

She loved her husband too much to live with him like this, but she had no place to go. She had trapped herself in a loveless marriage.

When she walked into the dining room, her husband seated her at the table as if all was normal between them. The majordomo and the footmen served dinner as if all was well with the world.

Amber knew better, though. Her world had fallen apart because of her husband's lack of trust in her.

"Where is Caroline?"

"She ate earlier," Miles answered. "I wanted to dine alone with my wife."

"Caroline is your daughter and should share meals with you."

Miles changed the subject. "When are you planning to invite the Squelch sisters to tea?"

"I changed my mind about that," Amber answered, giving him a sidelong glance. "I am not interested in Stratford society."

"You have no interest in decorating a nursery, renovating the east wing, or inviting my villagers to tea," Miles said. "What *does* interest you, my love?"

Love?

That one word—so carelessly spoken—exploded within her, unmasking a lifetime of bitter rejection.

"Do not use that word," Amber cried, bolting out of her chair. "You do not love me. You never wanted me here. You tried to get rid of me." She pointed at the portrait of Brenna Montgomery. *"You love her!"*

Amber whirled away, intending to flee the dining room. The majordomo stood there, inadvertently blocking her escape. "Get out of my way," she shouted and, when he moved, ran from the room.

Surprised by her outburst, Miles stared after her. He stood, his first instinct to go after her. Then he realized that would probably make matters worse.

Pebbles dismissed the two footmen with a nod of his head. Then he said, "You are not making any progress with her."

"Go away," Miles said, "or I'll terminate you."

Pebbles sat at the table and drank the princess's wine. "I have known you since the day you were born," the majordomo said. "The fire destroyed your first marriage, but you are destroying this marriage."

Miles looked at him but said nothing. His attentive silence gave the majordomo permission to continue.

"Lady Brenna's portrait hangs in every chamber," Pebbles said, gesturing to the mantel. "Everywhere she looks, Her Highness sees Lady Brenna. She cannot even eat without seeing the late countess, whom you were still mourning after four years."

Miles poured his majordomo another glass of wine. "I think I have lost her love."

Pebbles drained this second glass of wine and gestured for another. "For a smart man, you are a blockhead. If she didn't love you, Her Highness would not be so hurt by your failure to trust her, which incited you to plan divorce and keep her baby."

"How do you know that is the issue?"

Pebbles rolled his eyes. "Servants listen, my lord, and servants talk."

"How do you suggest I solve this problem?"

"You need to make the princess feel loved and cherished."

Miles nodded. "How do you propose I do that?"

Pebbles shrugged. "You are the earl, my lord, not I."

An hour later, Miles climbed the stairs to his wife's bedchamber. He did not know what to do to make her feel loved and cherished. He only had three words at his disposal . . . *I love you.* Whether she believed him or not was another matter. If he said those three words to her enough, perhaps she would believe him. Sooner or later.

Miles tapped on the door.

No answer.

Entering her chamber without permission, Miles crossed the room to the bed where she slept. He pulled the coverlet up to keep her from catching a chill.

He loved her.

These damn, cursed scars. The scars had ruled his whole life for more than four years. He believed she had chosen Sergei because the Russian had no scars. What a fool he had been.

Miles left the bedchamber and walked downstairs to the kitchen, surprising his staff. "Pebbles, I would speak with you."

"Yes, my lord." The majordomo followed him into the corridor outside the kitchen.

"Remove Lady Brenna's portrait from the dining room and the library," Miles instructed him.

"What shall I put there?"

Miles shook his head. "Nothing. I plan to commission an artist to paint Amber and Caroline."

"I will take care of it immediately."

"Thank you." Miles touched the older man's shoulder. "And thank you for the advice."

Pebbles cocked a brow at him and drawled, "Does this mean I am no longer in danger of termination?"

Miles smiled.

Amber ate a late breakfast in her chamber and then skipped lunch as she had done the previous two days. Her outburst embarrassed her. She didn't want to see her husband or the servants who had witnessed her loss of control.

Sitting on the chaise in front of the hearth, she noticed the book she had left there. *Studies in Aristocratic Finances in the Sixteenth and the Seventeenth Centuries*. This was the book she had used as an excuse to see her husband when he was avoiding her. Now she was avoiding him.

Checking the hour, Amber grabbed the book and headed for the door. She would return it while her husband ate lunch.

Amber walked into the library and stopped short. The enormous chamber was as dark as it had been on the first day she had ever seen it. Someone had closed the window drapes. Only the fire in the hearth cast light into the center of the chamber.

Setting the book down on a table, Amber walked to the hearth. Her gaze never left the empty space where Brenna Montgomery's portrait should have been hanging.

Amber stared at the barren wall. She could not imagine what had happened to the portrait.

And then faint, muffled noises coming from her husband's study penetrated her consciousness. On silent feet, she crossed the library.

Unaware of her presence, Miles sat facing the closed drapes. His head was bowed and his shoulders slumped.

He was weeping.

For her?

It could not be.

Amber didn't know what to do. She listened to his quiet sobs, each tear he shed melting the ice around her heart.

"Miles?" Amber knelt beside him and touched his hand. "What is it?"

Miles lifted his head and looked at her through tear-blurred eyes. "I doubted my own worth, not you," he told her. "I didn't trust your love because of my scars. I convinced myself that you loved Sergei because he had no scars."

"Oh, Miles," she moaned, and lifted his hand to her lips. "Come with me."

Amber led him to the window and opened the drapes, bringing sunlight into his study. She lifted the mask from his face and kissed his scarred cheek.

"I love you," Amber said, placing the palms of her hands on his cheeks. "I love all of you. Both sides of your face. *Even your scars.*"

"I love you, Amber." Miles crushed her against his

body. "I have loved you since the first day you walked into my life. Believe me. *Please.*"

"I do believe you."

Seven months later

"I cannot believe how much he's grown," Miles said, studying his two-month-old son cradled in his mother's arms.

"Alex is destined to be as big as his father," Amber agreed.

"He has a long road to travel before he grows into his name."

"Royalty always carries a long list of names."

Alexander Rudolf Miles William George Montgomery stepped onto the world's stage on April twenty-third. Her husband's birthday, Shakespeare's birthday, Saint George's Day.

His father was so happy he told his wife to name their first son. And then regretted it.

His wife named her son in honor of her father, her favorite cousin, her husband, William Shakespeare, and Saint George. She thought the name fit her son perfectly.

On that idyllic June afternoon, the Earl and Countess of Stratford sat on a bench in their garden and admired their son. Alexander Rudolf Miles William George slept peacefully, oblivious to the admiring gazes of his parents.

"My lord?"

Both Miles and Amber looked up. Their majordomo hurried across the lawn toward them, a courier following behind.

"A messenger from the Russian ambassador," Pebbles said.

Miles looked at the courier, who handed him a large, intricately carved box with a mother-of-pearl lid.

"Czar Alexander sends his regards and this gift to Princess Amber Kazanov." The courier passed him a letter. "Ambassador Korsekov sends the earl this."

"Thank you." Miles lifted the box and the missive out of the courier's hands and then instructed his majordomo, "Take the man inside for a hot meal and a place to perch."

"Yes, my lord."

"A gift from your father and a letter from the ambassador."

"Open the ambassador's letter first."

Miles broke the missive's seal and perused the short letter. Then he chuckled.

"What is so amusing?"

"Do you want to know how the villains were punished?"

Amber tore her gaze from her son and looked at her husband. "Does the punishment fit their crimes?"

"Czar Alexander forced Fedor to relinquish control of the Kazanov fortune to your cousin Vladimir," Miles told her. "Then he found the plainest, most contrary, unmarried lady he could and ordered Sergei to marry her."

Amber smiled with delight. "And Gromeko?"

"The czar liberated the count's slaves and forbade him to engage in the slave business," Miles answered. "All three are forbidden—upon pain of death—to leave Russia."

"I am truly safe."

"Your father is protecting you."

Amber smiled at that. "Open his gift."

Miles set the box on the bench and lifted the lid. Inside on a bed of purple velvet lay several items.

"This appears to be a legal document," Miles said, unrolling a parchment sealed with the czar's insignia. "Brace yourself, my love. Here are two proclamations, one in Russian and one in English, acknowledging Amber Kazanov as his true daughter. Though you and your progeny have no legitimate claim to the throne."

Strangely, her father's public acknowledgment did not make her as happy as she would have thought. She looked down at her son. "I told you what a special boy you are, the *official* grandson of Czar Alexander of Russia."

"Here is a ruby and gold ring with the czar's insignia," Miles said. "Look at this." He held up an exquisite jewel-encrusted gold chalice."

"How nice," she said, making her husband laugh.

"Darling, that is the understatement of the year." Miles lifted two sealed missives. "One letter is addressed to his grandson to be opened when he reaches his majority. This one is addressed to you."

"Tell me what it says."

Miles gave her a puzzled smile. "You do not want to read this letter yourself?"

"As you can see, my arms are filled with my son," Amber answered. "Holding Alex is more important than reading a letter from a father I have only seen once in my entire life."

"Your father apologizes for the trouble his neglect caused," Miles told her, perusing the letter. "He wants to assure you that he cared deeply for your mother and would have protected her if he had realized what Rozer Kazanov planned to do. He considers you "a child of his heart" and invites us to visit him whenever convenient."

Amber nodded absently, as if an invitation from the czar of Russia was insignificant.

"What do you want to do about the czar?"

"I will write him a letter and send him a miniature of our son."

"I am willing to travel to Moscow."

"I am *not* willing to travel so great a distance with my

children," Amber said. "Nor am I willing to leave my children in the care of others. The future will be soon enough for a visit to Moscow."

"Your father may not be alive at some future date."

"Then so be it." Amber looked at her husband. "Czar Alexander had twenty years to be my father. I do not intend to lose one moment with our children."

Miles leaned close and planted a chaste kiss on her cheek. Then he stood, walked the short distance to the rosebush, and plucked a rose for his wife.

"Ouch!" cried the rosebush.

Miles stepped back, startled, and then realized the rosebush sounded like his daughter. He peeked behind the bush and saw his daughter hiding there.

Caroline laughed at her prank. She ran across the lawn, calling, "Mummy, can we make a happiness cake?"

"Run inside and instruct Just-Pebbles to tell Mrs. Meade to gather the ingredients. Be sure you tell him what flavor you want."

"His name is just Pebbles," Miles said, sitting beside her again and offering her the rose.

"I called him Just-Pebbles. Is advanced age affecting your hearing?"

Miles smiled and put his arm around her shoulder. He kissed her temple, inhaling her lilacs-and-sunshine scent.

Amber lifted his mask with her free hand, planted a kiss on his scarred cheek, and then set the mask in place again.

"I love you, my husband."

"And I love you, my wife."

Amber gave him a flirtatious smile. "Do you love me enough to let your stallion cover my mare?"

Miles shouted with laughter and then leaned close. "I thought my sweet filly would never ask."

Amber looked down at her son. "Your father just called you a foal."

"You are incorrigible."

"You love me anyway?"

Miles grew serious. "I love you enough to defy fire."

"I love you in equal measure," Amber vowed, her eyes glistening with unshed tears.

"You would defy fire to save me?" he asked.

"Without hesitation."

"Do you love me enough to let *me* bake the happiness cake?"

"*No.*"

Please turn the page for an exciting sneak peek of
Patricia Grasso's next historical romance
SEDUCING THE PRINCE
coming in April 2005!

Chapter 1

London, 1821

"I forbade you to write that book."

The petite redhead stood to confront her husband. "I do not take orders from you."

Albert Merlot, the Earl of Brentwood, scowled at his wife and marched across the study. He stopped short when the Great Dane beside her growled.

"Good boy, Horatio." Dementia patted her dog's head and gave her husband a challenging smile. "Well, Bertie—"

Regina Bradford, the Countess of Langley, lifted her gaze from the paper. Tapping the quill against her lips, she let the warm breeze from the open window glide across her face.

A solitary bird serenaded the world from a branch in the silver birch tree. The perfume of roses, bluebells, and iris wafted into the study and mingled with the scent of ink.

After dipping her quill in the ink, Regina resumed writing. The quill scratched across the paper, an oddly comforting sound, more soothing than rhythmic pattering of rain against a window. Lying beside her chair, a Great Dane snored and twitched in sleep.

Regina stared out the window again. The singing bird winged away from the silver birch and glided through the air past her window.

A yearning swelled within her. Regina longed to soar like an eagle, a hawk, or a merlin. She would even settle for the smaller wings of a wren, a dove, or a sparrow. Whenever she felt trapped, she could fly away to freedom.

"Are you writing again?"

Regina ignored her husband's question, but a spark of irritation flickered to life inside her. The Great Dane lifted its head and growled low in its throat, bringing a smile to her lips.

"I forbade you to write that book."

Regina stared at what she had written. Apparently, she was writing what she knew.

"We have had this conversation a hundred times." Regina stood to confront her husband. "I do not take orders from you, Chuck."

"Do not call me that," Charles Bradford ordered. "I dislike nicknames."

"Yes, I know. *Chuck.*"

The Earl of Langley marched across the study toward his wife. He stopped short when the Great Dane sat up and growled again.

"Good boy, Hamlet." Regina stroked her dog's head and gave her husband a challenging smile.

"I'll shoot that dog some day," Charles said.

"You will be signing your own death warrant," Regina said, her tone and expression pleasant.

Anger mottled her husband's complexion. "Are you threatening me?"

"Take it as you like it."

"I don't like *it* at all with you," Charles said. "That

grotesque mane of red curls gives you a clownish appearance."

"I know you prefer blondes, especially named Adele," Regina said. "And I thank the Lord every night for His blessing."

Charles ignored her insult. "Be prepared to leave in the morning for the Duke of Inverary's estate. Remember, mingle with the other guests but do not argue with your betters."

"I told you I would not accompany you to the duke's," she reminded him.

"I cannot attend His Grace's party without my wife," he said. "Besides, I have already accepted for both of us."

Regina felt her irritation growing. Why did his wishes hold more importance than hers? She loathed venturing into society, where she was an unwelcome intruder.

"Once we arrive," Regina complained, "you and your mistress will disappear, and I will be alone for four days. I prefer staying home with my son."

"Your inability to conduct yourself properly in society does concern me," Charles said. "People will tolerate your presence if you keep your thoughts to yourself."

Regina felt like screaming, her irritation mixing with angry frustration. Not surprisingly, her husband refused to understand her feelings.

"I am *not* going anywhere."

"You will accompany me," he threatened, stepping closer, "or you will be sorry."

The Great Dane's growls drew their attention. Hamlet stood beside his mistress and bared his fangs.

Regina placed her hand on the dog's head. "Slowly back away, or you will be the sorry one."

Charles inched backwards, his gaze never leaving the dog. "Wipe the damn drool."

Regina looked at Hamlet. Great globs of drool flowed from both sides of his muzzle. She took a handkerchief from her pocket and crouched beside the dog to wipe the drool.

Then she stood and faced her husband. "Very well, I'll bring my writing."

"My wife will *not* publish a book."

Regina smiled sweetly, her blue eyes sparkling with amusement. "One word to Hamlet, and your widow will be publishing a book."

"Are you threatening me again?" Charles stepped forward, glanced at the dog, and thought better of it.

"You married a wealthy merchant's daughter for money," Regina said. "My father forced me down the aisle to secure a title for the family. Now I intend to get what I want."

"Which is?"

"Independence."

Her husband laughed without humor. He walked toward the door where Louis, his valet, waited for him.

"Charles?"

He turned around. "What?"

"If Hamlet dies before old age," Regina warned, her hands clenched into tiny fists at her sides, "you will soon follow him into the hereafter."

Depleted of energy, Regina plopped into the chair and stared out the window. She hated Charles Bradford and others of his ilk, high society and low morals.

She had married the earl to please her father. Another futile attempt to win his love. Her father blamed her for not being the son he wanted.

"Just like your mother," her father would say before shaking his head in disapproval.

If he felt that way about her mother, why had he married her? Or had he been unable to forgive her for dying without giving him a son?

In her mind's eye, Regina conjured her mother's image, a woman she had known only from a portrait. Riotous red curls, like her own. Blue eyes sparkling with humor, like her own. Ambiguous smile on full lips, like her own.

She wished her mother had lived. Life would have been different.

Two birds flew past the open window. She had never felt like soaring more than she did at this moment.

"Reggie?"

She looked over her shoulder.

Ginger Evans stood there, a worried expression on her face.

Regina did not know how she would have survived if the other woman had not agreed to live there after the death of her father. More like sisters than friends, the two women had known each other since childhood.

"You heard our latest argument?" Regina asked.

Ginger nodded and stroked the Great Dane's head. Hamlet returned the affection by licking her hand.

"Louis won't forget you insulted His Lordship," Ginger said.

"What can my husband's valet do to me?"

Ginger shrugged, always more cautious than her old friend. "I will take good care of Austen and Hamlet while you are gone."

"Are the household accounts finished?" Regina asked.

"Completed and balanced," Ginger answered, her pride in her mathematical abilities apparent. Like her late father, she was a genius with numbers.

"Did you manage to squirrel away anything for our escape fund?"

"We don't need to do that anymore," Ginger said. "Our distillery investments are producing incredible profits. I took part of our gin profits and invested in Kazanov Brothers Vodka and Campbell Whisky. I needed to use a business agent, of course."

"Is there any risk?"

"I diversified our investments. If one fails, we don't lose everything." Ginger smiled at her. "Do you believe our fellow Englishmen will suddenly find temperance more attractive than drunkeness?"

"More people drink ale and beer," Regina said, her thoughts on increasing their profits.

"I am investigating other possibilities."

"I'm glad you agreed to live here when your father"— Regina paused for a fraction of a moment—"when your father passed away."

"My father did not commit suicide," Ginger insisted. "Someone murdered him."

"I believe you," Regina said. "I sent a note to that constable and asked him to call upon me the day after tomorrow. I didn't want Charles around."

"Thank you, Reggie. I don't know who would hurt my father," Ginger said, "but he would never have done that." Tears welled up in her eyes. "I want him buried in hallowed ground."

"Persuade the constable to investigate further."

"My lady?" The Bradford majordomo stood in the doorway.

"Yes, Pickles?"

"Your father is waiting in the drawing room."

Regina rolled her eyes and grimaced. She did not want another argument today.

"Your sentiments match mine," Pickles drawled, making the women laugh.

"Tell my father I will be along shortly."

"Yes, my lady."

"You must admit Reginald has been less critical since Austen arrived," Ginger said. "He only wants to visit his grandson."

"I wish he would visit from a distance."

Ginger smiled. "You can't have everything."

"Given a choice," Regina said, "I prefer my father to blond hair."

* * *

Damn her. She had gone too far this time.

Prince Viktor Kazanov climbed the stairs to his wife's bedchamber and fought to control his fury. If he failed to suppress his anger, he would probably strangle her. Going to the gallows for murdering his wife meant his daughter would be orphaned, and he would not allow that to happen.

Viktor paused outside the bedchamber, his black gaze fixing on the closed portal. Willing his temper to cool, he counted to one hundred and then added another hundred for good measure.

After taking a deep breath, Viktor barged into the bedchamber and slammed the door shut. The heady scent of gardenia, her favorite pefume, hit him with the force of a slap. His wife was preening in front of the cheval mirror, unable to part with her own image. She was a beauty—blond hair, blue eyes, long legs—but so too were the most venomous snakes.

"I prefer you knock before entering," Adele said, watching him in the mirror.

"I do not give a damn what you prefer." Viktor closed the distance between them.

Adele ignored him. She held an emerald and diamond choker in one hand and several long ropes of pearls in the other. Holding the priceless choker against her bosom, Adele studied her reflection and then did the same with the pearls.

"What do you think?" Adele asked, her gaze meeting his in the mirror. She turned to face him. "I was thinking the green of the emeralds seems more in keeping with a country house party. You know, all that springtime green landscape."

"We are not leaving until tomorrow. Why are you packing now?"

"I am preparing, not packing."

"That gown is cut too low for a country house party,"

Viktor said, inspecting her. "Or are you planning to wet-nurse your lover of the moment?"

"You are crude."

"And you are an embarrassment." His tone mirrored his scorn. "How dare you wangle an invitation for your lover."

"Are you jealous?" Adele arched a brow at him. "Really, Viktor, you haven't reached for me in four years."

"I prefer a cup that has not been passed around the tavern."

Adele reached to slap him, but Viktor grabbed her wrist. "Do not provoke me to rash action."

"Spare me your empty threats," Adele sneered.

"Revoke Bradford's invitation," Viktor ordered. "I do not want you whoring in front of my family."

"Enjoying a liaison is not whoring," Adele told him. "Charles's wife will be accompanying him. Why don't you try her? The prince and the merchant's daughter coupling in the woods. What irony that would be."

"You disgust me."

"That is your problem."

"I want us to take Sally away for the summer," Viktor said, knowing his suggestion would be rejected. "We could summer in the Cotswalds or take her to Scotland. Maybe even Paris."

Adele stared at him for a long moment. "I think not. Besides, why would you pass the summer with a woman you despise?"

"Sally needs her mother," Viktor said. "You have scarcely glanced in her direction since her birth. *Five years ago.*"

Adele gave him a feline smile. "*My* daughter will understand when she's older."

Viktor raised his brows at her. "What do you mean by that?"

"I was pregnant when we married," Adele answered, "perhaps Sally isn't yours."

"*Liar.* You would never have done anything to ruin your chances of marrying a prince, and saying otherwise could harm our daughter." Viktor shoved his hands in his trouser pockets to keep from shaking some sense into her. "I would kill you, Adele, but you are not worth the trip to the gallows."

"You are hardly celibate," she said. "I've heard naughty rumors about you and Vanessa Stanton."

"We have an agreement," Viktor admitted. "Which was made *after* your lovers crowded our marriage."

Adele shrugged. "I am a lady who likes variety."

"You are no lady." Viktor lifted her left hand, slipped the jeweled wedding ring off her finger, and pocketed it. "I do not want you wearing a token of my former love while you service other men."

His insult hit its mark. "I do *not* service men."

"What do you call a woman who spreads her legs for any man who asks? When I divorce you, I will keep Sally as English law states. You, my dear, will become a social outcast as English custom dictates."

At that, Viktor walked to the door.

"You would not dare create a scandal," Adele called, alarmed.

Viktor paused, contempt etched across his expression. "I wish you were married to your grave."

Regina carried her one-year-old son into the drawing room. Ginger walked behind her, followed by Hamlet.

"Good afternoon," Regina greeted her father and Forest Fredericks, her father's business associate.

"I didn't come here to visit the dog," Reginald Smith snapped.

"I'll take him," Ginger said, and turned to leave. "Come, Hamlet. I'll give you a treat."

The large well-lit family drawing room exuded a cozy, bookish informality, which Regina loved almost as much as the study. With bookcases built into the walls, the drawing room had been decorated in red with touches of black and ochre walls. Richly patterned kilims, paisley upholstery, Persian rugs, patterned drapes, and leather-bound books warmed the room. Of course, her father preferred—

"The Countess of Langley should entertain in the formal drawing room, not the family parlor," her father said.

"I prefer this room to the formal coldness of the other," Regina said, determined to avoid an argument. At least, she would try. "I only entertain people I like in this room."

"We're flattered," Reginald said, his tone sarcastic. "Aren't we, Forest?"

Thinking an argument seemed imminent, Regina looked at Forest Fredericks, who winked at her. She smiled at the man whom she had always considered an uncle. If not for Forest and Ginger's father, she would have felt completely unloved.

Short and slight, Uncle Forest had a receding hairline and the beginnings of a pot belly. He wore thick spectacles that slipped constantly, which he pushed up with an index finger. Behind those spectacles, Forest had the warmest brown eyes and kindly expression.

In fact, Forest Fredericks was the opposite of Reginald Smith in looks, bearing, and personality. Her father was reasonably tall, just under six feet, and had black hair tinged with silver. The attractive widower had refused to remarry, though, certain that interested women wanted his money.

"How are you, Uncle Forest?"

"Quite well." He pushed his slipping spectacles up.

"Give me my grandson," her father ordered.

Regina passed him the boy. Austen stared at his grandfather's somber expression and reached to touch his face.

"Gapa," Austen said.

"He knows me," Reginald said, his dark eyes gleaming with pleasure.

How many years had it been since pleasure had registered on her father's face? She had no memory of his ever smiling at her with approval.

"The boy bears a remarkable resemblance to you," Forest said.

Regina covered her mouth to keep from laughing. She looked at her father's business associate and wondered how he could say that without laughing. She supposed Uncle Forest was merely flattering her father. Many people did that to deflect his sarcastic gruffness.

Except for the black hair and brown eyes, Austen looked nothing like his grandfather. He was the image of her husband, who also had dark hair and eyes.

"I am glad you decided to visit today," Regina said. "Charles and I are leaving tomorrow for the Duke of Inverary's country house."

"You are traveling in the highest circles," Reginald said, seeming pleased. "Mind your manners, missy."

Regina felt the familiar spark of irritation. She was a grown woman of twenty-two. Did her father believe she could not conduct herself properly, or was he trying to start an argument?

"You aren't taking Austen?"

"Austen will remain in London with Nanny Sprig and Ginger."

"Then visiting my grandson today or tomorrow matters little," Reginald said, his gaze on the boy.

Seeing his daughter mattered little to him.

Regina flinched at his sentiment but steeled herself against the pain. After a lifetime of callous disregard, Reginald Smith still possessed the power to hurt her.

"Well, I am happy to visit both Regina and Austen," Forest interjected.

Regina managed a faint smile. "Thank you, Uncle Forest."

"How is Ginger feeling these days?" Forest pushed his spectacles up with his index finger.

"She still believes someone murdered her father," Regina answered. "Bartholomew Evans loved his daughter too much to commit suicide."

"Bart hanged himself," Reginald said bluntly. "There was no evidence of foul play. None whatsoever."

"I find this subject distasteful," Regina said, glad that her friend had not heard her father.

"The subject or my opinion?"

"Both." Her father was the most insensitive man she had ever met. Except for her husband.

"You will certainly enjoy yourself at the duke's party," Forest said into the lengthening silence.

"I will not enjoy myself," Regina said. "Upon arrival, Charles will disappear with his mistress."

Forest Fredericks blushed with embarrassment and pushed his spectacles up.

Reginald chuckled, drawing her attention. "Men will always be men and take what is offered. That's the way the world wags."

"Not my world." Regina lost her temper. "How can my own father condone such immoral behavior? You disgust me almost as much as my husband."

"I should have known that red hair would give you a fiery temper." Reginald shook his head in disapproval. "You remind me of your mother."

"Those famous last words," Regina said. "If you wanted a title so badly, you should have married Bradford and left me in peace."

"Watch your mouth, missy," Reginald warned. "You're not too old—"

"Spare me the fatherly discipline," Regina interrupted. "If you cannot show me respect, then expect none in return. Do not bother visiting me again."

"Charles will have something to say about that," Reginald said.

"Chuck cares only about drinking, gambling, and whoring," Regina told him. "Stop blushing, Uncle Forest." She looked at her father again, adding, "My husband doesn't care if you never see Austen."

"He does if he wants my money."

"When you die," Regina said, "Charles will inherit all your money through me. I guarantee nothing will be left for Austen. All will have been wasted on cards, gin, and whores."

"You always did think you knew more than your father."

"Perhaps I do."

"I have taken precautions against your husband's spending habits," her father informed her.

"What do you mean?"

"Forest is the executor of my estate," Reginald answered. "Charles and you will receive generous allowances, but Forest will control my assets until Austen reaches his majority. Hopefully, your husband will have drunk himself into the grave by then."

"With all due respect to Uncle Forest, I am capable of handling my husband and my finances," Regina said, fuming at his high-handedness. "Ginger Evans has inherited her father's genius with numbers. If I cannot control my own money with her assistance, give it to charity."

"The money is *mine*, not yours," Reginald exclaimed. "You ungrateful wretch. I found you an earl to marry, and your son will be an earl."

"You chose yourself a son-in-law," Regina said. "You traded me for a title."

"You will thank me—"

"—for dying and leaving me in peace."

"You will regret those words some day."

"I can manage the regret, if not my own finances."

"Regina, perhaps we could have a private word," Forest said, ending the all-too-familiar bickering.

"I don't need her permission to do what I want," Reginald insisted.

"You do, if you don't want her to give Austen's inheritance to charity." Forest pushed his spectacles up and gave him a pointed look. Her father nodded a reluctant agreement.

Regina followed Forest into the corridor. "Both Ginger and I adore you," she said, "but we can take care of ourselves."

"I understand your feelings on the matter," Forest told her. "Reginald does not comprehend that women are different these days. Your father can be inflexible." He smiled to soften his next words. "Inflexibility is a quality you have inherited from him. Once he's gone, I will relinquish full control of the money to you. Of course, I will expect to advise you for a period of time."

Regina knew that was the best she could do. Her father had never had any faith in her abilities because she could never be the son he had wanted. In his eyes, his daughter was *only* a woman.

Regina inclined her head. "I will accept his inheritance."

They returned to the drawing room.

"Regina agrees to accept the inheritance and your plans for it," Forest told her father.

"Should I thank her for agreeing to take my money?" Reginald grumbled. "How did you manage that, Forest?"

"Regina is an intelligent young woman." He pushed his spectacles up. "Though, you refuse to recognize her worth."

Reginald stood, kissed his grandson's pudgy cheeks, and passed him to her. "Do not worry overmuch about your husband's mistress," he said in an awkward attempt to soothe her.

"I pray each night for Adele Kazanov's continued

good health," Regina said, her blue eyes sparkling with amusement.

Reginald gave her a decidedly unamused look and then followed Forest to the door.

"Father?"

He paused and turned around.

"Resembling my mother makes me proud."

ABOUT THE AUTHOR

Patricia Grasso lives in Massachusetts. She is the author of thirteen historical romances and is currently working on her next romance, which will be published by Zebra Books in April 2005. Pat loves to hear from her readers and you may write to her c/o Zebra Books. Readers can visit her website at www.patriciagrasso.com

Discover the Romances of
Hannah Howell